sava saheli singh

TIM MAUGHAN

INFINITE DETAIL

Tim Maughan is an author and a journalist who explores issues around cities, class, culture, globalization, technology, and the future. His work regularly appears on the BBC and in *VICE* and *New Scientist*.

INFINITE
DETAIL

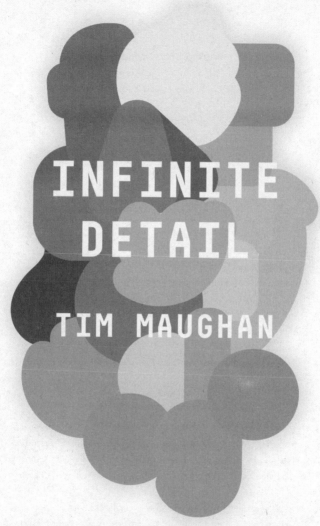

INFINITE DETAIL

TIM MAUGHAN

MCD × FSG ORIGINALS

FARRAR, STRAUS AND GIROUX NEW YORK

SCI
FIC
MAU

MCD × FSG Originals
Farrar, Straus and Giroux
175 Varick Street, New York 10014

ASCII illustration on page 222 by David Palmer.

Library of Congress Cataloging-in-Publication Data
Names: Maughan, Tim, 1973– author.
Title: Infinite detail / Tim Maughan.
Description: First edition. | New York : Farrar, Straus and
    Giroux, 2019. | "MCD x FSG Originals."
Identifiers: LCCN 2018033385 | ISBN 9780374175412 (pbk.)
Subjects: GSAFD: Dystopias.
Classification: LCC PR6113.A924 I54 2019 | DDC 823/.92—dc23
LC record available at https://lccn.loc.gov/2018033385

Designed by Abby Kagan

Our books may be purchased in bulk for promotional, educational,
or business use. Please contact your local bookseller or the Macmillan
Corporate and Premium Sales Department at 1-800-221-7945, extension
5442, or by e-mail at MacmillanSpecialMarkets@macmillan.com.

www.fsgoriginals.com • www.fsgbooks.com
Follow us on Twitter, Facebook, and Instagram at @fsgoriginals

1   3   5   7   9   10   8   6   4   2

for sava

INFINITE DETAIL

1. AFTER

The pathetic tinkle of the shop's bell announces their first visitor, the first believer of the day. The first of the regulars, the tired-looking mothers and lost children, the ones that come in just to catch a quick word with Mary, to thank her, to nervously leave offerings on her desk, to smile their awkward, uncomfortable smiles. The ones that just pop in to stare at the sad, pale, distant, generic dead faces.

"All right, Janet," Tyrone says.

"Hello, Tyrone." Janet flashes him a nervous smile from beneath her cowl of lank, greasy hair, her face gaunt pencil marks on torn gray paper, almost merging into the crowds that watch them from the walls. It's enough of a smile that he knows she's genuinely pleased to see him, like his unprompted words to her are some minor but important victory, one of the few tiny sparks of life that separate her from Mary's drawings.

"Is she busy?" Janet's eyes twitch anxiously around the room, her grip tightening on the oversized blue IKEA cube bag that bulges with unknown junk.

Tyrone glances over at Mary. She's sitting there as always, at the back of the shop, teenage eyes peering at him over the kaleidoscopic mass of debris that litters her desk—cans full of pens, crayons, paintbrushes, and sticks of chalk, broken toys. Worthless trinkets and colorful fragments of junked history that threaten to dwarf her barely teenage frame. Gifts from believers. She smiles back at him over it all, through those heavily paint-splattered glasses of hers, lowers her eyes back down to her desk. He can't see what she's working on from here, the paper protected from view by castle walls of priceless detritus, and in all truth he doesn't care. He knows exactly what it is, the same thing she always draws.

He knows it's the face of another dead person.

Most likely, he thinks, it's the face of another dead white person. They always seem to be white people. Dead white people. He's seen so many of them now that he struggles to tell them apart. College likes to joke that it's because all white people look the same, but Tyrone knows that's not true. It's something else, perhaps how Mary always draws them—sad, pale, distant, generic. Or maybe that's just how dead people all look.

"Nah, she's just drawing. Go say hello, innit."

Mary squeezes ghosts from sticks of chalk, traces lines of memory in pastel.

"Hello, Mary."

Mary looks up, over the brim of her glasses, and her heart sinks slightly from awkward discomfort as she sees Janet's nervous face looking back at her; feels her disturbed, overfocused eyes drilling into her skull. It's not that she dislikes her, it's not that she dislikes any of the believers—Tyrone and Grids's word, not hers—it's just their unfailing intensity that puts her on edge. She doesn't blame them; when she can see past the thousand-yard stares and the sense of odd displacement she can see the hurt, the pain, the struggle to cope with the shock. Plus it's her fault they're here, that they come to see her. They come because of what she does, what she is.

Grids tells her she's a celebrity. He says people need celebrities, especially now. He says there used to be too many of them, but then they were all washed away with everything else. Mary's not too sure about this, not sure she wants it, but she remembers his words at those times when she wants to avoid the people like Janet, to avoid the devotional gazes and awkward exchanges, to run from the responsibility.

"Morning, Janet, how you doing?"

"I'm o-kay." There's a high-low timbre to that last word, a noncommittal tone shift fishing for concern. Mary ignores it, not wanting to get sucked in. She always tells Tyrone she likes his music, his ancient tapes, and it ain't a lie, but the real reason she lets him play it in the shop all day is because it sucks the silence out of the room, fills the awkward vacuums, lets the pauses slip by more easily.

Janet ain't stopping, though. "What are you drawing? Another one?"

Mary looks down at the pale paper, the reverse of a two-foot-wide segment torn from the back of a Land Army recruitment poster, and for the first time this morning she feels like she really sees it. Formless pencil marks. Thick, dappled, inconsistent lines in chalk dust. Powdered history deposited on the texture of cracks from her unwashed hands. She looks, but remembers none of it, as though she had no part in its creation.

"Yeah. Another one."

"Oh, I brought you something!" Janet rummages in the pockets of her torn, stained, but still defiantly pink anorak, and then in the pockets of her baby-blue jogging bottoms, the faded trousers so short that the gray elasticated trim grips her ankles, exposing two-inch bands of pale skin marbled with blue veins as they fail to reach the rainwater-grayed, blood-flecked bandages that she wears because the ships carrying socks from China and India stopped coming.

Eventually she gives up and turns to the inevitable, muttering to herself as she opens wide the long-broken zip mouth of the IKEA bag, the blue plastic cube straining along its frayed seams, where it looks in places like single white fibers are the only things maintaining its hull integrity. Mary fears it might explode, either from pressure buildup or Janet's fevered rummaging, and fill the shop with even more historical residue, the same sedimentary layer of scraps she's been trying to dig her way out of all her life.

"Here! Found them!" exclaims Janet, just a little too loud, a little too excited. She thrusts forward a fist of brightly colored tubes, of various widths and lengths, her face full of glee and accomplishment. Mary takes them, smiles with forced appreciation, and thanks her as she cradles the gift in her open hands. Broken crayons; empty plastic pen shells; leadless, splintered pencils. Useless, all of it. But Mary feels some warmth from the gesture, sincerely, understands what these discarded odds and ends represent to some, the value they have in their irreproducibility, their nostalgia, their power as memory triggers. She understands these things way too well, and as she stares at her open palms the vibrant chalk dust that patterns them turns black and impossible to remove, as memories of scrabbling in the dirt, digging with broken fingernails in the shit, flood her senses.

She wants to throw them back in Janet's stupid fucking face.

She doesn't, she just smiles, thanks her again, gently lays them down on the desk. Memories fade, but the private stench, known just to her, still lingers.

Janet, about to speak, looks pleased enough, though, happy her gift has been welcomed, and Mary remembers Grids's words. *Give them what they want.*

"I was just wondering, if maybe—" The same question, every day. Mary knew it was coming.

"I was just wondering, if maybe, if you were out today, and you saw our Mark—"

"Janet—"

"You know, maybe you'll see him out in the street, y'know." Janet points toward the front of the shop, the light filtering in through the half-boarded-up windows. "Maybe if you see him out there you could tell him something for me?"

"Janet . . . we've been through this before. You know I can't say whether I'll see him. I can't always choose who I see."

"I know, my love, but you might—"

"I . . . I might, yeah, but it's not very likely. And even if I did, I can't talk to him."

"But you could just tell him—"

"Janet. I can't talk to Mark. He can't hear me, Janet." Mary swallows hard. "I can't . . . he's dead, Janet."

"Yeah, but—" Janet is unflustered, not even decelerated, by this statement of unquestionable fact.

Mary decides to let her finish. The path of least resistance.

"Yeah, but if you do see him, yeah? If you do, can you tell him just one thing? From me?"

"What's that?" Mary asks. Polite, redundant. She knows the answer.

"Just tell him his dad is sorry. Please?"

The doorbell again. Two people this time, a couple, presumably. Newbies. Husband and wife from the looks of it, father and mother most likely. Old. Well, old for around here.

They also look shit-scared. Tyrone is used to old white people looking at him and being shit-scared, but he's pretty sure they were shit-scared before they even knew he was there. It's in the way they stand next to each other, almost too close. Huddled. Tyrone guesses they're not only not from around here, but have probably never been to the Croft before. The armed security on the gate, the explosions of graffiti across bombed-out architecture, that ever-present edge of tension in the spice-scented air. It can be a pretty shit-scary place, your first time.

The guy, gray hair, gray face, gray clothes—old, washed-out, hand-repaired, but still maintaining some aging artifice of respectability—stops glancing around the shop and looks directly at Tyrone. It's clear he wants to speak, but isn't sure where to start. Tyrone decides to put him out of his misery.

"Morning. What can we do for you guys today?"

"We . . . well, my wife . . ." The guy pauses, glances at the woman, who is still staring, silently, at the dead faces on the walls. "She wanted to come down here, she'd heard the stories. She's . . . curious." His voice trembles with fear run through with skepticism.

Tyrone nods, smiles. The stories. "Of course. Where you guys from?"

"Bath."

"Wow, that's quite a trip. You drove?"

"God, no." The man laughs, politely. "God. No. We got the train."

"Oh, they running?"

"As far as Keynsham. We walked from there."

"Nice day for it." If in doubt, mention the weather.

"Yes, yes, it is." The man smiles, the fear edging away slightly. "So . . . I'm sorry. What's the setup here exactly? How does this . . . work?"

Tyrone takes a breath, prepares the spiel, but he's hardly got the first syllable out when he's interrupted.

The woman floats one hand in front of her mouth, fingers and lips both trembling, as she steps away from her husband, her gaze fixed on a spot on the wall. On a face. Her other hand darts back behind her, blind fumbling to grasp the man's arm, and when it finds his elbow it grabs hard, holds tight. Tyrone is unsure whether it's to get his attention or to anchor herself, to make sure she doesn't stray too far.

"Diane . . . ?" The man sounds breathless, startled. He glances from the viselike grip on his arm to her face, unable to make eye contact as he turns away from her, transfixed. Tyrone watches the fear return.

"It's him." The woman takes the hand from her mouth to point weakly, the shaking increasing in frequency, as it spreads up her arm to her larynx, modulating her words. "It's him, Alan. Look."

The silence unnerves Mary. Tyrone has stopped playing the old jungle tape he was listening to—he always does when they get an ID, without her ever asking, out of respect for the customers—and she wishes it would come back.

She closes her eyes for a second, wills it to return.

Nothing. Just silence.

Eyes open again. They're still here. Alan and Diane, peering at her from the other side of her desk, over the multicolored walls built from trash and gratitude. Mary has to look away from them both again—it's too intense, Diane's expectation, Alan's skepticism, their combined fear. It amplifies her constant discomfort, heightens it. She can feel their fear merging with her own, infecting it, making it stronger.

So she looks down at the desk, at the picture they handed her, that Tyrone had taken down from the wall for them. A man's face—no, a boy's. A teenager. Pale, young. Glasses. A scruff of blond spiked hair drawn in yellow chalk, freckles spotted on cheeks in brown felt-tip. A child's scrawl, a child's face. She remembers when she first saw it. She remembers them all.

"So this is your son?" Mary's voice is small, tiny, but it shatters the silence.

"Well, it . . . it bears a resemblance to—"

"It's him," Diane interrupts her husband, her voice as small as Mary's, but the conviction demanding attention.

"Darling—"

"It's him, Alan." She smiles, almost imperceptibly—at her husband, moisture in her eyes, her hand gripping his. It's enough to silence him, to make him swallow back his doubt, just seeing her like this, and he squeezes her hand in return. She turns back to Mary. "It's him, that's Ian. Our son."

Mary attempts to smile back at her, to transmit warmth, understanding. She has no idea if it works. Tyrone is much better at this stuff. It's a shame he can't do the rest of her job.

"And you've not seen him since . . ." Mary pauses, picks her words. "Since that night?"

Diane looks wordlessly down at her lap. Alan moves forward to fill the silence.

"No, we've . . . not. We've had no word from him since then. I mean, not even that night—about a week before. We've not heard anything from him since . . . since every-thing stopped working."

"Of course. And he lived round here?"

"No, but not far. In Bedminster."

"Southville," Diane corrects him. From the corner of her eye Mary sees Tyrone, always eavesdropping, smile and shake his head.

"Sorry, yes. Southville. Just off North Street. He was sharing a house there. He was a student."

"Medicine," adds Diane, a brittle shard of pride. Dead, buried significance.

"But he was here that night?" Mary asks.

"I . . . we believe so. We . . ." Alan's face suddenly becomes more sullen, his eyes fall. "We couldn't get here. Not straightaway. Not . . . not for months, in fact. I don't know if anyone realizes, but things were pretty bad in Bath, too. I mean, it must have been pretty bad everywhere. When we got here his house was deserted. There was no sign of him, just a few of his things. Not many. A few clothes. All the electronics and devices, obviously. Everything else was gone . . . the house had been broken into, so . . . what I'm saying is, I don't think he took the rest of his stuff with him . . . it must have been stolen and . . ."

He stops talking, like the words have just dried up. Mary recognizes the guilt, the regret, the helplessness, recognizes it all from Janet and every other parent that's walked into the shop before them.

"It's okay." Diane squeezes his hand, looks back at Mary. "We were looking for months. Eventually we found an old uni friend of his. She thought he'd come up here. But of course we couldn't get in here back then, it was all shut. But that's what she said, that he'd come up here. I mean, that's what people did, didn't they? People came here that night?"

"I believe so, yes." Give them what they want.

Diane forces a smile. "You're too young to remember, of course." She nods at the picture in front of Mary. "You drew him, though?"

"Yes. I'm afraid I ain't a very good artist."

"No . . . it's great. Really. It's a very good likeness."

"Diane—"

"Alan, please. It's him. Look. Please."

Alan glances at Mary's pastel scrawl, and then straight at her, like it hurts his eyes. "It could be him, yes. I guess . . . just . . . I'm sorry. What does this mean? If it is him, does this mean you've seen him?"

"Does it mean he's dead?"

Mary takes a breath, tries to smile. This is always the hardest part. Harder even than showing them.

"I ain't completely sure what it means myself, to be truthful." She fidgets nervously with one of her oversized hoop earrings. "Sometimes I see people, out in the street. Nobody else can see them. They're not fully there . . . just . . . half there."

"Like ghosts? You see ghosts?"

"Diane, please—"

"Let her answer! Are they ghosts?"

"I'm not sure. Maybe. I guess that depends on what you believe a ghost is. All I know is that they were here that night, and they're not always dead. I think you have to be dead to have a ghost."

"Not dead?" There's an echo of hope in Diane's voice.

"Not always, no. If I see someone, out in the street, then I come back here and I draw them. Put the picture up here, in the shop. Sometimes they come in, the people I've drawn, or someone that knows they're alive—and then I give them the picture. For free. These pictures here, they're all waiting to be collected."

"So . . . that's it?" There's an edge of anger to Alan's voice, just faint, hidden below the frustration and loss, like he's about had enough. "We have to wait, to see if he just happens to pass by and pick up his picture? That's the only way you know if he's alive or not?"

"Alan—"

"No," Mary says. "It's not the only way."

Tyrone puts the money that the old guy gave him in a scratched black metal box. It had been hard work getting it out of him, which isn't a surprise really—twenty quid ain't no joke, man—but Tyrone knew he'd fold and agree to it. Just had to see the way he looked at his old lady. Like he'd do anything to make her happy, even if it was only for a few moments, and involved him spending a month's wages on some heavily dubious bullshit. He watches Mary lead the couple—holding hands now, like small children—out into the pale daylight.

He takes the knife, its handle bandaged with black tape, out of the box and chucks the jungle tape he'd been playing in there, just to be sure. Five snags, no breaks. Yet. Irreplaceable. More valuable than the two tenners he just dropped in there, to him at least. He locks the box and places it on a high shelf, pockets the key, tucks the knife into the back of his jeans. Turns around to check the shop, sees Janet standing there, still. Staring at the uncollected faces. The dead ones.

"Janet. Yo, Janet. C'mon girl. Gotta go. I'm locking up."

Janet turns slowly, thousand-yard stare. "Sorry, Tyrone, I didn't realize." He holds the door open for her as she exits, flips the cardboard sign to CLOSED, and secures the locks and bolts.

"It's a'ight, Janet. Is just a quick thing. We'll be open again later."

It's bright outside, and he finds himself squinting against white sunshine. It's pretty quiet out, still early. Airborne reggae vibes drift across the street from somewhere, pulses and tones, like the jungle tape stripped of its urgency. Sheltering his eyes, he can see Mary leading her two punters down the street, down the main drag of Stokes Croft itself, toward the open gates. He'd better catch up, she's moving fast. Mary doesn't like to hang around when she's doing her thing.

"Is she gonna show 'em?" Janet asks him.

"Yeah. She is."

Janet's little face lights up. "Maybe she'll show me Mark again, afterwards?"

Tyrone looks at her. "You got twenty quid, Janet?"

Janet stares at him, glances down at her impossibly full IKEA bag, and then back at him. "No."

"Then she ain't gonna show you nothing. Look, I gotta go with her, make sure she's okay, all right? I'll catch you later, yeah?"

Tyrone doesn't wait for her to answer, just picks up the pace, closing the distance between him and Mary without looking like he's hurrying. It's been raining overnight and the pictures have washed off some of the walls as usual, running across the pavements and into the drains at the curb in crisscrossing tracks of dull translucent color, so it looks like the buildings themselves are bleeding out, melting. He half expects that if he traces the drying paint flows back he'll find the empty, see-through wireframe of a building, drained of all pigment.

But he's not got time. The last thing he needs would be Grids turning up when Mary looks like she's wandering around the Croft on her own. He checks up ahead; she's stopped now, about twenty feet short of the gates, the two punters still holding hands, their bemusement and discomfort openly betrayed by their body language even at this distance. When he's about ten feet away from them he slows, stops. Best to give them some space, at least the illusion of privacy.

From out of the shadows of the buildings on the far side of the street he sees a hulking figure moving toward him, slowly. Ozone gives him a half nod and a fist bump as they meet in the middle of the road, his other hand resting on the dull metal and plastic of the counterfeit Kalashnikov rifle that dangles from his neck. Tyrone looks at the huge aging gun, thinks of the tape-wrapped kitchen knife stuck in the back of his jeans, and remembers exactly where he stands in the pecking order.

"Easy, Ty."

"How's things, O?"

Ozone shrugs. "Yeah, good. On gate duty, innit."

"Anything exciting? You shot anyone this morning?"

Ozone laughs, rolls of fat under his neck rippling. "Nah. Nobody comes down here anymore, man, you know how it is. Not anyone wanting any trouble. Saw them two come through earlier, though." He half nods at Mary's punters. "Lord and Lady Marks and Spencer."

Tyrone snorts. "Yeah, they come just to see Mary." He slips into a sketchy, exaggerated posh accent. "All the way from Bath, don't you know."

"No shit. No wonder they looked fucking terrified when they saw me."

"To be fair, fam, you a scary-looking fucker even without that thing."

Ozone smiles, a blend of amusement and pride. "True."

Sweat patches spread from Ozone's armpits, turning the already grayed cotton of his once-white T-shirt even darker.

Tyrone's sure he can see them moving, growing, as he stands there.

"You all right, man? You look hot."

"Yeah." Ozone wipes sweat from his shaved head with his forearm. "This weather, man. Done with it."

"Don't say that. Gotta stay like this till after the weekend, man, at least. Carnival, innit."

Ozone sucks his teeth. "Fuck that. Can rain all weekend, far as I care. Then maybe no one will turn up."

"Fam!"

Ozone laughs, ripples his neck, gently taps the gun with two fingers. He glances over at Mary again. "How long she gonna be, man? You know she got big visitors today?"

"Oh yeah. Like Grids will let me forget."

Three faces stare at Mary, the first two full of fear, embarrassment, awkward impatience.

The third, scrawled on the paper in her hand, is seemingly blank of emotion.

Mary stares at it, traces her own badly daubed lines until she has a full image of it in her mind. Focuses, blinks.

Above her the sky starts to darken, mid-morning sun settling into evening gloom. Buildings morph and shift, subtle changes to both their 3D architecture and 2D surfaces. She always tries to avoid looking at the buildings, the displacement is too disorienting, plus if she focuses on them too much they all go kinda weird, like they're not really there, not really solid, like they're made up of some patch-work collage of old photos, the lighting and coloring on them never quite fitting together, so much so that she finds herself questioning what's real and what's not even more than usual, and she's trained herself to stop doing that. Best not to know.

The sky, the buildings. Only one place left to look. She holds her breath, looks down at the ground. She knows what's waiting there.

The lines of paint running into the drains turn red, scarlet trickles of blood filling indents in tarmac, pooling, a spiderweb network of bloodstains that weaves around shattered glass and dislodged masonry to link the bodies, the remains, the limbs together. Then the sound comes in, sudden, fast—there's always a delay, but it always surprises her, catches her unaware. At first it sounds muted, like she's been deafened, that fuzziness you get the day after standing near the sound system rigs for far too long. And then it whooshes in, like air filling a vacuum, the mix packed so chaotically, so densely, that it almost knocks her off her feet. Alarms, screams, sobbing, yells—from above, the low drone of engines and the ever-present skittering roll of drums.

In front of her stand Diane and Alan, oblivious to it all, even the thick, black, acrid smoke that is pouring from the broken shell of the overturned police van that lies just a few feet to their left, oblivious as the smoke spirals around them, engulfs them. They seem only half there to Mary, like they've been badly cut out from one old newspaper photo and stuck, with a child's blissful lack of care for perspective and lighting, onto another one, ripped from a story about a lost cat and pasted into a story about some terrible event in some savage, distant country, their pale faces lit by a sun she can't see.

She gazes past them, back toward the freshly hollowed-out shell of the wall-like 5102 building as it leaks more smoke and spits flames at the darkening sky, lost figures stumbling about in the thick haze of dust and airborne debris.

And then, from near her feet, voices. Faint, distorted, panicked.

move her we've got to move her get her out of the road we

no no moving her is worst thing we can do jesus just hold this here no here hold that

here christ what was that we need an ambulance she needs a fucking ambulance

they won't let any in they won't let them in just don't let go they've got to they've got to got to fucking let them in now get that fucking mask off her jesus

"He's here," Mary tells Diane and Alan, barely more than a whisper.

"Where? Where is he?"

"Diane, calm down—"

Mary crouches in the street, brings her face almost eye to eye with the boy. It's definitely him from the picture, she can be sure of it now, and she realizes his expression isn't blank, it's intense concentration. He's on his knees, his arms disappearing into a mess of red that Mary can't bring herself to look at directly, she's just aware there's a body there, motionless, a person, parts that should be there gone, face covered by a paint-spattered gas mask. Next to the boy kneels a girl, sobbing, her clothes soaked in crimson.

"He's here," Mary repeats, louder. "Right here. Kneeling on the ground."

"I've had enough—"

"Shut up!" Diane drops to the ground, crouches next to Mary. Her hand lightly strokes the tarmac, feeling its way, as if she's trying to read some message encoded in the compacted black gravel, but from Mary's view it looks like she's rooting around in the corpse's abdomen. She feels sick.

She stands again, focuses. She pauses time.

Or, more accurately, she pauses one of the times. *Then* time. The time from that night. Smoke stops swirling, becomes sculpture, strangely flat, two-dimensional. Paper fragments, burnt and fluttering from the sky, suddenly hover in the air, still. Around her, the bodies that have somehow remained upright become statuesque, broken and disfigured.

Diane is still crouched in the road, unaware of how close she sits to her frozen son.

"What's he doing?"

"He's trying to help people. People are hurt, and he's trying to help them. To deal with their wounds." She feels sick again.

"Oh, c'mon now." Alan has heard enough. "We already told you he was studying to be a doctor, you're just using—"

"Shush!" Diane holds her palm up at her husband, silencing him. "Is he . . . is he alone?"

"There's a girl with him. About his age. Blond hair, pretty." She's lying now, slightly. She can't see the girl's face; it's blurred. They sometimes are. Give them what they want.

"It's Sarah!" Diane is suddenly on her feet, clutching Alan's arm. "It must be Sarah!"

"Di—"

"Can you . . . can you tell us anything else? Can you describe him? What . . . what's he wearing?" The pleading eyes. Mary has seen them on every parent that's passed through the shop.

She looks down at the three figures, flinches at the perfectly spherical blood drops suspended in the air around the boy's bruised face, inspects his clothes—clearly unchanged for days, ripped and worn, splattered in blood and vomit and shit.

"He's wearing a black coat, large hood with a fur collar. It's nice. Looks warm."

"Yes . . ."

"And he's got a bag . . . a bag with him. It's full of bandages, medical stuff. He's using it now, to help someone."

"What color is it?"

The bag is so soaked in blood she can't make it out at first.

"Green . . . and brown. Patterned. Camouflage. Yeah, it's camouflage-patterned."

"Ian . . ." Teardrops roll slowly down Diane's cheeks, and Mary finds herself surprised by how the fluid motion contrasts with the freeze-framed world around her. The man, however, isn't moving at all, as though he's become infected, become part of the *then* world, frozen.

"Alan . . . it's him. That's his bag. You bought it for him . . . he insisted on camouflage . . . you wanted to get him a leather one but . . ."

The man still doesn't move, the blood drained from his already pale face.

Enough. Mary has had enough. Time to end this.

She unfreezes *then* time.

There's a roar behind her, and she turns to look. Clouds of smoke roll toward them from the direction of the gates, but it's white this time, not black, and it stings the eyes and faces of those running to escape from it. Some of them wear gas masks like the corpse on the floor, to protect them from just this, but still they run out of the smoke.

Mary knows what they run from—she can hear it: the shouts, the thunder of hoofs on concrete—she's seen it before, too many times, she doesn't need to see it again. She takes her glasses off.

"It happened here," she says.

"What?" The man finally speaks. "What happened?"

Tyrone yawns, stretches his arms out to his sides.

"C'mon, girl, this is long. Wind it up."

"What, she don't usually take this long, then?" Ozone has never seen Mary do her thing before, Tyrone realizes.

"Nah, she usually like—oh, here we go. Done."

From their respectable distance they watch the man crumble, fold in half. The woman tries to catch him, supports him for a painful second, but she can't hold him, and he's down on his hands and knees in the paint-stained road.

"Fuck, man. What she say to them?"

"Well, if you believe any of this shit," Tyrone says, yawning, "then she just showed them where their son died."

2. BEFORE

T his your first time?"

The guy's eyes seem too close together.

"In America? Yeah. Yeah, it is."

He nods, seemingly at the space itself. Pale fluorescent light falling through conditioned air. Government-issue beige walls.

"Ah. So definitely your first time in here, then."

"Yeah."

Pause.

"Not me."

Rush sighs, hopefully to himself. He glances at the guy. Shaved head coming back through as blond stubble, orange tan sitting uncomfortably against the beige. Forehead stacked with lines from too much sun, time, or both. Eyes definitely too close together.

"No?"

"Nope." No pause at all this time, almost comically fast. Impatient. "Not me. Not my first time at all."

Rush notices his knee is bouncing. Feels his heel pounding against the floor. He makes it stop.

"In fact, happens every time I fly back into the country. And that's a lot."

"Really?" Rush's interest perks up. "You on a list?"

"Nope."

"Oh." Interest gone. They took Rush's spex and his watch, along with his carry-on bag. There are no clocks in here. How long has it been?

"No prints, that's the thing."

They took his passport, too. "Sorry?"

"No prints, see?" The guy waves his right hand at him, wiggles his fingers.

Rush recognizes the words, but right now they make no sense. How long has it been? "I—"

"No fingerprints." The guy is unbuttoning the sleeve of his shirt, and gently but purposefully pulling it up, an act often and proudly repeated, it's clear. Plastic is revealed, 3D-printed prosthetic pink, a municipal flesh tone that sits far more comfortably with the official beige than the present color of this guy's real skin.

The guy flexes his arm and plastic carapaces shift

against one another. The faint sound of motors whirring now that Rush knows to listen for them.

"Lost it in Nigeria, back in '17." The guy's southern drawl is instantly more pronounced. "Was contracting for a Chinese mining company. Boko Haram. IED. Middle of nowhere. Sonofabitches hid it in a goat carcass by the side of the road. Roadkill. Middle of fucking nowhere." He shakes his head.

Rush feels that familiar, sudden wave of embarrassment and guilty repulsion wash over him. "I didn't realize, I'm sorry—"

"Oh, don't be. Not your fault." The guy starts to roll his shirt back down. "You weren't there."

Rush smiles, shakes his head, looks at the ground. His knee bounces again. He wonders how his skin looks against the beige.

He tries to summon moisture to his dry mouth, takes a breath, puts on his best British accent. That's meant to be worth something here, right?

"Excuse me, I was just wondering—do you know how much longer it will be?"

She looks up at him from across an expanse of IKEA farmed pine, his skin color and accent triggering a wave of cognitive dissonance to flicker across her face. Her skin pale against the beige. She stares into mid-space, focusing on text he can't see.

"Rushdi Manaan?"

"Yes."

"You shouldn't be too long. They're just running some background checks. You'll be out within a couple of hours."

"Okay." He tries to hide his shock at a couple of hours. How long has it been already? He ramps up the Englishness. "I was just wondering if it would be at all possible to send a message? It's just my friend was meant to be meeting me, and he'll have been waiting for quite some time now. It would be great if I could just let him know it won't be long now?"

"Well—"

"Sorry—I know it's an awful lot to ask. But I'm worried he might leave. I've already put him through an awful inconvenience asking him to come and meet me, the poor thing. You'd be doing me an awfully big favor if I could just text him, even."

She smiles, unable to resist the accent, that use of "awfully." Bingo. Americans, it's like they're hardwired for it. Instant backdoor access.

She leans forward, lowers her voice, sliding open a drawer full of spex. All brands, all designs, all looking at first glance like innocent pairs of glasses. She pulls out a pair of Amazon Basics.

"These yours?"

"Yes." He's surprised to see them just sitting there. He'd expected them to have been taken off and plugged into some DHS laptop somewhere, been torn down by forensic software. Not that they'd find anything. He knows better than to get on an international flight without wiping all his devices first.

"Okay, take them into the bathroom." She motions over to the long window that runs the length of the room. "Go in the stall, so nobody sees you. No voice, no video. Text only. No pictures, okay?"

He nods.

"I really shouldn't be letting you do this. Be quick, okay?"

"I will. Thank you. So much. You're awfully kind."

She smiles, charmed again. "It's my pleasure."

In the bathroom he realizes that the long window is a two-way mirror, which seems pointless as all the cubicles—sorry, stalls—have doors anyway. Whatever. He'd abandoned the idea of there being any logic to security theater years ago. The idea she'd just hand him his spex like that because of his accent was bullshit too; she probably gives them back to anybody who actually asks. Unofficial policy, for practical sanity, to stop everyone kicking off all the time. It's no big deal being in here, really. Security theater. Bullshit and ritual. Fear and flag-waving. He shakes his head and ducks into the stall.

He thumbs the power on the spex, checks the LED is green for charge, and slips them onto his face. Blinks his PIN. The glasses struggle to find a data connection at first, but then handshake with some unfamiliar U.S. provider. Probably costing him a fortune.

The space around him erupts with windows, missed calls and notifications, and he brushes them aside to jump straight into his messages app. There they are, thirteen unreads from Scott. Cartoon speech bubbles.

He's still here. He waited. He's worried. He misses him. He cares.

He came. And he waited.

He's real.

Rush subvocalizes a reply.

—*hey hey im here im here im ok*

A few tortured seconds' wait for the reply to come back. Then the typing animation.

—*wtf where the fuck are you*

—*homeland sec. holed up in some beige office. omg you should see this merc guy thats in here with me*

—*!!!are you ok? are they going to let you out? are you hurt*

—*IM FINE!! dont worry. they say theyre just doing background checks, and ill be out in a couple of hours. theyre just fucking with me.*

—*jesus fucking christ the cocksuckers*

—*yeah. well, i guess i know whether im on a list now or not :/*

—*ha yeah I guess. are you sure you're ok?*

He cares.

—*im fine, really. dont worry. im just sorry, i feel terrible*

—*sorry for what?*

—*for you coming all this way, and then having to wait for hours because of my bullshit*

—*well, what else was I going to do on a saturday afternoon?*

—*I'm sorry :(go home if you like, i can get a cab when i get out*

—*what? dont be crazy. I'm not going anywhere.*

—*thanks. i miss you.*

Instant send regret.

Pause.

The typing animation.

—*I miss you too*

He misses him.

—*I gotta go. They let me have my spex but only so i could msg you quick. I gotta give them back*

—*They let you have them? weird*

—*yeah i know rite. its all bullshit. they got me in the bathroom so nobody can see*

—*the bathroom? is there a mirror there? send me a selfie*

—*i can't, she said strictly no photos*

—*ah c'mon quick just a quick one, I want to see you*

He wants to see me.

Rush steps out of the stall, stands in front of the mirror, and his heart sinks.

—*I look terrible. so tired*

—*im sure you look just fine. just take it. I want to see my boo!*

Rush straightens up, tries to suck in his gut, ineffectually plays with his hair and beard. Tries to choke back self-doubt. Sighs.

Tries to look just right; not too much smile, not too much pout. Both make him look cheesy. Blinks the selfie icon. The countdown.

3

2

"Jesus Christ CODE RED CODE RED WE'VE GOT A BODY IN THE RESTROOM WITH LIVE SPEX," the mirror yells at him.

1

The artificial shutter sound, a quick preview flash of his terrified face.

"REQUEST IMMEDIATE BACKUP, REPEAT, IMMEDIATE BACKUP TO THE HOLDING AREA BATHROOM," bellows the mirror.

Rush thinks he might have shit himself.

The guard comes through the door, all dark blue uniform and Oakley spex and something that Rush can't decide is a truncheon or a baseball bat.

"TAKE THE FUCKING SPEX OFF AND DROP THEM TO THE FLOOR DROP THEM NOW."

The spex clatter on the floor as they hit.

"HANDS ON YOUR HEAD HANDS ON YOUR HEAD MOTHERFUCKER."

Rush's head feels clammy to his touch, his hair greasy. He can feel himself shaking.

Two more guards enter, then more, navy and Oakleys

and truncheons all pushing past one another. He sees a gun.

"Where did you get those spex from? You know their use is prohibited in here. Where did you get them?"

Rush gibbers something.

"You'd better tell me quick, son." More guns appear.

"THE DESK! The des—the lady on the desk! She said I can use them! They're mine, but she said I could message my friend quick!" Despite the circumstances, he's suddenly horrified at how pathetic he sounds.

"Sandra? This true?" Voices shouting back into the beige.

"Huh?"

"You say this body could use his spex?"

"The English guy? Yeah, sure. He's fine."

A look of what Rush can only read as disappointment falls across the faces of everyone in the bathroom apart from him. Truncheons and guns go limp, shoulders relax. Muttering. Uniforms start to shuffle out the door.

"Sorry, man," says the guard. "Didn't mean to scare you."

Rush feels like he's going to pass out. Hands still on his head, he nods toward the spex on the floor.

"Oh yeah, sure. Just give 'em back to Sandra when you're done." He turns to leave. "Next time, do us all a favor? Go in the stall."

— — — —

Frank's cart is perfectly organized, and fuck you if you say otherwise.

He knows what's in every bag, and how many. One hundred cans in each. Got his Cokes separated out from his Pepsis, too, the beer bottles and the plastic bottles all separate, sorted by distributor. Used to be you could just bring them down here to Thrifty Redemption on McDonald and they'd sort them for you—they'd weigh them and then give you a price, and you'd just take that and go and that was it. Now it's all machines, and if you put the wrong can or bottle in the wrong machine then you don't get squat. The machines know, see. They can tell which distributor the can is from as soon as you drop it in that hole right there at the front. Put the wrong can in the wrong hole and you get nothing but that buzzing sound, and no way of getting your can back.

Which is why Frank likes to have his cart perfectly organized. All sorted before he turns up here. Too many canners don't know shit these days and just turn up with everything random, and that's why there's long-ass lines at Thrifty like there is today.

Frank's cart is big, too, one of those green Whole Foods ones, but with the electronics and the screens and all that shit ripped out. Got it fixed up so it don't know where it is anymore, so it can't whine to the cops about not being at Whole Foods. It's a good cart and he likes it, nice and big and the wheels ain't too lousy, tend to go where they're meant to be going, and the brake works still. He's got it piled up today, eight bags. Five stacked so high in the cart that he's gotta lean around to see where he's going, another three tied on to the sides. Eight bags with a hundred cans or bottles in each. Six cents per unit. Six bucks per bag. Forty-eight bucks in total. Not bad for a Tuesday.

He should be happy but now he's pissed because the line for the machines is too long, and it ain't moving. And it's hot. He's tried shouting up to the front of the line but it didn't achieve anything. Some sort of commotion up there. He's just going to have to go up there himself and sort it out.

So he pulls his cart out of the line and heaves it up there—no way he's leaving it behind so these cocksuckers can start going through his bags. He catches some shit as he pushes it up there for cutting the line, but he gives back as good as he gets, telling them to chill the fuck out. He'll get back to the end of the line, just as soon as he's figured out what's wrong. Chill the fuck out.

There's some kind of clusterfuck going down at the machines, though, when he gets there. Like four canners all shouting at one another. Couple of old Chinese broads, this black dude, and this other Mexican cat he knows called Max.

"What the fuck's the holdup?" he asks him.

"Machines are fucked, man," says Max.

"What you mean? Fucked how?"

"Fucked. Every can I put in, just get the buzzing." Max turns around and tries to calm down one of the Chinese ladies, who is losing her shit at him for holding everything up. Frank knows how she feels.

"Then you're putting them in the wrong machine."

"No, I'm fucking not, man," Max says. "Seriously. The machines are all fucked. You don't believe me, you try it, man."

So Frank pulls a Coke can out of the top bag on his cart, and heads over to the big gray plastic monolith of the Coke recycling machine. He's about to drop it in the hole on the front when the other Chinese woman starts shouting at him about cutting in, but he tells her to shut the fuck up and drops it in anyway.

The machine buzzes angrily. Text flashes across its front.

Can has already been deposited. No redemption.

Which doesn't make any sense.

"This don't make any sense," he says. He turns to Max. "It says the can was already deposited?"

"Yeah, that's what it said about all mine."

"Where they from?"

"Usual places. Prospect Park, Flatbush Ave."

"Street trash or residential?"

"Both."

"You talk to Al?" He nods over to the entrance of Thrifty.

"Al's not here. Talked to that kid of his. Says he don't know anything about the machines. Says the machines manage themselves, or something."

Frank stands there for maybe half a minute, thinking, while the others continue to squabble.

"You know what I think, Max?" he says, eventually.

"What?"

"I think these machines are fucked."

Scott's mouth tastes of stale coffee and mouthwash.

Rush doesn't want to imagine what his tastes like. It wasn't meant to be like this. After seven and a half hours on the plane he was meant to go into the bathroom to freshen up, brush his teeth, change his shirt. Get those nice Samsung spex out of his luggage. Instead he got thrown in a beige holding room for six hours. Now he looks and smells and feels like shit and just wants to go home.

But he's here. And he's real. And he's kissing him again.

They stop, pull apart, and nervously smile at each other.

"I look terrible, sorry."

Scott blushes. "You look fine. You look great."

It wasn't meant to be like this. For months Scott had been teasing him, talking about when they'd actually meet, talking about if he'd pass the "airport test." He was meant to be ready, prepared for it. At his best.

Scott kisses him again. Coffee and mouthwash. He never wants it to stop.

It does, eventually.

"So?"

"So?"

Scott seems slightly shorter than the mental image he's built from virt and social, slightly pinker. Less composed. Real.

"How did I do?"

Scott laughs, blushes again. "Flying colors."

They make out on the bus from Newark to Times Square. Scott wanted to get an Uber or a Google, but Rush wouldn't let him, partly on principle but mainly because it's too expensive. The bus takes way too long, but neither of them cares.

They make out in the Port Authority Bus Terminal, under AR billboards that try to steal their attention from each other, so they take off their spex, which were bumping when they kissed anyway.

They make out on the Times Square subway platform while waiting for the Q, Rush freaked out by the cockroaches that scuttle around their feet but fascinated by the people walking by. Scott says that before you come to New York all you know of it are movie stereotypes, then when you get here you realize they're all true. On the way into the station they'd had to hold hands as they passed through the turnstiles, Scott explaining it was so the city could see they're together, and charge him for Rush's fare. The idea made Rush uncomfortable, but holding his hand felt so right. He's made a career out of telling everyone that cities know too much, but right then he didn't care that this one knew they were together, or who it told.

They make out on the Q. It's packed with rush-hour

commuters, but Scott manages to move him over to the door so that when the train bursts out into daylight on the bridge he can see the view. As they skim across Chinatown's graffiti-spattered rooftops and the towers rise behind them Rush can't believe he is finally here. Nobody else on the train—even Scott after a while—seems to care, all lost in their tablets and spex, grasping a brief window of network access, gazing at their own private vistas. He notices Scott is wearing plastic gloves, must have slipped them on when he wasn't looking, and sees a few other people on the train are, too. He asks Scott about them.

"Anti-bac nanofiber. They're just to keep my hands clean down here. I won't touch anything down here. It's so fucking gross."

"Really? Didn't take you for a germophobe. Guess I'm learning something new about you every day."

Scott laughs. "I'm not a germophobe. It's just it's gross down here. Filthy. You don't know who has been touching what, where their hands have been before."

"Still sounds paranoid to me." He's teasing him.

"Maybe, maybe I am being paranoid. But trust me, I touch my face way too much. Don't want to transfer anything. You wouldn't want me spoiling this perfect complexion, now, would you?"

They make out in the diner, where Rush nibbles at some fries while Scott forces him to download the NYC app. Rush really doesn't want to, because it's the literal fucking antithesis of everything he is and does, and Scott says,

I know but it'll make getting around and buying stuff easier, and Rush says, I know, and that's the exact fucking
problem, and then Scott asks him if this is their first fight.
It's not.

They make love in Scott's bed, in the corner of his tiny
but neat studio, which he pays too much rent for, because
it's tucked away on the third floor of one of those beautiful
brownstones in Brooklyn that the female leads in rom-coms
can somehow always afford to have all to themselves, on
just their salary, despite the fact that they're social-media
marketers or virt designers or something else that involves
working in an office. Nobody, Scott tells him, that works
in an office can afford one of these whole buildings.

After they make love they hold each other, and Scott
starts to cry. Rush panics.

"What's wrong?"

"Nothing. Nothing at all."

"Then why are you crying?"

"Why do you think? Just because. You're here. You're
real."

Later on they head out to a party that Rush can't be bothered with. He's thirsty, still adjusting to the late-summer
heat, so he picks up a can of Coke from the corner bodega,
along with some cheap Peruvian beers for the party. Reluctantly he pays for it with the NYC app.

They walk. A few blocks later he drops the empty can

in a recycling bin, which chimes gently at him. His spex make a *kerrching* sound.

"What was that?"

"Huh?"

"The bin?"

"'Bin'? Oh, the trash! You just got your six cents." Scott smiles.

"Six cents?"

"Your deposit for recycling the can. Buy something with the NYC app and then when you toss it in the recycling here or at home you get your deposit. It's pretty neat."

"It—what? How long has this been going on?"

"It's pretty new, actually. Been running in some neighborhoods for a while but only got turned on in Brooklyn last week."

"The city does this? They basically track every can of drink in the city?"

"I guess. They got some tiny chip in the cans now. I think the city did it in partnership with the drink companies. And Google."

Rush is kind of stunned, in that resigned-stunned way only professional cynics can be. "So . . . let me get this straight. The city—and Coke and all these companies, and Google—know every time I buy a can of pop, and where from, and every time I toss it away, and where? They basically know every time I have a drink, and where I am? For which they pay me six cents?"

"I guess so, if you look at it that way."

"That doesn't bother you?"

"Not really, I think it's kinda neat. It's not just them, you can see all of it, too. The NYC app lets you sync it with your health app stats. It's great for watching your calories, you know?"

"Jesus wept."

"Plus last week, there was a story on *Gothamist* where they said the police had arrested this guy because they used the trash can data to prove he was lying about where he was the night this girl got attacked."

"The police have access to it too? Of course they do. Perfect."

"Jesus, Rush, you do worry. Too much." Scott grabs his hand and pulls him along. "C'mon, we'll be late."

Every time Frank pulls something out of this trash can it buzzes angrily at him, the same buzz the machines at Thrifty do when you put in the wrong can. It doesn't make any sense, and it's pissing him off.

It's hot on Vanderbilt, and he can feel himself sweating under his beanie. He could do with a drink. A beer would be nice. But he's broke, got no money because the machines at Thrifty are still on the fritz. Same with the ones down at Cash 4 Cans on Linden. They're all fucked. For three days now. Al came back to Thrifty, tried giving them all some bullshit excuse that nobody understands about how the machines are changing, how it was all changing from this to that, and with the networks and everything, and how things are smart now, and how now you could only get shit redeemed if you bought it yourself. Which doesn't make any sense to Frank, and is pissing him off.

His cart is overfilled, more bags than he's ever shifted at once. At least 160 bucks in there. It's getting hard to push around, tricky to see where he's going. Not that he minds, but others seem to get pissed with him easily when they're standing in his way.

He's just pulling a plastic Sprite bottle out of the buzzing can when who should show up but Max, pushing an empty cart. Empty!

"Hey, Max, your cart is empty!"

"Yeah, man, just emptied it." Max looks happy. "Gonna go eat, man, get some food, ya hear me?"

"The machines working at Thrifty again?"

"Nah, man. Not Thrifty. Not Brooklyn. Everything in Brooklyn is fucked, man. None the machines in Brooklyn working."

"Then where'd you take 'em, man?"

"Chinatown."

Frank's heart drops. "Chinatown, Manhattan?"

"Yeah, man, Chinatown, Manhattan. You know that place, just off Canal. You know that old place, man. Just over the bridge."

"Yeah, I know that place. Fuck. The machines working there?"

"Yeah, man, the machines are working there just fine.

Just like normal. Someone said they ain't been updated yet or something? I dunno. But whatever's made the machines in Brooklyn all fucked, it ain't happened there yet, man."

"Okay. Well. I guess I'm going to Chinatown tomorrow, then." The place will be closed by the time he'd get there tonight, he'll just have to talk nicely to the super in his building again, hope he lets him keep the cart in his lockup for one more night. He can't keep it in his apartment when it's full like this, it makes all the roaches come out. And then his sister and her kids start fucking going off. Like they don't go off enough already as it is. It pisses him off when they're always going off. Plus they're just looking for another reason to kick him out on the street again.

"Okay, then. Chinatown, Manhattan. Tomorrow." Frank sighs loudly. "I fucking hate Manhattan."

Everyone at the party, apart from Rush, obviously, is super fucking white. That kind of Brooklyn white that he can't really understand, where white people openly talk about their white things—their yoga and taxidermy classes, or growing organic cilantro (which he thinks is the same thing as coriander?) and how hard it is being a journalist because you're expected to have thoughts and feelings on everything and that can just get to be too much sometimes, you know?—without any kind of apparent shame at all.

Their host is cosplaying as an 1890s London sex worker, and Rush can't decide whether she thinks it's funny, edgy, ironic, or all three. After a painful ten minutes talking with her he decides she probably hasn't thought about it much at all, as on hearing his accent she launches into detailing her love for Empire-era "England," despite him mentioning his Pakistani heritage at least twice.

Her apartment is full of shit. Mason jars and antique trinkets, perfume bottles and too many candleholders, like flea market trash excavated from a dead civilization's landfill. What really creeps him out are the stuffed animals that inhabit the walls and shelves like cursed ghouls: twisted ravens and squirrels in top hats; dead cats with glass eyes sipping tea in waistcoats; a huge, once-elegant Komodo dragon reduced to a petrified, defeated corpse. It makes Rush's skin crawl, this twee, whimsical celebration of death, like the ultimate flaunting of privilege for those to whom it is never more than a distant concern.

It baffles him, what brings these people to live in New York—a city filled with every culture, with every nation, a massive machine built from people and architecture, that gives birth to new cultures, new conflicts on every street corner, a city that every day fights with the future—what brings them here just to bed down in Brooklyn and create enclaves where they fetishize someone else's past? To lock themselves away and surround themselves with their own kind? What brings them to cities at all, only to seemingly reject the exhilaration and machine chaos of urban life completely, obsessing instead over the faux authenticities of the organic and the artisanal? Wouldn't they be better in the country, out in the wilds and swamps of the south, where they could kill and stuff whatever they like, and mount it on their walls, while they fixate over their home-made preserves and cross-stitch cushions, like some kind of post-Tumblr Amish sect?

Rush doesn't get answers to any of this, because he's too cowardly to bring it up in person. Instead he makes quiet small talk with some guy named Steve, who is apparently one of the east coast's leading puppeteers.

"This your first time in New York?"

"Yeah. First time in the U.S., in fact."

"Nice. How you finding it?"

"Oh, I love it, it's great. So much energy. The architecture is just fantastic. Manhattan is beautiful."

"Yes. Yes, I guess it is. You stop noticing it after a while." Steve sips his wine delicately. Rush can't decide how old he is; he could be fifty as easily as he could be thirty-five. Something artificial, sculpted about his appearance. "Where are you staying?"

"Park Slope."

"Ah, of course—with Scott, right? Nice neighborhood."

"Yeah . . . yeah. It is. It's . . . kind of fancy. Not exactly the Brooklyn I was expecting."

Steve looks puzzled. "I'm not sure I follow?"

"Well . . . I was saying to Scott, if I wanted to be surrounded by obnoxious white people I'd have stayed in England."

Steve looks even more puzzled.

"I'm kidding," Rush says.

Steve laughs politely, followed by an awkward pause. "This is your first time meeting Scott?"

"IRL? Yeah. Yeah, it is."

"Excellent. You make a cute couple. How long have you been together online?"

"About four months now."

"Oh, not long at all. Me and my wife remote-dated for nearly a year before we met."

"Oh, really?" Rush feigns interest, it's hardly unusual these days. It felt like most of his friends had remote-dated for at least six months before meeting. It was appallingly on trend. "Is she here tonight?"

"Huh? Ah, no. At home, looking after the kids."

"Ah."

"How long are you here for?"

"Just a week this time, sadly. I'm very tied up with a big project at home, means I can't stay away for long."

"That's a shame. It'll be tough going back. It always is after the first meeting, if it's gone well."

Rush looked across the room, to where Scott was laughing with a small group, unrestrained and unbridled by anger and cynicism. "Yeah. Yeah, it'll be tough."

On entering, all the guests had to put their spex in a bowl in the kitchen, which of course is an upturned jaguar skull. Rush is hovering around it, trying to resist pulling his out and venting, when this guy appears next to him. Slightly nerdier than everyone else at the party, awkward but with that sheen of smart-kid arrogance that makes Rush's skin crawl even more than decorating your home with dead squirrels.

"You're Rushdi Manaan, right?"

"Yeah. Sorry, have we met?"

"No, but I'm very familiar with your work." He extends a hand. "Chris Mattis. I write for *VICE*."

"Ah." Shit.

"I heard you had a little trouble getting into the country this week?"

"Not a big one for small talk, huh, Chris?"

Chris smiles. "Pretty brave of you really, coming here."

"To Crown Heights? Seems like a nice neighborhood."

"You know what I mean."

"Actually, no, Chris. Not sure I do."

"Well, I'd have thought you'd be pretty high up Homeland Security's stop lists, what with the Republic being attached to that Boeing e-mail leak last month. Rush-zero-zero, the legendary smart city hacker. And that's without even taking into account how often your name has personally been attached to all those high-level Anon and Dronegods ops."

It was the first time anyone had mentioned the Republic to him in days. "You shouldn't believe everything you read on the Internet, Chris. In fact, I hear some of the people that write for the Internet are completely full of shit."

"You've got joint nationality, right? Joint British-Pakistani? That's pretty brave in itself, leaving the country when the U.K. government is canceling British passports for joint-national activists left, right, and center."

"Well, I like to live life on the edge. I feed off the danger and excitement." Rush takes an exaggeratedly deep breath. "It keeps me alive."

Someone walks into the party wearing a Marie Antoinette wig and carrying a cake.

Chris smiles again. "It really must. I'd love to sit down with you while you're here, chat some things over with you."

"Yeah. I bet you would. But this, right now, here at this party, this is off-the-record, right?"

"Of course, completely off-the-record."

"Okay. Great. Just so that's cleared up. Seeing as we're off-the-record, can I tell you something quick now?"

"Sure."

"Thanks. Thanks, Chris, I appreciate the chance to talk to you off-the-record, to let me give you my honest yet unquotable opinion on something."

"Of course."

"Thanks, thanks again. Off-the-record: I think you're an insufferable little shit."

Rush finishes his beer and drops the empty bottle into

the kitchen's recycling bin. It chimes and the city pays him six cents.

Frank fucking hates cops.

Now he's got two of them busting his balls, 'cause he pushed the cart through the emergency exit at Seventh Avenue and all the fucking alarms went off. Like they always do. Just happened to be these two fucking cops standing around playing with their balls this time.

What the fuck else was he supposed to do? Can't get a cart through a turnstile. Won't fucking fit. Gotta go through the emergency exit. That's what it's there for. So that's what he did. Problem now is that his cart is on one side of the barrier, and he's on the other. And there's two fucking cops and the closed exit between them.

"C'mon, officer—"

"You got money, go through the turnstile," says fucking cop A.

"But that's my cart, officer. That's my cans."

"No, they ain't," says fucking cop B, squinting at the cart through his fancy sunglasses. "Those cans don't belong to you. They've all been redeemed already."

"What you talking about? They're my cans! Of course they're my cans. I collected them."

"Sorry, old man," says fucking cop A, "these cans are already in the system as deposited. They ain't worth shit to you now. They're just trash."

"I just notified MTA Cleaning and Removal," says fucking cop B. "They'll have a unit down here in eight minutes to take it away."

Frank panics. "No! NO! NO! Fuck you! Nobody's taking my cans! They're my fucking—"

"Okay, okay, calm down, I SAID, CALM DOWN." Fucking cop A puts a hand on Frank's chest. "You want your cans, even though technically they ain't your cans anymore, you go through the turnstile and get them. But from what I can see you ain't got no subway credit, so unless you got cash to get back there and get a single-fare ticket, you ain't getting your cans back."

"Cleaning and Removal Unit ETA: seven minutes," says fucking cop B.

Frank stares through the scuffed mesh of the emergency exit at his cart. It's there, just there. Nearly two hundred bucks' worth of cans. His cans. His eyes start to fill with tears.

Fucking cops.

Scott had jokingly told him not to get into trouble, it being his first day out in the big city on his own. He'd laughed. What did Scott think was going to happen?

Now he's got some homeless-looking guy all up in his face pleading with him, while these two pissed-off-looking cops are eyeballing him from a few feet away.

"Please, man!" The homeless guy seems frantic. "Please!

You gotta help me, I just gotta get through the turnstile, that's all! They got my cans through there. Look! That's my cart!"

He's pointing at this big shopping trolley on the other side of the barrier, full of what looks like trash. Rush is having trouble keeping his eyes off the cops, though. He knows they're watching him, both with their own eyes and those they wear for the city. He knows how quickly they could know exactly who he is, how little effort it would take them. Literally just the blink of an eye.

"I'm sorry, I got no cash . . ."

"Don't want cash, just get me through the turnstile!"

"But—"

"Just hold my hand! C'mon, man! I gotta be quick, they gonna take my cans away in a few minutes!"

The homeless guy runs over to the turnstile, looks back at him, sad puppy eyes full of tears, holds out his hand. Black fingernails and peeling gray Band-Aids. "Please! Just hold my hand!"

Rush looks at him, glances over at the cops, one of whom still seems to be watching him.

"For fuck's sake," he whispers under his breath.

He walks over to the frantic guy, takes his hand. It's warm, clammy, rough with cuts and calluses, sticky with trash residue.

He thinks back to the guy with the robot hand and no fingerprints, Scott's little anti-bac gloves, cockroaches at Times Square.

They cross through the turnstiles together, hand in hand, like lost children. The city knows they're together, and it gently chimes its awareness in Rush's ear, flashing a double fare deduction across his spex.

The guy sprints ahead of him, gets to his shopping cart, starts fussing around it, checking it's all there. Rush ends up helping him down the stairs to the platform with it—nearly dying twice—and onto a Q heading into Manhattan.

"What you got in this thing, man?"

"Cans," the old guy says. He must be in his late forties at least, Rush guesses. "Mostly. Bottles as well. Both plastic and glass. Gotta take 'em to fucking Chinatown to be recycled."

"Really? You can't do that in Brooklyn?"

"Nah, all the machines are fucked in Brooklyn."

"Machines?"

"Yeah. The depositing machines. They all fucked. Take your cans but don't give you the money back. They're fucked."

Rush looks at him, looks at the cart. Blinking through menus in his periphery, he pulls up a home-brewed RFID-reading tool. Suddenly the cart is covered in hundreds of little labels, tiny floating tags, one for each can and bottle. Each has two numbers, twelve digits long, that he can't understand but knows the city can. He guesses the first one is written on the can's chip when it's bought, the second when it's tossed. Cross-reference those with the city's database of NYC app users and bingo, instant tracking of every can bought from shop to being recycled. It's elegantly simple, he has to agree, but hardly secure. The potential for abuse is huge.

"Hey, you know these cans can't be recycled, right? What I mean is they won't give you money for them. They've all already been deposited."

The homeless guy shakes his head at him. "That's what everybody keeps saying, but they wrong. They fucking wrong. These are my cans. I found 'em. I dug them outta the trash. I been doing this for fifteen years now, collecting cans, and I've never heard of this 'they ain't your cans' bullshit. These are my cans."

"Fifteen years?"

"Yes, sir. Been a canner for fifteen years now."

"That's how you make money? I mean your only way?"

"It is right now, yes, sir. Canning is my job. Full-time."

"There a lot of people doing it? There a lot of canners out there?"

"Hell yeah, there's hundreds of us. Thousands, maybe. City is full of 'em. Used to be a lot of people did it as a part-time thing, but more and more are going full-time, it seems. Especially since there's no work for cabbies now, y'know? I used to know a lot of cabbies that would just do a little canning on the side when work was slow and all, but now they gotta go full-time, they says. Say nobody wants anyone to drive a cab anymore. I ain't worried, though."

"You ain't worried?"

"Nah, man, I ain't worried. About the competition, I

mean. I'm good. Best canner there is, no shit. Because I'm organized, understand? I'm organized. My whole cart is organized. I know where everything is in there, and how many there is of it. And fuck anyone that says otherwise. Plus there's enough cans to go around."

"Yeah?"

"Hell yeah! Canning is a growth industry. I been doing this fifteen years, and every year I seen more cans than before. There's always going to be canning, as long as there's people that want to drink. They'll never stop that. Never take that away from me. They might not need cab drivers anymore, but they'll always need canners." He smiles, for the first time.

Rush isn't sure what to say to him. He sighs and looks at the cart, and the hundreds of floating tags reappear. His heart sinks.

He knows he shouldn't get involved, not here and now, but he can't help it.

He rummages in his bag, pulls out a small wand-like thing, something he'd wired together himself from cheap Chinese-made components and duct tape. He pairs it with his spex. As discretely as possible he waves it slowly over the cart.

"Hey, man, what the fuck you doing?"

"Shhh, be quiet a sec."

The first exploit he tries fails, but to his amusement the second one works straightaway. He tries not to laugh to himself. He passes the wand over the cart again. As he does

so the labels change color, emptying themselves of numbers, resetting to their default, untagged state.

"There you go, man. Sorted. They should all work now
when you take them in."

"The cans?" The guy doesn't look like he understands
what Rush is saying.

"Yeah, the cans. I reset them all. They'll work now.
They're yours."

"Yeah, okay." The guy looks at him like he's mad, talks
to him like he's a child. "Thanks, man, thanks for that."

The next stop is Canal, and Rush helps the guy get his
cart off the train before jumping back on. He waves at him,
smiling, as the doors close. The guy waves back, shaking
his head like he still thinks Rush is crazy.

Rush laughs to himself, smiles, and steadies himself
against the lurch of the train as it pulls away by grasping a
nearby pole with his unprotected, naked hand.

Frank gets to the recycling place just as they're
loading the last of the machines onto the back of the truck.

"What the fuck are you doing? Where you going with
the machines?"

One of the laborers, some Mexican-looking guy, turns
to face him. "No more machines, old man. They out of
service now."

"Out of service? Here, too? When you bringing them
back?"

"Never. We ain't never bringing them back. That's it, man. New system, no need for these old machines. They redundant."

"But I just brought these all the way over from Brooklyn . . . How am I going to get my money for them? I need some cash! There's like two hundred bucks here!"

"No cash," the guy says, as he jumps up onto the truck's front platform, where its cab should be. "No cash for recycling, just credit. You gotta get the app now."

"This doesn't make any fucking sense," says Frank.

"You gotta keep up, man, gotta get smart," the guy shouts down from the truck as it starts to drive itself away. "The city is changing."

Frank watches the truck roll past him, watches it pull out onto Canal Street. Looks over at his cart. He walks over to it and starts to push it away.

"Fuck you," he says, to anyone that can hear. "Fuck you and your changing city."

3. AFTER

This guy comes and sits next to her, the feet of the plastic chair squealing against the floor as he pulls it out from under the table. She'd mentally tagged him a couple of times already, as she'd scanned the crowd in the café, his eyes fixed on hers, his gaze never backing down when she met it.

Now he's leaning in, as if he knows her, with some unjustified familiarity, uninvited intimacy. Rotten-egg breath and matted beard hair barely hiding inflamed, peeling skin.

"You getting weird looks, girl?" he says.

"Only from you." She fixes him with a stare, and again

his gaze stays firm, unwavering. A half smile breaks out across his face as he studies her.

"You think you can walk around a place like this without being recognized? You're the buzz of the services. Everyone's talking about you."

She breaks his gaze, scans the café again. Here and there a pair of eyes catch hers, but unlike his they look away the instant she meets them. Disheveled figures hunched over Formica tables. Ripped coats bleeding filling from elbows, cloaks improvised from stained blankets. This used to be a Costa Coffee, she remembers. She stares at the repeating coffee bean motif engraved in the walls, like ancient hieroglyphs that get harder to decipher as time passes. There are kids alive today that have never seen a coffee bean, she thinks, probably never will.

Magor Services. They used to stop here on trips into Wales, when Claire would force them to take a break from the city for a few days. Flash back to cappuccinos and Kit-Kats, panini and impossibly pure water wrapped in plastic bottles. Rush and College leaning over laptops, unable to let go. There used to be a McDonald's here, too, she thinks. Maybe a KFC. Some noodle place. A WHSmith selling print magazines that she never saw anybody buy. Back then this place had a purpose, a little node of brands and consumption for when travelers on the M4 needed a break, back when the supply chains still flowed and before the motorways were deserted.

She turns back to the guy. "I think you've got the wrong person."

"Have I?" He reaches into a pocket, retrieves a ball of paper. Unravels it, places it in front of her, attempts to flatten it out with mud-stained fingers. A badly photocopied face stares back at her, smeared and stretched out of proportion, but still too familiar.

"They're everywhere," he says. "All over the place. Every wall between here and the border. It's a wonder the LA's got that much ink and paper. And they're using so much of it on your face. They must really want to find you."

The face is young, and she had shorter hair then. It's a head shot rather than a mug shot, posed rather than forced; staring off into the distance, into some lost future, rather than directly into the camera. It used to be her, that image. Her on social media, her on artist profiles, her in high-end print magazines that she never saw anybody buy. She wonders where they found it.

WANTED, the text above the image reads. Below it, ANIKA BERNHARDT. WANTED FOR TERRORISM AND CRIMES AGAINST THE COALITION. CASH AND RATIONS REWARD FOR ANY INFORMATION LEADING TO HER ARREST.

She sighs, choking back panic. Takes a breath. Picks up the chipped mug of lukewarm mint tea and downs the dregs. Pushes the sheet of paper back across the table to the guy.

"I think you've got the wrong person," she repeats. She stands up to leave.

He shoots a hand up, grabs her arm just below the elbow. Holds it, too tight.

"Get your fucking hands off me," she tells him, calmly.

"I just thought you'd want to know, LA patrol just turned up. Parked up out on the slip road there. Only one guy got out and he headed straight in here. Probably a piss break."

She looks out of the café's grease-smeared windows, squinting. She can just make it out. Land Rover, camouflage colors.

"When?"

"Just a few minutes ago." He lets go of her arm. "Just before I came over. Maybe he left already. Just be careful. The people here, you might be a hero to them, but they're hungry. They've got family to feed."

She nods at him, grabs her bag from the floor, pulls her hood up, and leaves.

Head down, hood up. Weaving through bodies.

Out of the café.

Into the corridor.

And straight into the Land Army trooper.

They pass each other silently, in slow motion.

He's young, they always are.

His eyes are brown, tired. They meet hers for a second as they pass. Some flicker across his face. Maybe recognition. Maybe disgust. Maybe fear.

But he keeps on walking.

So does she, until she reaches the doors, where she pauses. Staring out across the chaos of the car park, toward the green-and-brown Land Rover.

He could be on his radio right now. Calling in the sighting. Or maybe he'll piss first. Or get tea. Either way, once he tells them, the whole forecourt will be crawling with troopers before she can get out of here.

Or maybe he won't do anything. Maybe he didn't recognize her. Maybe he doesn't care. Maybe he just wants to piss and get tea and get home, no hassles.

Maybe.

She pauses. Thinks. Tries not to panic.

Reaches out a hand to push open the heavy glass doors.

Freezes, pulls it back.

Turns on her heel and heads back into the crowds.

The men's toilet stinks of piss and shit, like it's not been cleaned in three years.

Half a dozen faces turn to meet her, startled to see a woman in here.

Before anyone can speak, she puts a finger to her lips, mouths Everybody out.

Taps are turned, dicks are zipped away. The men start to shuffle out past her, except for one. He pauses, looks her in the eye. Turns and points at an occupied cubicle.

She nods back at him and he leaves. As he passes he

whispers to her: I'll make sure you're not bothered, as long as I can.

She nods at him again. Doesn't move until the door closes behind him.

Silently she repeats the mantra in her head, as she quietly stalks the line of cubicles, checking for feet under doors.

She closes her eyes briefly, slows her breathing, recalls the Bloc mantra.

With zero bandwidth there is no calling for backup.

With zero bandwidth the advantage is ours.

With zero bandwidth there is no many.

With zero bandwidth there is no legion.

With zero bandwidth we are singular.

With zero bandwidth there is no time to hesitate.

With zero bandwidth there is only opportunity.

With zero bandwidth opportunity is our only weapon.

Nothing, nothing until she reaches the stall the guy had pointed out. Two black boots, scuffed and split. Camouflage fatigues pulled down around ankles.

With zero bandwidth there is only opportunity.

With zero bandwidth opportunity is our only weapon.

As quietly as she can, she slips into the adjacent stall, closes the door. Drops her bag on the filth-stained floor. One foot up on the toilet as she gently pushes herself up, so she's peering over the flimsy hardboard divider.

He's young, they always are. But he looks even younger from this angle, looking down on him shitting, vulnerable, like a kid on a potty. He's reading a book, she can't see what it is. Some disintegrating paperback, loose pages sticking out at wrong angles. There's no gun, that she can see. He probably left it back in the jeep. There's no radio that she can see, either. And if there is, he's not using it to call her in. No guns, no radio, just some kid, maybe seventeen years old, trying to get some time for himself, trying to escape in a book, trying to take a shit.

And then he looks up.

"What the fu—"

And she drops on him, her boot hitting his face with enough force that she's pretty sure the crack she hears is his jaw breaking.

She lands better than she hoped, steadying herself against the wobbling stall wall.

To her surprise and his credit, the kid tries to get up. She breaks his nose with her palm getting him to sit back down.

Time to finish this. She glances around, looking for her bag. Not here. In the cubicle next door. Fuck.

The kid has clearly got some spirit. Or, more likely, he knows what's meant to be coming and is shit-scared, because he tries to get up again. This time he throws himself at her, wrapping his arms around her waist and sticking his head into her stomach, like some angry rugby tackle. Anika doesn't see it coming at all, and it's enough to wind her, pushing her back hard against the closed cubicle door. She grabs him by the hair and pulls him off her, kicking him in the chest to put him down, before dropping to the floor, grabbing him by the hair again, and smashing his head into the toilet bowl.

Once.

Twice.

Maybe four times.

She stops. There's not much left of his face, or the toilet bowl, and for long seconds she's dazed, looking at the mess, trying to work out what's blood and what's shitty water, what's porcelain fragments and what's teeth.

Then she snaps out of it, gets moving. Tries to open the door but she can't because his foot is jammed against it. His boots look relatively new, like maybe just ten years old. Maybe she should take them? It'd be a good motive, too. She's seen people beaten to death for less than a pair of boots. Far less.

No fucking time, Anika, snap out of it. She forgets the door, pushes herself up off the cistern, drops down into the next stall. Grabs her bag off the floor and pukes in the toilet. Brown liquid, stringy spit, and the taste of overstewed mint-and-nettle tea. She realizes she's sobbing.

Out in the corridor the guy is still keeping watch. They nod at each other silently and she leaves, bursting out into the daylight of the car park from a side exit. Head down, hood up.

The forecourt is like a shanty town, stalls and tents, tarpaulins draped between dead cars to provide shelter. She can smell food cooking and she thinks she might puke again. Music coming from somewhere, breakbeats and bass hits. Some woman ranting to anyone that will listen about how the air is cleaner now, since the crash, clean of Wi-Fi and cell signals. It's safe to breathe again, she says, embrace the clean air, fill your lungs. Anika wonders how long she's been here, how long any of these people have, if any of them were here when it happened, stranded when their phones died and their cars stopped driving themselves, and that's why they stayed, stranded on this concrete island.

No time to ask. Head down, hood up. She's past the shantytown and into the larger car park, walking the aisles and scanning license plate numbers looking for the one she's memorized, trying to stay calm.

Her hand is in her bag, holding the grip. Any second now, she thinks. Any second now they'll find the body, and then there'll be shouts and screams and running and gunfire and—

This is it. White Ford Transit van. Ancient, pre-automation. Matching registration number. Some guy leaning into the open hood, tweaking the engine, his face hidden. Oh, please fucking god, tell me it fucking works.

"Neal?"

He looks up, narrowly missing banging his head, turns to face her. White, old but fresh faced. A little too friendly, somehow.

"Anika? Ah, you made it." He extends a hand stained with motor grease, and before thinking she meets it with one smeared in blood. She catches him nervously glancing at it.

"Does it work?" is all she can say.

"Huh?"

"The van. The engine? Does it work?"

Neal laughs, glances over his shoulder. "Oh yeah, she works. I mean, she's a bit temperamental and—"

"We need to go. Now."

"Oh, okay, well, I—"

"Now. We need to go now." She gestures out toward the motorway. "There's an LA jeep parked up there. Did you see it on your way in?"

"Yeah, I think so—"

"Well, if they see me, they'll kill me. And then they'll kill you."

Neal sighs, the friendliness fading from his face. "Right. Okay. Shit. Dave said this would be fun."

"Dave paid you already, right?"

"Yeah."

"Then we go. Right fucking now."

He closes the hood, wipes his oily hands on a rag, and opens the passenger door for her. Yellow foam spilling from split, fake leather seats. The faint smell of mold.

"After you," he says.

▬ ▬ ▬ ▬

A few minutes later, after Neal coaxes the van into life, they're slipping out of the car park, onto the access road to the motorway. Right past where the LA jeep is parked.

"I'm sorry, no other way out," Neal says through gritted teeth.

"It's fine." She sinks down into her seat, pulls her hoodie up as much as she can. "Just, y'know, let's not hang around."

As he pulls the van onto the motorway she glances out at the parked patrol. The guy back in the café was right, it's a Land Rover, but it's not army issue. It looks like a farmer's old jeep that's been badly sprayed forest camouflage colors. Land Army stencils on the side. Towheaded kids, no older than the one bleeding out in the toilets, smoking a joint, laughing, cradling assault rifles. It suddenly all looks like a joke to her, like apart from the guns it's nothing more frightening than some out-of-their-depth kids. It reminds her of being told, back at the camp, that it's all the Land Army is: bored farmers and starving country kids, trying to stay alive and playing army. Kids angry at the cities, blaming the cities for everything, for all that went wrong.

Maybe they're right, she thinks.

But then all she can see is the labor camps, the starving children being dragged from their homes by LA troopers, the fields of crops being burned just to prove a point.

And then they're away, past the patrol, out on the M4. Heading east.

She lets herself relax, just slightly. Neal chuckles next to her, shakes his head.

"I tell you what, girl, I hope it's worth it."

"What?"

"Whatever you're going to Bristol for. I hope it's worth all this shit."

"Yeah," she says. "Yeah. So do I."

4. BEFORE

Dumb City: The Neighbourhood That Logged Off
7 July 2021
Neeta Singh
BBC News magazine

In a hip neighbourhood in Bristol, a controversial group of anarchists are rebelling against the smart city by blocking out the internet. Neeta Singh visits the People's Republic of Stokes Croft to find out what life off-grid looks like in the centre of one of the UK's most connected cities.

The whole world around me is cycling with colours—every building down this busy Bristol street is covered with

animated patterns: flocks of birds scroll across their surfaces; intricate, alien-looking plants burst forth from the
architecture; and stylised faces look down on me with cool
disdain. And I can't share or tell anyone about it: my
timelines aren't working. I can't connect to Facebook, Twitter, Instagram, or even my Gmail. In fact, I can't connect to
the internet at all. I can't even send a text message or
make a voice call. My spex have been completely hijacked
by secret, almost mystical, technologies hidden in the
buildings around me, and I've no choice but to try and enjoy
the ride.

Welcome to the People's Republic of Stokes Croft, a two-
mile-long digital no-man's-land right in the centre of Bristol,
one of the UK's leading smart cities. Part hippyster commune, part permanent art installation, and part political
protest, the Croft (as the locals call it) claims to be a refuge
from the physical and digital surveillance we associate with
everyday life both in major cities and online.

"Your first reaction might be 'oh god, I can't connect to
anything,' but the reality is that *you've* actually disappeared,"
explains Rushdi Manaan, anti-surveillance activist and the
PRSC's most infamous founder. "When you step into the
Croft here you vanish not just from the internet, but also from
the cameras and sensors that now watch us everywhere
else we go in the city. Your spex and your phone might not
be able to access the usual networks and services you use,
but that means they can't find you, either—they can't track
what you're doing, can't record your every movement—both

in the real world and on the internet. Only here can you be truly sure of some privacy."

If Manaan's name sounds familiar, it's because it's been associated with controversy for years. The academic researcher turned activist has evaded being sent to prison on two occasions, when his name was allegedly tied to high-level hacks and email leaks at Apple and Uber. He's been accused of being amongst the highest ranks of hacktivist groups such as Anonymous, Dronegod$, and BaeSec—which he strongly denies—and flirted with legal issues again a few years ago when he posted a series of tutorials online that explained how to create DIY tools for hacking and spoofing common smart-city monitoring systems. With the PRSC, though, he may have created his most controversial and rebellious project yet—an entire neighbourhood that rejects the digital status quo of surveillance, the internet, and big data.

"Everywhere you go, even in your own home, you're not only being watched by cameras, but you're generating data," Manaan tells me. "We've reached a point, in cities like Bristol, where we're in a state of total surveillance. Where every square inch of the built environment has been mapped, is being watched. And I don't mean just by cameras, the city is also covered in sensors—from LIDAR through to embedded microphones and pressure pads under the pavements that can measure how many people have walked past.

"And all that's before we start to even include what we do online, how big data companies like Google or Facebook track us across the internet, from site to site and service to service. Everything we do creates data that these companies monitor and collect, and use to track us and to try to predict what we do."

This is nothing new, I suggest.

"No, of course not, it's been this way for at least two decades. But in the last few years those two areas of surveillance—online and off—have merged in ways we couldn't even have imagined ten years ago." He points at my spex. "We're all carrying—wearing, even—hugely powerful devices that create and gather data simultaneously about our physical and digital activities. It's increasingly hard to separate the two. What we're trying to do here is to create a space where people can escape from all that."

I ask him whether he isn't painting a rather dystopian picture—it's not as though all this monitoring and data collection is being done by one Big Brother–style organization. And isn't most of it done for our benefit and convenience, to improve the quality of our lives?

He laughs. "Well, that's a moot point. Do you know who is tracking you online, when you are looking at your timelines, shopping, walking down the street? I mean, you can guess—it might be Google or Twitter or Amazon or whoever—but do you know what they do with that data? Who they sell it to? Who they let have access? What it's used for? Also, we've known for over ten years now—since Snowden—that many of these companies are actually sharing that data with governments, and that organizations like

GCHQ and the NSA have ways of compiling and mining it to create scarily comprehensive ways of watching every aspect of our lives.

"As for the convenience thing—well, that's a matter of opinion. Sure, the city or the internet knowing what we're doing, or predicting what we want, might make our everyday life seem easier, but at what cost? How much control are we actually giving up? How much are our lives and habits being shaped by these conveniences, by letting these networks and the algorithms that control them make decisions for us? Are they really convenient for us, or for the networks? Again it's an issue of transparency—we can't really see what is going on, so how can we know the decisions are being made for our benefit? How can we argue with them, question them? We're constantly told that the internet is freeing and democratising, but all these decisions are being made from the top down—from big companies, big data, and big government. That's what the Croft is about—showing that there's an alternative."

And that's the other part of what the People's Republic of Stokes Croft is about—it doesn't just kill your access to the internet and other networks, it also provides you with an alternative. When I first crossed into the Croft's supposedly designated area (more on this later), not only did all my internet, wifi, and cellular data die—but I also received a message asking me to install a special app. With some slight unease I agreed, and my spex went into what Manaan calls "big data hibernation mode"—all its other apps, as well as a large chunk of its OS, are frozen. "It's necessary to do this because it's not just apps and websites that constantly collect data, but your spex's OS itself is constantly monitoring everything and reporting back when it can," he explains. "Even cutting it off from the net isn't enough to stop it—we had to find a way to stop it watching altogether, otherwise as soon as you leave here and reconnect it just reports back everything you did while you were here."

With my spex under the control of Manaan's app—called Flex—I was instantly connected to another network. The Flex network appears like normal wifi access at first, but it's radically different: for a start it has no connections to the internet at all. "This is a MESH network, it's completely decentralised. Instead of connecting to a router or a central server to access it, you connect directly to other Flex users over Bluetooth, and through them to everybody else on the network. It's very localised—in order to connect you have to be within fifty or so meters of someone else that's connected. But if you are then you can potentially reach everyone else in the network. So even though it's hyperlocal there's no limit to how many people can join, or how big the network can grow—this is networking on a community scale."

For Manaan this kind of networking is a viable alternative to the corporate-dominated, top-down network model of the internet. As such it provides a lot of familiar services and applications—messaging, a Twitter-style social networking timeline, forums, wikis, voice, video and avatar-based calls, and file sharing. Again this is all decentralised. "There are no servers here, no data centres or cloud storage. The file-sharing system is pretty sophisticated but very easy to use—you can share pretty much anything, from web pages to streaming video and full VR environments, but it has to be stored locally on your spex or another device running Flex. We just set this up and let users do what they want with it. We've spontaneously ended up with dozens of photo-sharing groups, radio stations, and mixed-reality gaming campaigns. And it's all come from within the community."

Despite Manaan's claims of transparency, he's surprisingly cagey about how the technology that keeps the Croft running actually works. "I can't talk about it too much right now, because we've got security concerns of our own, but we have a set geographical boundary in the neighbourhood, and within that we use certain frequency-jamming technologies to block all conventional wifi and cellular signals. The Flex network actually runs across direct Bluetooth 4.0 connections between spex, so we don't jam that frequency, obviously."

Beyond this, Manaan doesn't want to reveal much more about the nuts and bolts of how the Croft's "digital boundary" works, not just because of his security fears, but also because of possible legal ramifications. "At first glance it probably uses the same jamming technologies employed by law enforcement agencies in the Middle East and some parts of the US," Dr Erin Pletz of Bristol University tells me.

"These are usually mounted on jeeps or riot vans, and are activated at scenes of civil unrest in order to stop protesters communicating with each other over social media, etc. While it's thought the British police has trialled these systems, I don't think any forces have them on active deployment. The legal status around using them is extremely fuzzy—there are no fixed laws as yet about how and when they can be used, or who can use them—especially private individuals.

"What interests me more is how the People's Republic of Stokes Croft got hold of the technology in the first place," Pletz continues. "Buying it would be hard and expensive, and probably more illegal than using it, as I believe it's classified as a weapons system at present. It's not unfeasible, though, that they may have built it themselves. It's certainly possible to do so, with a mix of off-the-shelf and 3D-printed components. The know-how is available online if you know where to look."

Certainly a do-it-yourself attitude seems prevalent amongst the community in the Croft. "It's really the essence of what we're trying to do here," Manaan tells me as he shows me around the neighbourhood, pointing out the several boutique 3D print and bespoke component shops. "We're all about finding alternatives to top-down approaches to technology, so it's unsurprising that we've attracted people that want to start businesses and workshops along these lines. People also come here because they know they're not being watched—people who perhaps want to tinker with existing technologies without large companies or lawyers breathing down their necks. They value the freedom we offer."

Another group that clearly values the freedom here are artists. Built on the reputation of the likes of Banksy and 3Cube, Bristol has long been considered Europe's graffiti and street art mecca, and long before Manaan and his crew arrived, Stokes Croft was one of its hot spots. There is barely a patch of wall down the whole street that isn't daubed in paint, with the whole fronts of some buildings transformed into massive murals. This is nothing new, Stokes Croft has looked like this for decades—but put on a pair of spex running Flex and the art comes alive in ways that seem to warp reality. Buildings strobe with colour while tentacles of paint slither out of the architecture to splatter unsuspecting passersby, herds of rainbow-coloured zebras run alongside passing traffic, and vast, ancient-looking trees explode through rooftops to dominate the skies. They're the kind of augmented graffiti hacks you might have seen in cities all across the globe, but on an unprecedented scale. "What we do is basically impose zero limits on what artists can create and post," explains the Dutch artist Anika Bernhardt, the Croft's "uncurator." "As long as they stick by a handful of community-agreed guidelines, artists can put art—both digital and paint—basically wherever they like. They're free to post over or alter other people's work, even; in fact, we actively encourage it. It's very much a free-for-all. My job here is less being curator and more a logger or archivist—

instead of deciding what art is shown here, I just make a record of it."

I'm intrigued by the way she talks about encouraging artists to post over others' work. Isn't that hugely frustrating to the original artist? Isn't it just a form of vandalism? "We don't like to use that word here," Bernhardt tells me. "We want to break that association that art is something that needs gatekeepers, that has to be restricted to galleries. Plus, we have ways of recording all the art, so that it's instantly retrievable." She demonstrates this to me, using a part of the Flex app that allows us to delve back in time. It's a dizzying effect—almost as surreal as the street art itself—as she appears to rewind time, the faces of the buildings changing rapidly around me as murals and AR projections shift and change in reverse. "You can stop at any time, pause everything, and really focus on a work that grabs your attention. You can peel back the layers of the graffiti and find what was there before."

Already an established installation and performance artist in Amsterdam and online, Bernhardt first came to Bristol to research the work of the city's infamous AR street artist 3Cube, but fell in love with what was happening in the Croft, so decided to stay. She's now been here nearly two years. "It was wonderful, what was happening here—just so exciting. It's really playful, and I think that's incredibly important. It's important that we make cities playful. People think we're Luddites here—that we're anti-technology—but in fact it's quite the opposite. We're celebrating technology.

"The whole smart-city idea is so top-down, it's nothing more than a suite of products sold to cities by large companies. It's a one-size-fits-all model—it works on the idea that all cities are the same, that they have the same problems and situations. That's just not true. Cities are different, just as the people that live in them are different. What we're doing here is showing how technology in cities can belong to the people that live there, that they can come along and shape how it works and what it does. What better way to do that than through art?"

As exciting a picture as Bernhardt paints, the People's Republic of Stokes Croft has remained unsurprisingly controversial. While there's been an attempt by Bristol City Council to maintain its liberal approach to art experiments such as this, it has butted its head against Manaan's community a number of times, as have the local police. Most of this is over the disruption to surveillance in the neighborhood, and the worry that it's creating a "crime blackspot." Local media and some of the more conservative members of the council have focused on this, demanding that the network jammers be shut down. Although he wasn't available to comment for this article, Chief Constable Chris Walker has previously voiced concerns about the area becoming "a physical manifestation of the dark web: an area that attracts the worst kind of criminals and preys on the most vulnerable. This is not what Bristol needs, and I personally will not let it happen."

"The stories of drug dealers, child pornographers, and

malware manufacturers around here are nonsense," says Manaan. "It's nothing more than media hype, lazy journalists and politicians looking for an easy, fear-mongering story. Look around, this is clearly a happy, vibrant, and safe place, that's incredibly well integrated with the local community."

In many ways however, it might actually be community integration that poses the biggest threat to the PRSC. Stokes Croft has always been a controversial street anyway—a vein of bohemian gentrification that runs through St Paul's, an area that has traditionally been dominated by South Asian and West Indian families. It's been a conflict for years, but the PRSC seems to be making the situation worse. From talking to just a handful of people at random, it was clear there were strong tensions in the neighbourhood.

"It's a pain in the bloody backside," I'm told by Jiten Patel, who has run a newsagent's and off-licence on Stokes Croft for 25 years, right in the middle of the jammed zone. "I've had to replace all the bloody wireless gear in my shop, the tills, the stock-checking wands, the security cameras and alarms, everything. Either replace it with wired gear or find stuff that isn't blocked. Rush and his lot helped me do that, sure, even gave me some bits and pieces, but still it cost me money. I can't use the internet on my phone while I'm here, I have to use this ancient laptop that's on a direct wired connection. It's a pain. I mean they're nice kids and that, and it brings in new customers because a lot of people come down here to have a look at the art, but it's a pain largely. We've been here, my family and me, for over forty years, and nobody asked us first. They just went ahead and did it.

"I worry about the crime angle too," Patel adds. "It's not affected me personally yet, but you hear stories. I worry it's not safe out there with no CCTV cameras. I can't hail a cab from here either, I have to walk to the end of the street—both Uber and GoogleCabs pass through here but they can't stop. Also it's dirty, the streets. The road-cleaning robots can't come down here anymore, because of the jamming. Now I have to go out and clean the street in front of my shop myself—I don't mind as such, but my council tax is meant to be paying for those robots, you know? It's bloody stupid."

Another problem is that as tight as Manaan's digital boundary might be, there's some obvious seepage into neighbouring streets. "Half the time the wireless in my own house doesn't work," I'm told by Chantelle Andrews, who lives nearly half a mile outside the jamming zone. She works as a driver for a local on-demand delivery service, and she says it's highly disruptive to her job. "I have to get up early in the morning, get in my van, and drive out of the neighbourhood to pick up my jobs for the day. It's also the only way I can get phone calls and messages. If any work comes up that means picking up or dropping off in the Croft itself, I usually have to just turn it down. It's affecting my daughter, too—she's zero hours, working freelance retail, so none of the apps she uses to bid for jobs work at home. She has to walk for half a mile just to get reception. I don't think it's fair, to be honest."

Even some of the Croft's newest residents, brought here by the freedom promised by the PRSC, have run into problems. Tara-Jane Allbright is a jewellery designer that moved into one of the communal art spaces last year. "I sell most of my work via Facebook and eBay, so I've had to do a lot of adapting. In some ways it's great—I separate out my creative work here in the studio, where I've got no internet, from my admin and shipping work, which I do when I go home on my wired connection. But it means I can be slow to deal with customers' inquiries, which has led to some problems."

I put all this to Manaan—is there not a danger that the Croft is actually just becoming another form of gentrification, foisting itself upon unwilling surrounding communities? "I don't think so," he says. "We try and work very hard with local communities, and we're always checking and monitoring exactly where the perimeter is, and finding ways to make it tighter and more accurate. This is an experiment, we freely admit that—it's not perfect. It's a work in progress. As such there's always going to be conflicts, problems and issues that need to be smoothed out. But I've got faith that we can deal with things sensibly, and through consensus. It's what this place is about, really—freedom, as well as bringing people together.

"It's important to try and remember what we're trying to do here," he continues. "This is an experiment, a statement. People don't realise how reliant we are on the internet now. If it disappeared tomorrow there'd be chaos. It's not just that you wouldn't be able to Facebook your mates or read the news—everything is connected to it now. The markets would stop trading. The economy would collapse. There'd probably be no electricity, no food in the shops. Vital equipment in hospitals would stop working. It's not just your phone or your spex—cars, busses, trains—everything would grind to a halt. It'd feel like the end of the world. We're just trying to show people how dependent we've all become on something that we don't own, that isn't controlled by us. We're just trying to show people that there are alternatives, different ways of doing things."

5. AFTER

Vibrations jerk Anika awake, and for the nth time she feels that fleeting half second of panic and disorientation, and then curses herself for nodding off again. Her hair sticks to her face where it's been sandwiched between her skull and the van's window, but she doesn't move straightaway, the cold of the glass pressing against her forehead strangely calming.

She brushes aside enough of her fringe so that she can peer out the windscreen, just in time to watch the ancient shard of the Purdown communications tower slip past on the right-hand side of the motorway; its strange, distinctive stack of concrete disks still looking like abandoned

Cold War space hardware, still transmitting nostalgic futures from its mess of long-dead aerials and dishes.

Fuck, she realizes, we're here.

And she's right, within seconds they're hurtling down a concrete corridor, the motorway snaking down into northeast Bristol, and she feels her stomach flip, unsure if it's the altitude drop or her nerves—another flash of panic, but minus the disorientation. She knows exactly where she is.

As if on cue the walls drop away and they're on the fly-over above Eastville, and through the grease mark her hair has left on the window she can, for fleeting, fragmented seconds, see into the rooms of the houses, can glance across the dome of the mosque. It always fascinates and horrifies her how close the top stories of the buildings here are to the elevated motorway, how if she could freeze time she could reach out and touch them, leap across onto someone's roof, through someone's open bedroom window, find somewhere to curl up and sleep. She always thought this, every time she drove back into Bristol this way, tired and wanting to get home, fascinated by the seemingly arm-length proximity to the road, horrified by whatever interpretation of progress was used to justify slicing through a community so brutally.

And then the buildings drop away, and for a second she's disoriented again, until she twigs that she's looking down on Eastville Park—or at least what used to be called that—the first thing she's seen so far that seems to have changed in the last ten years, its green expanse of trees gone, flattened, turned into rows of crops, patchworked into segments too large to be community allotments or private vegetable gardens, and she sighs to herself, numbly fighting back the anger and disappointment.

"You're awake, then, eh?" Neal flashes her a smile as he guides the van straight over the top of the Eastville roundabout, no need to pause for the nonexistent traffic. The roads have been basically empty since they left the services, and cleared everywhere—just the occasional abandoned car dragged onto the hard shoulder, the odd encampment of parked-up nomads.

"Yeah, must've nodded off again." She forces herself to smile back at Neal, who seems mainly harmless.

"Well, nearly there now." Past the silhouette of his head she catches a glance of the blue-and-yellow bulk of IKEA, the superstore looking mainly intact from up here. Now the towers are rising out of the mist to their left, gray and red brutalist monoliths, drying laundry flicking pixel-speckles of color across their faces. So little has changed, she thinks, although she can't shake the feeling that something is missing, that there's some stark, unidentifiable emptiness.

"Long time since you been back, yeah?" Neal asks her.

"Yeah. Long time. I got out just before things got bad."

"Well . . . I reckon you picked the right time to come back. City is getting back on its feet, they say. Most people got power, most the time. They mainly got the solar back working, see?" He nods at the roofs of the houses to their right. "But it was tough for a while, yeah. Really tough. Wise decision."

"Wise decision?"

"Staying away, until now. You made a wise decision. Things weren't good, not for a long while. Better now though, mind."

Anika looks back out her side window, unconvinced. Perhaps she's left it far too long. Her stomach flips again, and then—as she stares at the empty spaces between the road and the buildings—she realizes what's missing.

"The trees. All the trees are gone."

"Yeah. Yeah. Well, like I say, was bad, first few years. Especially first couple of winters. Terrible, it was."

Anika doesn't catch his drift at first. "And . . . the trees?"

"Well, they burnt them all, my love." Neal takes his eyes off the road to glance over at her with palpable sadness. "For heat."

The next thing Anika knows, they're off the motorway and slap-bang right into the town center, and she's pushing herself back into her seat and holding on for dear life, her left hand grasping the door handle while the fingertips of her right try to pierce the seat's upholstery as Neal guides the van through a mass of crisscrossing cyclists, trading curse words and hand gestures with them through his open window.

No motorized traffic at all, no cars or vans apart from them, just bikes. Fucking hundreds of bikes. Fucking hundreds of people, in fact, far more than Anika imagined—somewhere in her head she expected to come back to empty streets, abandoned buildings, silent post-apocalyptic wastelands. But the opposite seems true, like the city has been pumped full of people, and all of them apparently on bikes right now, in the town center, trying to get run over by Neal's van. And then—just as Neal narrowly avoids wiping out what looks like a whole family balanced on a single bike, a mother with a baby hanging off her, an older child sitting on the handlebars and a third riding pillion—something else hits her. They're all so young. Children, mainly. Even the eldest faces she clocks as they whiz past seem to be barely out of their teens.

"So many kids," she says.

Neal laughs. "Yeah. Well, I guess that's what you get after a decade of no TV or contraception."

Anika laughs back, nods. "How's the life expectancy?"

Neal inhales hard. "Not great, to be honest. Hospitals are a fucking nightmare, can't get to see a doctor, zero sup-plies. Seriously, anything happens to you, you're best try-ing to sort it out yourself, you get me? So life expectancy . . . well, I dunno. I dunno an official age or anything. But put it this way—I live down in Hanham and I'm one of the oldest down my ends."

"How old are you?"

"Forty-five."

"Ouch. You look like you're doing all right, though?"

"Yeah . . . I guess. I try and look after myself, y'know? It's tough, though. I mean, you never know what's gonna come along, do you?"

Anika doesn't answer.

"I mean . . . like I say, winters were bad. Still can be. A cold comes along and everyone gets it . . ." He stops himself, obviously pained. "I seen whole streets die, whole families. Not just the olds but the little kiddies, too. Just from a cough, y'know? I mean, it's a bit better now, mind, now we got some food and that. Vegetables again, like. But still. Come autumn, someone starts coughing and you see the whole street paying attention."

He cuts himself off by violently veering to the left, like he's missed a turn, and Anika realizes that's exactly what's happened as he mounts the curb and punches the van through a hole in a nearby building. It takes Anika a minute to work out what the fuck is going on, but as they're submerged in interior darkness she realizes they've just entered the Cabot Circus multistory car park. There'd been no indication it was there, she realizes, no street furniture, no signage, no entrance barriers. She wonders if they'd all been burned for heat too.

Next thing she knows they're hurtling up the huge spiral ramp, and she's gripping the seat and handle again— partly out of fright at Neal's slightly too fast velocity, partly because the strobing effect of the sunlight as they spin past the ramp's columns threatens to induce seizures. She closes her eyes to block it out, but then the dislocated motion of the climbing, twisting van turns her stomach and she opens them again, realizing just how unused to traveling in cars she's become.

Then they're off the ramp, and Neal finally seems to cut his speed for the first time since they left Wales, easing them around pillars and parked cars—most of them looking to Anika like they've been here awhile, abandoned. Cars and vans much newer than the antique Ford they're sitting in now: driverless cars, fuel-cell-powered, digitally controlled. Chinese, Korean, Brazilian designs. All useless now. Some of them have been stripped for parts, some have been burned out, others converted into what looks like living spaces; she catches the glimpse of curtain fabric in windows, notices how some of the cars have been moved to create walls, defenses. Security. It's like a small town on this level, streets formed out of spaces between the abandoned machines, lit by repurposed headlights, paved with tarpaulin and piss and oil. She can smell it.

"Right, that's the exit over there," says Neal, pointing toward an impossibly dark-looking corner. "When you open the door I want you to just walk straight there, don't stop and talk to anybody, right?"

"Right."

"Oh, and I nearly forgot." Neal turns to her, flashes his Jack-the-lad smile.

"What?"

"Welcome home, girl."

"Yeah. Cheers."

Neal makes her memorize the day and time he'll be heading to Wales again, just in case she wants a ride, and then she leaves him to fend off the scavengers and traders clamoring to see what's in the back of his van. She makes it to the exit unhassled, drops down a couple of flights of scruffy steps until she hits level three, makes her way past blackening walls and the broken shells of parking ticket and vending machines until she finds the curved glass bridge that leads over to Cabot Circus proper. She's not actually been this way that many times, no need—never owned a car, and lived just down the road anyway—plus she always hated Cabot, a pointless, overcomplicated senses assault you avoided until you had no choice.

Despite her unfamiliarity, she doesn't pause too long on the bridge, mindful of Neal's advice—she stops just long enough to glance at the street below, surprised at how little has changed. The buildings, huge cubes of flat concrete, still stand, even some of their windows still intact, more drying laundry fluttering from balconies. At least they're being used, she thinks, these redundant office blocks and hotels apparently repurposed as living spaces. Necessarily, it appears. The biggest change is still the bikes, flowing through the streets like floodwater—there's so many of them, so many people, that it starts to spin Anika out as she watches them swarm below her, their unflinching movement and the bridge's transparent curvature conspiring in vertigo. She closes her eyes again briefly, steps away from the rail, reopens them, and focuses on the floor until she reaches the other side.

Cabot Circus, third floor. It's like stepping out into the upper level of a huge, angular amphitheater—Cabot always seemed ancient to Anika, like it's stood here for centuries, despite her knowing full well it's barely twenty-five years old. Before it was here Bristol's central retail district was a disorganized mess, intersected by roads and traffic, meaning any shopping trip involved multiple road crossings, snarl-ups, gridlocks, and the occasional dead child. The obvious answer would have been to pedestrianize a chunk of it, but people—especially Bristolians, it seemed to Anika—loved their cars back then, so instead they demolished a chunk of it and built an out-of-town shopping mall in a middle-of-town space.

She leans on the railing, stares down into the pit lit by pale sunlight falling through the grease-smeared glass of the huge structure's once-futuristic matrix of a roof, shadows projecting a faint grid onto everything below. Again she's surprised by the sheer number of people—there's a fair few wandering around on this level and the one below, but the ground floor is heaving, thick with bodies, a never-ending, swirling whirlpool of people. She smiles to herself, seeing the truth in Neal's joke—you can try to starve a population, deprive them of health care, power, and data, but you can't stop them fucking.

The smile grows into a self-deprecating chuckle; and she's strangely embarrassed that part of her had imagined walking out into some huge abandoned space: a bourgeois science-fictional fantasy of a long-lost civilization where she's the special one, the only survivor that could see past the crass commercialism of the masses and got out in time, the intrepid, educated explorer unearthing this forgotten, archaic relic of barbaric capitalism, an empty cave filled with unfamiliar, alien branding.

Instead, most of the branding has gone, ripped down from the fronts of shops and disposed of with the same startling ease with which the digital entities that owned them blinked out of existence, their physical manifestations grinding to a halt as the data that kept them alive simply vanished. Like a splintered army lost too deep into enemy territory, their supply lines were overrun and their troops had deserted their positions, going permanently AWOL as they slipped away into the surrounding forces.

But Cabot itself still remains, and, free of the branding and mission statements and retail management strategies, it seems, to Anika's curiosity, to be flourishing: parents wander around in their charity-shop mélange of found clothes, dragging children in oversized T-shirts printed with images that have been long separated from their fleeting cultural significance—what they used to call refugee chic— stopping at the stalls that would previously never have been allowed to litter the elevated walkways that line and cross the complex's central atrium. She finds herself heading down the steps of a long-motionless escalator to the floor below, eager to explore, drawn to join in, wanting to experience what appears to be the decentralized, community-driven anarchic economy they'd spent so many late, stoned, enthusiasm-soaked nights dreaming of in fevered, utopian discussions.

Instead, standing in the silence of the first shop she passes, she finds inevitable disappointment. For a start, the nameless store has barely any stock, and what is here is a disorganized mess of broken, discarded junk piled up in boxes or spread randomly around the half-bare shelving—at first glance she thinks it could even be the ramshackle debris left over from the original store's ransacking, but soon she realizes the truth is even more depressing. For that to be true there'd have to be some shred of purpose, form. Between embarrassed glances she starts to think that maybe it's just her own deep-rooted, bred-in consumer expectations clouding her assessment, so she tries to throw them aside and embrace the nonconforming landfill-mined chaos of scuffed plasticwear, broken crockery, torn clothing, dead electronics, and crumbling paperbacks—but it's impossible. There's not just a lack of organization here, it's a total absence of function, value. She gingerly lifts an empty beer bottle from a detritus-strewn shelf, and where her fingers disturb its dusty surface they reveal glimmering deep brown, something she realizes she's not seen for years.

Sculpted, manufactured glass; industrial machine art designed to capture light and catch the eye. She can't hold
back the sense-memory-fueled smile, as she twists it in her
hands, trying to ascertain the brand—but the label is gone,
leaving behind no identifying traces on its surface, so blank
that even the machine that made it would struggle to clas-
sify it, the only thing resembling a bar code being the
streaks of white paper and residual glue left behind as the
label was torn away.

Nobody has attempted to remove them, to clean them
off, as though they still have some mystical value, some
symbolic link to the label itself—the most valuable part.
Disappointed, she replaces the bottle, and as she glances
around the near-empty shop she realizes that the missing
label is actually the center of all this, of what's happening
here. This isn't so much a thriving, defiant artisan economy as a desperate clinging to the past, a once-significant
tribal ritual still guiltily rehearsed by repentant believers,
sneaking back into the same temple where they burned all
the icons.

She leaves the shop, drifts anxiously along walkways,
confused and distracted. Below, on the ground floor, the
crowd still churns, more human bodies in one space than
she's seen in years, their combined mass emitting a constant low, dull drone, conversational white noise echoing
off the empty architecture. There's something restrained to
it, Anika senses, as if something is holding it back, keeping
it in check.

On the way down there she pauses where a group has gathered, and gently pushes through to see what they're watching: a shop window full of color and movement, its entire frame filled with antique LCD televisions; the huge, bulky physical displays that had been going out of fashion when Anika was a kid, old enough to be unconnected, unsmart, uninfected. She still feels a curious thrill to see moving images again, despite the lack of sound, the low resolution, and the honeycombing effect the chicken wire lining the windows has, like she's watching everything with an insect's compound eyes. One screen is showing an old soccer match, another what looks like an ancient sitcom, the others all flickering with movies that seem familiar in their nostalgic anonymity: giant robots, space battles, food fights, car chases, period costumes. The kids at the front of the crowd giggle and point, whisper to one another. Scrawled in pink paint directly on the window, free of the chicken wire, is the first thing Anika has seen that resembles a sign in any way:

WE BUY SELL ANY:

DVD'S

BLURRAY'S

VHS

CD'S

TAPE'S

SWAPS POSSIBLE, NO CREDIT

THIEVES WILL BE SHOT

It's the first shop Anika's seen that appears to have a purpose, to have something of real value for sale. It's also the first shop she's seen with an armed guard on the door: a bored-looking teenager propped up on a barstool blocks the way in, a farmer's double-barreled shotgun resting lazily across his lap. He looks like he'd hardly cause her any real problem, but like the rest of the crowd watching through the chicken wire she decides against going in.

She drops down another static escalator to the ground floor, straight into the thickest crowds, and into a wave of unexpected panic. She's not been surrounded by so many people since that last night in Bristol, she realizes, and it's unnerving in its similarity—the tension on faces, the stains on unwashed clothes, the stench of unbathed flesh.

But there's something else she can smell, and as she works her way to the outside of the crowd it grows stronger as everything starts to fall into place. She couldn't see it from the balconies above, but the shops down here have had their windows removed and replaced with counters, the crowd snaking out from its central mass, tentacle-like, into huge queues at each one. She's standing in the center of a circular food market, each counter identified in huge letters, in the Gill Sans font Anika recognizes all too well— VEGETABLES, FRUIT, DAIRY, ALCOHOL, and, in similar but smaller letters below, NO PURCHASES WITHOUT ADEQUATE RATION COUPONS.

The smell now is intoxicating, that marketplace scent she's not experienced for close to a decade: the musk of unrefrigerated meat mixing with the acrid twang of decaying vegetation. She can't see much by just peering into the crowd, and her urge is to push through, to see it, to drink it all in, but something stops her.

Between every couple of shops, towering above everyone's heads on platforms built from scaffold and repurposed motorway signs, stands a Land Army trooper. Woodland camouflage jackets, SA-80 assault rifles, shaved heads turning slowly to survey the patiently queueing crowds.

Hanging from the wall behind each trooper is the first true branding Anika has seen since stepping foot in Cabot Circus, the familiar Land Army poster—the instantly identifiable Coca-Cola white-on-red colors, the stylized crown, the same huge Gill Sans lettering:

KEEP

CALM

AND

CARRY

ON

LOOTERS WILL BE SHOT

Anika feels the people around melt away, feels suddenly, horrifically exposed. She drops her eyes to the filth-strewn marble floor, pulls up the hood of her jacket, and heads for the exit.

Outside in the open air for the first time, she relaxes, slows her pace, silently curses her own naïveté. She pulls back her hood, lets the warm sunlight stroke her face as she stares up at the sun bursting over the concrete canyon walls of Bond Street, imagines impossible cinematic lens flare. It's quieter out here, just the lessening flow of passing bikes. She probably panicked back there; the chances of anyone recognizing her are much slimmer in Bristol. Still, it feels safer out here.

She takes a deep breath.

She should never have come back.

She's not going to find what she hoped for.

Fuck it.

Fuck it all.

But.

But.

There's only one way to be sure.

Anika stares at the sun again, squinting up through smashed hexagonal geodesic wireframes and bird-shit-smeared glass, watching seagulls trace invisible thermals as she tries to ignore the building in front of her, its huge mass mockingly goading her onward.

She walked here, almost on autopilot, until she found herself at the Bearpit roundabout, a century-old futurist's dream from a time when subterranean public plazas on the wrong side of town were a utopian urban planning solution rather than a crime scene waiting to happen. The entire center of the roundabout is sunk below ground level, and although open to the sky it was always a natural destination for those who wanted to conduct business unseen. Drunks, junkies, dealers, prostitutes, graffiti artists. There'd been the inevitable effort to gentrify it at the turn of the century, to bring in the obligatory performance spaces and organic hot dog stalls—they'd erected an angular, origamic sculpture of a twelve-foot bear, and then, as if blissfully drunk on nostalgic naïveté, they built a geodesic dome over the whole thing—but still the winos and the junkies found corners they believed were unseen.

She makes to leave the Bearpit via the opposite underpass to the one she entered through, but she stops on the way out. It's still there.

She would see it every time she passed through here on the way home. Everyone would, who came this way. She's surprised to see it, unsure why. Maybe she expected it to have been ripped down, smashed up. It's damaged, certainly, pierced by two bullet holes, smeared with filth, uncleaned. But it's still there, and Anika can't decide whether it's now defiant, ironic, or just in bad taste. Whichever way, it makes her pause, triggering emotions she'd not expected, can't control.

White stenciled text and a laurel wreath on a red board—the wood apparently spared from becoming fuel—the sign is unmissable, its message bold, even if the context is unclear.

STOKES CROFT—RELENTLESS OPTIMISM

6. AFTER

Mary doesn't often see anyone wearing a suit. Well, unless you count the tramps down in the Bearpit—some of them wear suits, but mismatched ones, jackets from here, trousers from there. The occasional tie. But all old, dirty, smeared in their own shit and piss. Plus Mary doesn't go down to the Bearpit very often. Grids doesn't let her.

Grids doesn't wear suits, she thinks, even though he's important. And isn't that the whole point of suits? To show that you're important? That you're different? That's what someone told her, that lots more people used to wear them, when lots more people were important, or had important things to do. Special occasions. She peers past her customer and toward the front of the shop—Grids is standing there, anxiously trying to look like he's not watching them, and even though this is an important thing for him, a special occasion, he's still not wearing a suit. Just his regular outfit, dark blue jeans, black T-shirt. The thin silver chain that always hangs from his neck.

The guy sitting in front of her now, though—now, he is very much wearing a suit. The kind of suit Mary has never seen before outside of old movies. Different shades of gray, varying textures—silk, wool. Mary wants to lean forward and touch it, to rub it between her fingers. But what transfixes her the most is his shirt—slashed down the middle by a streak of pink tie—and how white it is. Really white, clean white—not graying, grubby, but pure white. Mary's not seen anything like it before, an item of clothing that white, that clean. That pure. It looks like it could almost be new.

Not even Grids's trainers ever look that white.

The guy—Walker is his name—has picked a face from the wall. It was one of the really high-up ones—Tyrone had to stand tiptoe on a chair to get it down. Usually Grids would have used that as a chance to make some joke in front of his crew about how short Ty is, but he didn't today. Grids is being all serious today, polite.

It's a girl, quite young. Serious-looking. Pink hair and thick-rimmed glasses, like so many in the pictures are wearing. The face has been up on the wall for months, and Mary barely remembers drawing it, even though she recognizes the paper it's on—she had a few sheets of this gray, coarse stuff one of Grids's boys had brought her. Said he'd found it somewhere, suspiciously. It was torn at the edges, but big enough that Mary could rip it into smaller bits. She really liked it. It was nice paper, took chalk and felt-tip pens really well, like it was made just to do that. Plus she liked the feel of it between her fingers, rough to the point that it felt almost furry, like it was made out of compressed hair.

Mary feels the paper now, just one corner.

"Do you know her?" she asks Walker.

"This girl? No. I just picked her at random, from your many wonderful drawings. I liked her face." Fake smile flash. "Does that matter? Does it affect . . . what you do?"

His voice is authoritative, questioning. Mary recalls being back at the tip; the dismissive, patronizing tones of Land Army officers. She bristles defensively.

"No. No, it doesn't. Why should it?"

Walker smiles. "Forgive me. I'm just trying to understand your . . . ability. Do you need to have a connection to the person you're trying to trace? I mean . . . to be near someone that knows them, or knew them? Does that make sense?"

"No. No, not at all. It doesn't work that way."

He smiles again. "So tell me. How does it work?"

Mary takes a breath, embarrassed. She tries to mentally prepare herself, to say the words yet again. This is always the hardest part. Harder even than showing them.

"I ain't completely sure how it works, to be truthful." She fidgets nervously with one of her oversized hoop earrings. "Sometimes I see people, out in the street. Nobody else can see them. They're not fully there . . . just . . . half there."

Walker tries to hide a skeptical smirk. "You're saying you can see ghosts?"

"I'm not sure. Maybe. I guess that depends on what you believe a ghost is. All I know is that they were here that night, and they're not always dead. I think you have to be dead to have a ghost."

He leans forward. "So perhaps, what you see . . . it's maybe memories? Like people's memories, from that night?"

"Maybe. I guess so."

"And you can see these people, right? But only see them? You can't . . . touch them, or feel them?"

"I can hear them." Defensively.

"You can hear them when they speak?"

"Yes." She can hear them when they scream, too, Mary thinks. She can hear them when they call for help, when they beg for mercy. When they die.

"And what do they say?"

"'They'? They don't all say the same thing." She resists the temptation to tell him about the screaming, the dying.

"Of course." The fake smile, but this time shot through with a trace of genuine humor and what might even be respect. "But what about her?" He leans forward, and stretching one well-tailored arm across the wall of junk he taps the picture of the girl with the tip of one finger, three times. "What does she say?"

Tyrone, bored, sits and takes it all in. Weighs shit up. Analyzes.

This kid standing opposite him, cradling the assault rifle like a comfort blanket and looking nervously at the faces on the walls, is barely as old as Ty. Maybe fourteen or fifteen, his thrown-together uniform a mess of camouflage fabrics and drab, faded olive cotton. Land Army child soldier, here to protect this bigwig that's come to see Mary. He's got one of those little headsets, an earphone and a mic, fixed behind one ear. Makes him look almost futuristic, except that Tyrone can see the coiled wire snakes down to one of those ancient radio walkie-talkies on his belt, a massive brick of a thing, held together with curled, graying sticky tape and tightly tied string. Tyrone wonders if it works.

Though he's much more interested in the gun, if he's honest.

He nods at its squat bulk. "So, you use that much, then?"

The guy takes his eyes off the faces on the wall, flicks them down at Ty. "This? Only when I have to."

"You ever shot anyone?"

The guy smiles, somehow managing to look even younger. "Nah. Had to fire it above a crowd's heads once, though."

"Serious?"

"Yeah. All kicked off down at Cabot, in the food market. People fightin' over bread."

"Bet that got their attention."

"Yeah. Yeah, you could say that. They simmered down pretty quick."

Tyrone nods, sarcasm-tinged appreciation. "So what's it like, then?"

"What? Firing this?"

"Nah, I mean the Land Army, the whole thing."

The guy shrugs, stares out the shop window. "It's all right. I only been signed up about . . . about seven months now, I think? Yeah, it's okay. Boring a lot of the time, to be honest."

"Yeah, guess you missed out on most of the fun, huh?"

"Yeah. It's pretty quiet now. Occasionally something kicks off, something the magistrates can't handle on their own, and they call us in. Apart from that I'm usually just doing jobs like this."

"Like this?"

"Yeah, VIP escorts. But even they don't happen much these days. Spend a lot of time patrolling the downs, you know? Making sure nobody sneaks in and tries to steal crops."

"Seen. So, seven months. Why you sign up?"

The guy glances at him, and before he returns his face to the window, Ty sees the color drain from it, his whole expression drop. "Didn't have much choice, to be honest. Was in a kids' home up in Kingswood. Hit fifteen and they don't keep you on. Had a choice—sign up, go work on a farm, or get shipped out to one of the landfills." He shrugs again. "Signed up."

"Right." Tyrone tries to find the right words. "You got no family, then?"

The guy's eyes drop to the ground. "Nah. They didn't make it. You?"

"Same. Mum died just after. Lived with my aunt for a while, but she only lasted a few more years."

"Sorry."

"Yeah." Tyrone suddenly can't match his gaze, feels the hair pricking up on his neck, his skin temperature drop like he's been enveloped in a bubble of cold air. "Likewise."

Seconds pass like minutes, Tyrone trying to think of something to break the awkward silence. Luckily Grids wanders over from where he's been agitatedly hovering, shifting weight from foot to foot, trying to eavesdrop. The atmosphere is suddenly very businesslike.

"Right. They going out." He leans in close to Ty, drops his voice low. "Keep an eye on them. Like I said, Mary doesn't leave the Croft. She doesn't pass the gates, under any circs. Get me?"

"No problem, man. I'm on it."

"I fucking hope so."

▬ ▬ ▬

Anika didn't know what those long-dead futurists were thinking when they built the 5102, but she suspects they just thought it would look cool to have a road flowing under a building, a Fritz Lang–shot world of tomorrow where cars appeared and disappeared into the very fabric of the city, like trains disappearing into Alpine tunnels. Maybe that's all it was: just architects flexing their terraforming muscles by building urban mountains, not allowing their future city to be restrained by the limitations of such antique concepts as roads and streets.

Of course, what they'd actually created was a wall. A huge, ten-story-high wall with the smallest of gateways at the bottom, just wide enough for a single road—the A38 Stokes Croft—to slip through. The cynic, the class warrior still hidden deep inside Anika, would always whisper that it was intentional—that they had actually glimpsed the future, and knew exactly what they were doing—building a barrier with a single, controllable gateway to the badlands of St. Paul's and beyond. That they'd seen everything that would follow, from the race riots of the '70s through to the cataclysmic rebellion of the new century, and had built a wall to try to keep it out, a preemptive strike on the geography of the city's undesirables.

She knew that wasn't true. For a start, a true prophet would have seen how it would have been reversed, deflected back as defenses for the other side. A wall of protection, fortification—not exclusion.

At least for a while, before the tides turned again and it became the wall of a prison, a tomb.

It hadn't been called the 5102 when they built it, it was Avon House—the main offices for now-long-defunct regional authorities. It had sat derelict for years before being reborn as city-center apartments, part of that first wave of turn-of-the-century artisan gentrification that swept along Stokes Croft like floodwater, staining the buildings with graffiti and coffee bars as it receded.

And then, later, as Stokes Croft had grown beyond just being a street and had become a place, for Anika the 5102 had become not just a symbol, but home.

She honestly hadn't been sure, as she'd emerged from the shadows of the Bearpit, that it would even still be there. But here it is, the fortress wall, breached yet still standing. The star-shaped hole they punched in it reveals all Anika needs to know, as it exposes crumbling concrete floors and twisted metal entrails, the rotting honeycomb of an empty, abandoned hive. The building might still stand, but it looks like it's been bled to death.

Anika stands, stares up at it, unsure what to think. She remembers the last time she saw it, glancing back over her shoulder as she fled, smoke still seeping from broken windows and a handful of defiant residents still on the roof, waving their improvised red flags and raining tiles onto retreating, unseen aggressors. She remembers a shot ringing out, a sound like fractured air, and the mass of people around her ducking, flinching as one, a few standing out from the crowd as they remain immobile, numbed and unmoved, failing to hear it, failing to care, or just refusing to be shocked anymore.

Below the fractured wall she stares into the gloom of the underpass, the once-ever-busy road silent, the once-barricaded gateway clear. Well, temporarily, at least—someone has built a gate across it, two giant sliding doors welded together from scaffolding poles and chicken wire, mounted on what looks like a couple of dozen shopping cart wheels. Putting aside the fact it's wide open, it hardly looks secure, like it couldn't keep anything out—or in—just another symbolic barrier, a physical manifestation of a long-forgotten virtual boundary.

As Anika steps across the line between July sun and the shadow of the 5102's underpass she clocks the two guys—kids, really, less than half her age—standing just the other side of the darkness, both holding guns. Big guns, old AKs refurbished with printed parts, their dull metal color patchworked with sections of gray plastic. As gate guards they're both pretty shit, she figures—they've got their backs to her for a start, staring inward. She looks past them, into the Croft, follows their line of sight to a small group walking slowly but steadily straight toward them.

Four people, heading up the center of the mainly empty street.

They're led by a girl, young—younger than even these two kids on the gate. Dark hair tied back tight, hoop earrings, aging stormsuit a couple of sizes too big for her.

A man, older. Suited. Obvious VIP.

Behind them:

A black kid, apparently unarmed.

A Land Army trooper, full battle dress, assault rifle. Obvious VIP detail.

Anika instinctively flattens herself against cold brick, trying to merge into the shadows, become invisible, hood up. Hand in bag.

She closes her eyes briefly, slows her breathing, recalls her Bloc mantra.

With zero bandwidth there is no calling for backup.

With zero bandwidth the advantage is ours.

With zero bandwidth there is no many.

With zero bandwidth there is no legion.

With zero bandwidth we are singular.

With zero bandwidth there is no time to hesitate.

With zero bandwidth there is only opportunity.

With zero bandwidth opportunity is our only weapon.

When her eyes open again she's identifying targets— the suit and the trooper, calculating distances, angles.

The trooper first.

No, wait. The suit first. Too good an opportunity to waste.

With zero bandwidth there is only opportunity.

With zero bandwidth opportunity is our only weapon.

She's no idea how these kids with the guns are going to react. They're not LA but they've obviously got a job to do.

The suit, the trooper, then these two kids.

The girl looks like low priority. Collateral at best.

The kid at the back . . . the kid at the back is the wild card.

She closes her eyes again, measures her breathing. When she opens them again the group is closer. In line with her predictions.

The kid at the back . . . the kid at the back is the wild card.

The hand in her bag flexes, exercising fingers, regripping the metal and leather.

Wait.

Wait until they're close to the shadows.

"**Here.** She was here."

Again faces stare at Mary; the only one not expecting anything flutters in her hands, on that really nice paper.

What none of them, apart from her, can see is that she's already flipped across, back to *then*.

Everything is frozen. It's earlier than last time, before the explosions and the smoke. Before the blood.

She glances around, there's hundreds of ghost people here, out in the streets, their faces blurred. Different atmosphere, almost happy. She can see bodies in weird static poses, dancing interrupted by the cessation of time.

The girl she's looking for, though, she's here. She looks less happy.

There are three of them, in fact—three huddled together. On the left a girl, in the middle a boy, on the right the face from her picture. It takes Mary a few seconds to work out what's going on, but then it's obvious. The boy in the middle is injured—a blood-soaked scarf is wrapped around his left arm—and the other two are helping him to stand.

They look strangely out of place, serious faces contrasting with the street-party vibe that surrounds them.

Not contrasting as much as Walker's face, though, which looks alien here, wrong. The lighting not right, the perspective just off.

"She was here," Mary repeats. "She's helping one of her friends to walk. He's been injured."

"How do you know?" Walker asks.

"I can see her," Mary says, allowing deadpan annoyance to seep into her voice.

Walker is unfazed, fake smile gone, a sudden, surprising hint of genuine concern. "Can you hear her?"

"Not now. But everything is frozen now. There's no sound."

"Is it always like that, Mary? Are people always frozen when you see them?"

"No, not at all. Usually I can control it."

"Can you control it now?"

"Of course." Mary blinks, unfreezes *then* time.

The first thing that hits her is the noise only she can hear—that overpowering music, those low, thunderous bass sounds that Tyrone loves so much, rattling her glasses, drilling into her skull. That and the shouting and chanting, the drumming, the sounds of celebration and defiance.

And below that, muffled by everything else, the sobbing, the panicked chatting.

They're not going to let us out

They will

Ahhh god my arm god I think it's broken

We're best just getting to some first aid

Ahhh please

Be careful

They'll let us out really trust me

The two figures are moving now, shuffling really, slowed down by their injured burden.

"They're heading toward the gate." Mary is aware she's talking loudly, to be heard over the cacophony that nobody else can hear, worries it makes her look even more mad. She looks past the trio toward the gate, which is partly obscured by the fog-like mass of a boisterous crowd; she can only just make out Grids's guards with their antique guns and the darkness of the underpass through the dancing, cheering translucent bodies.

"Can we follow them?" asks Walker.

"Of course."

And then, before she has time to move, it feels like a third reality is intersecting with the two she's already struggling to control as something large and swift and purposeful suddenly moves in front of her, blocking her way.

"That's it, no farther. She ain't going no farther."

Tyrone is standing between Mary and the suit, his heart pounding.

"Ah, now . . . c'mon."

"No, man. No fucking dice. I'm on orders. She don't go through that gate, get me?"

"Now, please. We're only just getting started here." Walker steps forward, an arm passing by Tyrone to touch Mary gently on the arm.

Tyrone flicks the arm away, with enough force to shock the old suited fucker, enough that he nearly falls backward.

"Serious. Don't fucking touch her again."

Tyrone hears a click, ominous. He knows it's a safety coming off, he's watched enough DVDs, seen Grids's boys showing off their tools.

"And you're not going to be doing any more touching either, mate, step back." Behind Walker and to his left the LA trooper has his gun raised, aimed firmly at Tyrone. Right between his eyes.

Tyrone throws his hands up, instinctively.

Two more clicks, behind Tyrone. Ozone and the other guy—a white kid with dreads—are moving away from the gate, their guns raised.

"We got a problem, Ty?" Ozone says, tough-guy voice, but Tyrone can hear the quiver of doubt, fear.

"Nah. Nah, Ozone, there's no problem. It's cool. Everybody is cool. There's just been a little misunderstanding here, that's all. Nothing major. We all just going to walk back to the shop now, all friends, and we going to discuss this with Grids." He makes eye contact with Walker. "Ain't that right?"

Flash of fake smile. "Of course." Walker glances back at the young trooper, nods. In response the trooper slowly lowers his assault rifle. Ty checks behind him, sees the two guards doing the same.

As the rest of the group drift away and head back up Stokes Croft, Tyrone turns to Mary, puts one hand on her shoulder. She's taken her glasses off, and her eyes look damp.

"You all right?"

"Yeah." She smiles back at him. "You?"

"Yeah. Think so. Jesus, I thought it was all going to kick off then."

"I'm sorry, I—"

"Nah, nah, Mary. Not your fault. I need to stop putting ideas in people's heads."

Mary looks at him quizzically.

"I need to stop asking people with guns if they've ever shot anyone."

— — — —

Walker climbs into the back seat of the bust-up old Audi, the upholstery smelling of damp, mold, and dust.

"So?" His driver twists around a shaved head to show him a face mapped with scars, wrinkles, weariness. "How'd it go?"

His security detail slides into the front passenger seat. Doors clunk shut. The driver fights with the ancient ignition briefly and the car pulls away from the curb, starts to roll back up Stokes Croft.

"Well," says Walker. "It was certainly a pleasant day out. Always good to get out of the office."

"Get what you wanted, boss?"

"Not sure. Not sure at all." He sighs. "It all felt strangely . . . vague to me. I mean, the girl seems genuine enough. She's telling the truth, mad, or a fantastic liar. I liked her."

"How old is she?"

"Fourteen, apparently. Interesting accent, couldn't make it out. Irish?"

His security detail nods. "She's a Traveler originally. That's what the black kid told me."

"Ohhh, maybe she's got the gypsy magic, then." Walker wiggles fingers mysteriously. Everyone in the car laughs.

"So, assuming she's not put the curse on all of us, what do we do next?" says the driver.

"We tread easily, that's what. Don't get any ideas about charging in there, they're jumpy enough as it is. Plus I don't think even the girl knows what she's sitting on."

"Understood. But then . . . what?"

Walker is staring out the window, watching the walls and the graffiti and the gawping faces that haven't seen a motor-car in months strobe past. And then it's all gone, jump-cut away, as the car passes into the dark of the underpass.

They're in there just seconds, three at most, but in the dark Walker sees memories stir, swirl. A hooded figure, a woman's face, high cheekbones and eyes he recognizes from somewhere, staring back at him, impossibly familiar.

"Boss?"

"Sorry." He laughs, quiet and short, embarrassed. "It must be catching."

"What?"

"I think I just saw a ghost."

7. BEFORE

Another night, another party.

This time it's a spacious forty-sixth-floor penthouse teetering on top of a spindle in Manhattan's Financial District, the walls covered with art and the precisely conditioned air filled with inoffensive commercial hip-hop. Half the crowd here are finance bros of every gender, the other half their partners, all with the kinds of job you can do in NYC these days only if your other half is a millionaire hedge fund manager. Meatpacking District gallery curators. Life coaches. Personal stylists. Social-media brand managers. Artisan cupcake distributors. Food bloggers. Lots of food bloggers.

Rush has barely spoken a word to any of them, but he knows what they do just by glancing around the room. This is the opposite of that Brooklyn party—no upturned skull you have to put your spex in, far from it: not wearing them would seem not just unusual but suspicious. Rude, even. This is an unashamed networking opportunity, a chance for a sliver of the 1 percent to come together and reinforce the connections that make them what they are. Rush just has to look at someone and blink and there it all is, float-ing around their head, their digital exhaust fumes—their name, their occupation, their social-media feeds. Photos of their beautiful kids, snapshots from their holidays in Italy, sunsets from the decks of yachts. Perfectly curated and out on display, as immaculate and polished as their pantsuits and manicures. Scott told him he'd brought him here so he could check out the view, but he knew it was because he wanted to network himself, on the hope he might find a buyer for some of his art, that he might be able to fulfill that ever-present desperation to be accepted into a circle like this.

The view is impressive, though, there's no denying that. He's out on one of the apartment's two balconies, catching some much-needed air and space. Manhattan both towers above and falls away from him, spires built from concrete and capital giving way to valleys of brick and asphalt. The whole island rolled out in front of him in infinite detail: automated traffic and subway trains snaking across to Brooklyn through the exposed dinosaur rib cages of the bridges crossing the water to the east; to the west New Jersey's shoreline fading into sunset burned red. As he leans against the railing he's suddenly aware of being above this vital node in global infrastructure, of floating over a principal network point of global capitalism, and he can almost feel the data pulsing through the city, the buildings shaking from subterranean traffic as the cables that span the globe merge beneath their foundations. He breathes deeply to stave off a sudden rush of vertigo, and looks instead to the horizon, where the skeletal frames of the giant, automated cargo cranes of the Bayonne container port stand against the orange sky. Another network node, an input/output gate, where the capital becomes physical, and physical goods from unseen foreign factories flow into the system as freely as the data.

"Helluva view, huh?" says a voice beside him.

Average white guy, in an above-average suit. Immaculate hair. The very latest Apple spex. Rush smiles weakly. He can't bring himself to expend the energy on blinking to find out more, looks back out over the view.

"You could say that."

"Place must have cost John and Christie a bomb. Quite the spot." He takes a sip from his martini glass. "I'm Brad, by the way." He extends a hand.

Rush reluctantly takes it. "Rush."

"Good to meet you. How you know these guys?"

Rush glances back into the crowded apartment. "I, ah, don't really. I'm just here with my boyfriend." The word falls out of his mouth easily, but he's suddenly aware it might be the first time he's used it to describe Scott. He feels his face blush. "Scott? He knows them. He's sold them some of his work in the past. He's an artist."

"Ah. Gotcha. And you? You an artist too?"

"Oh, no. Not at all." Although he's wearing spex, Rush has got his privacy settings locked down tight. His social-media feeds—at least the ones that matter—are secured away from public eyes. Brad can blink all he likes but he won't see anything. He could, of course, take a snap of Rush's face and run it through Google, and blink through to any one of the top results: *VICE*, the BBC, the *Times*, even, then he'd know exactly who he was dealing with. But perhaps he can't bring himself to expend the energy either.

"I, ah . . . I work with computers." Rush laughs quietly. Doesn't everyone? "It's not very interesting, really."

"Fintech?"

"No. No, not at all. Security, mainly." He tries to deflect. "And you?"

"Ah, that's not very interesting either. I'm a trader. Y'know." He shrugs.

"Oh, really? I didn't think people did that anymore."

Brad laughs. "Touché. Yeah, it's all pretty automated now. Most of what I do is software procurement. I sit in sales pitches for new algorithms all day. Well, not all day."

"Really?" Rush knows a little about this stuff—mainly

the stories everyone heard about how fucked it all is—but it's fascinating to him. Fascinating and scary. "So that's high-frequency trading stuff, yeah?"

"Yeah."

"So how's that work?"

Brad takes a sip from his drink and glances over his shoulder, as if to check nobody is listening. His demeanor seems to change, he seems to relax, like's he's just dropped some front he's been carrying around all day. "Honestly? I've no fucking clue."

"Really?"

"Really. I got no fucking idea how it works." Brad's accent slips into something less refined, more honest. More Jersey Shore than Manhattan high-rise. The change is jarring. "I don't think anybody does. I don't even think the guys making the algorithms know. I mean, they come to sell me new ones and they don't have a clue what they do, or how they do it. I mean, they say they do—this one watches for buyers, this one finds leads, this one monitors Twitter, this one reads the *Journal* and the *Times*—but then you buy them, they install them for you, and they walk away. I don't think they know what they're doing in there. The algos are all in there talking to one another, they say. But they don't really know what's going on. Y'know?"

"I don't."

"That's the point. Nobody does. I mean, I know what my business is meant to be, y'know? I specialize in facilitating trades between various public exchanges and corporate dark pools. It's making money off other people's deals mainly, thousands of transactions a second and all that. Like, when I was a kid and I started at Citi it was different. I used to chase my own leads, I'd watch the markets all day. Shit, I even used to call clients on the phone. Now I just sit in the office and watch money scroll across the screen. I mean, that's if I've got meetings. Otherwise I can just sit in bed and watch it while I scratch my balls."

"Really. Wow."

"The whole thing is too complicated, man. I mean everything, y'know? It's impossible for any one person—the banks, the investors, the traders, the Goldmans, the kids writing the code—it's impossible for any of them to understand what's happening anymore. The markets are too big and they move too fucking quick. People might know what's going on in their little bit, in their tiny corner, but otherwise they're just sitting there letting the algorithms get on with it. Market basically runs itself. Just nobody knows how anymore."

"Shit."

Brad suddenly becomes animated, defensive. "I mean, don't get me wrong, bro! Don't get me wrong at all. I ain't complaining. Not in the slightest. It gets a bit dull, but you should see what I banked last quarter. No joke. I'd blow your mind telling you how much money went through my office last year. Trust me, I ain't complaining."

"I'm sure." Rush suddenly feels flushed with anger. Brad

seems nice enough—weirdly naïve, even—but Rush can't shake the realization that he represents everything he hates. All the greed and the ignorance, all the willingness to hand over control to the machines, to take away any sense of human self-determination and to put it in the arms of the network. And all just to keep a few people rich, to squander technology's potential for real change in order to make a quick, lazy buck.

He finds himself pondering whether he could grab him and tip him over the balcony, send his Armani-wrapped body tumbling down into the steel-and-concrete canyon below. But the railing looks too high, Brad too heavy. He looks like he works out, when he's not watching his money or scratching his balls.

Instead Rush returns to gazing out over the city, down onto the usually hidden rooftop infrastructure, countless uplink dishes and microwave relays, birds circling the thermals from air-conditioner outlets the size of tennis courts. Somewhere uptown two NYPD helicopters hover just above rooftop level, and as he squints in the dying light he can see a swarm—maybe a dozen strong—of small quadcopter drones descend from them, splitting up and peeling off as they drop into the streets.

"Looks like something's going down," says Brad.

"It'll be the protest."

"What protest?"

Rush turns to look at him, slightly incredulous. "You've not heard? It's all over the timelines."

"Ah, I never check them." He smiles. "Got my algos to do that."

Rush shakes his head, lets out a reluctant chuckle, then instantly feels guilty. "It's a Black Lives Matter march. They're protesting the shooting of a seventy-eight-year-old woman in Queens."

"Jesus. What'd she do?"

"Nothing." Rush grits his teeth. "That's the whole fucking point. She didn't do anything. Cops got a tip-off from their predictive software that there was a mugging in one of the housing projects in Flushing. Cops turned up and fired into a dark stairwell. Killed this poor old lady that was just minding her business. Going to the bodega to get some milk, apparently."

"Shit. When did that happen?"

"This morning."

"And it was the predictive software's fault?"

"Well, it was the fucking cops' fault for firing into a stairwell before asking any questions. But yeah, the software fucked up. It's been doing that a lot lately. Another one of your algorithms that nobody really understands how they work. Meant to predict where crimes take place based on all sorts of data: embedded sensors, social media, cameras, residents' profiles . . ."

"Sounds familiar."

"Yeah, same shit but this time instead of you losing some cash someone gets killed. Since the NYPD started using it in the spring there's been this huge increase in wrongful arrests. And at least four deaths that we know of. All African Americans. You know what they say about algos, they're only as good as—"

"—the data you put in 'em. Yeah. Hear that a lot."

"Right. Well, it turns out the data the cops have been putting into them is racist as fuck."

"So who are they protesting? The cops or the algo?"

"Both, I think. The cops mainly, for using it. But also I think the protest is going to swing past the offices of the company that makes the software. They're actually up near Times Square."

"Who's the company?" Brad asks him.

"Prescience. Start-up out of MIT originally." He can see Brad's eyes flicking and blinking behind his spex's lenses, googling as he speaks. "Big guns in the data-analysis biz. They started doing full, real-time analysis of Facebook and Twitter demographics. Helped your president win his last two elections, helped get those fascists in France back in power. Then they moved into predictive policing, but it's not been working out so well for them. Obviously."

Brad sucks his teeth. "That's terrible. Just awful. I mean, the cops have a tough enough job as it is."

Rush sighs, bites his tongue, fights back rage again. "Sure. Anyway, I think I might go down and check it out. Wanna come along? Show your support?"

"Ah." Brad smiles, nervously. "I'd love to, but I don't do well in crowds, y'know?"

"Sure."

– – – –

"Is that . . . is that real?"

"Yeah. Think so."

There is an original Keith Haring here. In the fucking bathroom.

Scott wraps his legs around the back of Rush's thighs, pulling him against him, their mouths and crotches meeting, the taste of vodka and salt, the sensation of hardness behind denim.

As they stop kissing Rush pulls away slightly, takes in the bathroom again. It's attached to the master bedroom and is about half the size of Scott's whole apartment. Scott is sitting on a marble countertop, between two sinks. Matching gilded faucets. Behind Rush there are two showers.

"I can't believe you're leaving so soon," Scott says.

It's true. He's only got a couple of days left before he heads back to the U.K. The last week had flown by, far too quickly.

"I know. But I've gotta. I've got to give that talk on Monday."

"The talk on the boat?"

Rush smiles at him, shakes his head. "The *Dymaxion* isn't a boat. It's a ship. A container ship."

"*The* Dymaxion, *it's a container ship.*" Scott mimics his serious tone back at him. "Oh my god, who *are* you? Where the hell did I find you?"

They both start laughing.

"Just cancel it," says Scott. "Stay here with me."

"I can't. I mean, I'd love to, but I can't. I promised. And Simon is a good friend."

"Your friends are weird. You've got weird fucking friends."

"That . . . that's true."

Fittingly, he'd first met Simon Strickland on the *Dymaxion* about five years ago, not long after Simon had bought her, saving her from being cut up for parts by Maersk in some Gujarat ship-breaking yard. He'd got her fixed up and she limped back to the U.K., where she'd floated off the coast of Dover for a few months while Simon had run his speculative-design summer school on board. He'd invited Rush along to teach classes on digital protest and activism. The ship was buzzing then, full of young design students and excited academics on the upper decks, workmen and maintenance crews on the lower ones. By the end of August she was ready to sail, and Simon had set off on his first supply-chain expedition, taking more students, artists, and paying customers back to the source of it all, the *Dymaxion* transformed into what he called "a floating Temporary Autonomous Zone meets nomadic design studio," the hundreds of containers stacked in its hold turned into dorms, art installations, and "experimental spaces." It was halfway between a floating conference center and one of those reconstructed tall ships they take kids out on for months to learn trade history. Rush imagines it was every bit as pretentious and annoying as it sounds.

"You having fun?" Scott asks him.

"Always." They kiss again.

"No, silly. I mean here. The party?"

"Ah." Rush looks past him, into his own eyes in the mirror behind him. He looks tired, he thinks. "Sure. It's okay. I was hoping we could get out of here, though."

"Oh, really?" Scott pulls him against him again. Vodka, salt, hardness.

"I was . . . hoping we could go check out the protest."

Scott's shoulders fall, defeated. He smiles. "God, you're so predictable. I thought you were being romantic, wanting to get me on my own."

"I am, I mean I do want to. Later. Sorry I—"

"Shhh. It's okay. I'm just teasing." Scott brings up a hand to brush the stubble on his face. Rush finds himself leaning into Scott's palm, like a cat trying to get you to stroke its face. "I think it's cute how involved you get in these things. How much you care."

"Really?"

"Of course. It's why I'm with you." He kisses him again, but gently this time. Tenderly. "I love it."

Rush catches himself in the mirror again, sees himself blush. "I was talking to some guy earlier. Out on the balcony. I think I referred to you as my boyfriend."

"Oh really? Is that what you're calling me now?"

"I'm sorry, I—"

Scott laughs. "Jesus. What are you apologizing for? So fucking British sometimes." He pulls him forward again. This time the kiss is harder, deeper. Lingering. When they separate their foreheads meet, resting against each other, noses nudging. For a second Rush thinks his legs will give way beneath him.

Scott unhooks his legs, playfully pushes him away. "C'mon, then. We can finish this later. Let's get you to your protest, boyfriend."

They move quickly and purposefully through the city, thousands strong, shutting down traffic as they flow around it. Streets full of driverless cars are paralyzed, unable to re-act to this many human bodies flooding their space. The few remaining yellow cabs, artifacts from a dying age, honk in support, their human drivers reaching out of wound-down windows to high-five protestors as they pass.

At Rush's insistence both he and Scott have got their scarves and hoods up to try to mask their faces from the police drones that float constantly above their heads. Most of the rest of the marchers have done the same: if not hood-ies or scarves then actual masks—3D-printed re-creations of too many other black men and women slain by the police, to keep their memories alive as much as to hide identities, as if vengeful ghosts have been summoned to march with them.

Pretty much everyone is wearing spex, too, which gives Rush some pause. When he jumps into the #blacklivesmatter hashtag channel he can see why they are: virtual protest signs appear floating above heads, demands and slogans, calls to action, tweets from supporters across the globe, and video streams from simultaneous marches in Atlanta, D.C., L.A. But Rush knows for sure that probably most of the protesters don't have their shit as locked down as much as he does, that they don't have the same levels of encryption as his custom OS, and that as well masked as their faces might be they're still leaking personal data, that just by using the spex they're betraying their identities to the drones sniffing the air above them.

It's not just NYPD drones buzzing around them, though—the protesters have brought their own, of all models and sizes, from tiny, cheap toys to prosumer hexcopters. Illegal to fly in NYC as far as Rush knows, they play a constant cat-and-mouse game with the cops: filming and streaming the crowds, blocking the NYPD drones' cameras, flashing arrows across LCD screens to show the marchers which way to go as the route dynamically changes to avoid blockades and police lines. Most important, they relay, from tiny Bluetooth speakers strapped to their undersides with string and sticky tape, the never-ending call-and-response chants that the marchers echo back at them.

NO JUSTICE!
NO PEACE!
NO RACIST POLICE!

WHOSE STREETS?
OUR STREETS!
WHOSE STREETS?
OUR STREETS!

The air is electric, and Rush can almost feel it pulsing through the ground, the same way he imagined he could feel the data flows earlier back in the penthouse—the ground and the buildings shaking again, but this time the marchers are the network nodes, pulsing through the city, reclaiming the streets and the infrastructure. It's intoxicating. He squeezes Scott's hand tight as they walk.

"You okay?"

"Yeah." Scott seems hesitant.

"You sure?"

"Yeah, oh yeah. I'm fine. I mean, this is amazing. It's just, it's so different from marches I've been on before."

"How so?"

"There's just so . . ." He pauses to pick his words carefully. "So much urgency, you know? And focus. I've been on Pride, and I went on the Women's March . . . but this . . . They were different, right? Like it felt like people were there to have fun. Like the signs all had jokes on them, people were partying, taking selfies. This, this feels like it's about something. Like I said, focused. Urgent. Angry. But with good reason. You know what I mean?"

Rush smiles behind his scarf. "I do."

"Plus, on those marches, there was never this many cops."

They turn a corner and hit a wall of dark blue, a line of police in body-warping armor, their chests and shoulders encased in black plastic, faces hidden behind tinted visors and apocalyptic breathing masks. Most of them hold batons, some shotguns. Behind them are parked two huge armored personal carriers, towering above the crowd like futuristic mobile fortresses, more cops leaning lazily from hatches and nursing assault rifles. Rush has seen crowd-control units back home before, on the streets of Bristol and London, but this is something else, something terrifying and barely believable, like an exaggerated dystopian sci-fi movie, or the hyperstylized cover of some comic book about a fascist police state.

Immediately the protesters' drones start to drop lower, arrows scrolling across their screens to shift the march's route, and new cues rattling from speakers to realign the chanting.

WHY ARE YOU IN RIOT GEAR?
WE DON'T SEE NO RIOT HERE!
WHY ARE YOU IN RIOT GEAR?
WE DON'T SEE NO RIOT HERE!

Rush spots a couple of cops behind the main line not wearing headgear, senior officers or strategic management agents, and blinks to grab images of them, storing them away to run through image-search algorithms later. *Until you can dismantle them,* he tells himself, *always use the oppressors' tools against them.*

Then they're being picked up by the momentum of the crowd again, as it communally senses that it's nearing its target, seeming to pick up speed. Suddenly they're turning off Forty-fifth—Rush has lost all sense of direction—and marching down Seventh Avenue, and they're here, swarming around gridlocked traffic and into Times Square. It's the first time Rush has seen it; Scott had refused to bring him before, saying it's not somewhere real New Yorkers go. It's just as awful and wonderful as he'd imagined.

Hundred-foot-high superheroes fill the air, punching their cartoon nemeses into skyscrapers that explode into glass-shard blizzards, only to be replaced by hundred-foot-tall anthropomorphic M&Ms, arguing and laughing and falling over, only to be replaced by hundred-foot-tall teen pop stars, peering down at him and smiling over the rims of the latest Samsung spex, only to be replaced by koi carp the size of humpback whales, lazily orbiting a Sony logo built from iridescent bubbles, only to be replaced by hundred-foot-tall NBA legends, slam-dunking—

Rush yanks his spex away from his face and the augmented-reality adverts disappear, the towering hyperreal simulations vanishing from the warm night air, but the screens are still there, still everywhere. Some are the size of apartment blocks, some mere tennis courts, but they're fucking everywhere, everywhere that isn't a shop front or a Starbucks, on every wall and building. They cycle through brand after brand, from Google to Coke, Delta to Facebook, Hershey to Tesla. Brands merge into faces: politicians, the celebrity president, bleached-hair Aryan news anchors, all peering at him over scrolling text. Share prices, breaking news, war atrocities, football scores, celebrity gossip, fake news and real lies. It's like somebody took the Internet, the hyperactive never-ending churn of the timelines, the constant scroll through Twitter and Facebook and Instagram, and made it real, physical, and nailed it to the walls of the fucking city.

Rush pulls his attention away from the lights and screens and tries to focus on the crowds instead, which are growing and thickening now, confused tourists and determined protesters circling around one another. Through gaps in the mass of bodies he sees police lining the square, more riot units, blocking exits. The drones still buzz above them, the whirl of their rotor blades drowned out by the amplified chants bouncing back from the crowd.

HANDS UP!
DON'T SHOOT!
HANDS UP!
DON'T SHOOT!

NO JUSTICE!
NO PEACE!
NO RACIST POLICE!

WHOSE STREETS?
OUR STREETS!
WHOSE STREETS?
OUR STREETS!

For what can only be minutes he loses Scott, his hand slipping out of Scott's as the crowd contracts around him, and he finds himself in a state of panic, wheeling around shouting Scott's name, and then he's there again, grabbing him, hugging him. The euphoric energy of the crowd is intoxicating, but for some brief minutes it was gone, replaced by fear and loss, and this overpowering sense—this pure, desperate fear—had taken over, this realization that he never wants to lose him, that he never wants to be apart. It's terrifying and reassuring at the same time, and he holds Scott close, pulls down both their scarves and kisses him, long and deep, as the crowd jostles them, the sounds of chanting and the rumble of drone engines echoing about them.

And then the lights go out.

For a nanosecond there seems to be nothing but stillness and silence.

Rush breaks off the kiss and they step away from each other, staring into the darkness.

The dead screens are the color of the night sky. Every streetlight and crossing signal is out, every shop front dark, every robotic car and bus ground to a halt. He slips his spex back on but there's nothing—his home-brew OS struggling to connect to nonexistent networks.

Something explodes next to them, the crowd nearly knocking him off his feet as they make room for something heavy that's fallen from the sky, a failed police drone smashed to fragments of plastic and silicone as it impacts the asphalt.

And then the silence is gone, the crowd erupting into spontaneous cheering, and Rush finds himself joining in, hands above his head, emptying every last trace molecule of air from his lungs.

He's lost in pure rapture, ecstatic in a moment of pure defiance, unsure exactly what has happened but thrilled to have been part of the ultimate, simplest act of resistance. At that point the details were unimportant, but he knew it was deliberate, that they'd shown him—shown everyone—that there was another, almost unthinkable way. They could just shut it all down. They could turn it all off.

From across the square, from multiple directions, there's the sound of breaking glass. Cheers and screams and shouting. Celebrations and anger. The piecing jolt of tear gas canisters being fired.

And then Scott is pulling his arm down, grabbing his hand and holding it tight, and dragging him through the crowd toward the subway entrance.

— — —

Two days later Rush stands in line at Starbucks on Fulton. He's waiting to place his order, absentmindedly scrolling through timelines and blinking through hacker rumor forums, trying to piece together who shut Times Square down, when somebody barges in front of him and grabs his arm.

"Rush? Hey, it's Rush, right? I got that right, yeah?"

Rush pushes his spex up onto his head, the excitable face in front of him coming into focus. "Um, yeah, it's—"

"Brad! Brad, man! We met at the party the other night!"

"Oh yeah, sure. Of course. How you—"

"Oh, man. I'm so pleased to see you. I was hoping I was going to bump into you, man. I owe you big." It is clear that Brad is fucking hyped about something. Hyped and loud. "You changed my life. Thank you!"

Brad is aware that the other customers in the line are backing away from them. "I—"

"The protests, man! Prescience! Black Lives Matter!"

"You—you went to the protests?"

"Ah shit, no, no. I didn't go. Can't do crowds. But after the party I went home. Stuck on the news, checked my feeds. Shit was crazy. And I started looking into Prescience, the company?"

"Okay . . ."

"Man." Brad pauses, takes a breath, tries to calm himself but fails. "The next day when the markets opened

their stock tanked. I mean it completely fucking flatlined.
It was fucking *amazing*."

"I'm not sure I—"

"I made a fucking killing, bro. A fucking killing."

Rush doesn't get it, but right now he's still trying to process the words falling out of Brad's mouth quickly enough, like he's on some archaic transatlantic delay. "You made a killing off of stock flatlining?"

"Yeah, man. Soon as the market opened I was ready. Had the algorithms primed and all set to go. Within twenty seconds they'd cleaned up the market of Prescience stock. I had cornered that shit. I had them in every exchange from here to Jersey, picking them up quick and stealthy before my interest meant they could start to rally."

"Okay . . ."

"And then, nine twenty-seven. BOOM." Brad claps his hands together. It feels like everyone in the store jumps, then turns to look at them. "In comes Google."

"Google?"

"Yeah, man, Google. The Goog, dude. See, because of you giving me that lead I'd read up. I knew Google had been eyeing a hostile for the last year. And I knew if shit went bad they'd be there to pick up the pieces. And BOOM. In they came."

"Oh." Rush's brain catches up and his heart starts to sink.

"I made so much fucking money, man."

"Right." Rush feels sick.

"And it's all down to you."

"Okay." Rush wants to actually throw up.

"The thing is, Rush, if I'm really honest?" Suddenly Brad seems serene, and Rush is legitimately unsure if that is better or worse. "It ain't even about the money. I was about ready to quit. I was about ready to get off the street and find something else to do with my life. I was bored shit-less. But then you gave me this . . . you gave me a lead. And I followed the lead! And it was such a fucking thrill! I am fucking born again, man!"

And then Brad hugs him. A big locker-room bro hug that squeezes the air from his lungs, and makes it very clear that, yes, Brad does work out.

"Thank you, bro, thank you. Look, I'm sorry but I gotta go. Meeting. But thank you, man. You saved my life. Thank you."

And with that Brad is gone, as quickly as he appeared, leaving Rush alone to deflect the judging gazes of every other customer in Starbucks, and dreaming that he could just shut it all down. Turn it all off.

8. AFTER

Tyrone stares down at his tattered Nikes as they carry him along the Croft. He's not sure the shoes will make it to winter, which worries him. Finding this pair was a chore, months of scavenging every shop from Cabot up to Whiteladies, while his bare feet became encased in an immovable cake of scabs, blood, dead skin, and concrete dust. He'd even snuck into Clifton—three times—past the magistrates and the Land Army patrols, because someone, some wasteman, had fed him some bullshit about how Clifton got all the good shit. Clifton, the fortified neighborhood up on the hill whose residents had somehow managed to hold on to enough scraps of their wealth and privilege even after the crash had come, even after the rest of Bristol had struggled and burned. He'd been fed some lie about how they had these special operatives that come down here and buy up anything of any value, secretly, as soon as it comes off the gypsy vans from the landfills. And that they've got secret maps for the docks at Avonmouth that show where there are still containers with stuff in them, whole containers half the size of houses full of pristine treasures from China—brand-new fresh kicks, unblemished, sealed in cardboard boxes, lovingly hand-wrapped in tissue paper. Shirts, socks, jeans—all new. Devices with the peel-off protective films still stuck to their lenses, screens, and surfaces. Unused tech, uninfected, hibernating in warm nests woven from bubble-wrapping and polystyrene beads. Brand-new stormsuits still sealed in plastic wrappers that release a heady aroma of synthetic cotton and chemical cleanliness when you tear them open. Detergent fresh. It's not a smell Tyrone can remember, but he tries to imagine it, sometimes.

Containers with stuff still in them. Tyrone snorts to himself, sucks his teeth. He went up to Avonmouth once, years back, with a crew from his old ends. All kids, hungry but dumb, believing the hype. Nearly killed himself scaling a twelve-foot chain-link fence for nothing. Nothing. Not a thing. Nothing in those containers but tramps and criminals sheltering from the winds that rolled in from the Bristol Channel. And they'd looked for hours, for a whole day, man—fuck, it's big up there. They'd got lost more than once in there, in the endless maze of streets and alleyways formed by the spaces between the containers—padding around aimlessly, staring at cliff walls that towered into the sky and blocked the sun, smothering them in cold shadow, walls built from uniformly sized giant bricks—all twenty feet long, ten feet high—but every color of the spectrum, symbols and logos sprayed on their faces. Not like down here, where all the walls are painted with constantly shifting color, cartoon energies, and explosions of love and anger—no, Tyrone was used to that, knew that, recognized it. Down here it's background noise: the desperate, frustrated, barely controlled outpourings of people, of humans, splattered onto walls in paint born from crushed plants and rocks. But it was different up there in the container streets, it was like everything meant something. Of course, Tyrone knows the shit on the walls down here is meant to mean something too—pause too long on the Croft or down in Bemmie and invariably one of the old heads will snag you, running a hand through their geriatric beards or scratching at the flabby skin under their threadbare Adidas while they point at the walls and tell you the stories of the artists, the stories of rebellion and passion, of protest and rivalry, of riots and turf war. Human meanings; unreliable, fragile, and malleable.

But not on the containers. Tyrone couldn't tell what the symbols meant. There were words—hell, there were individual letters—he didn't understand, didn't even recognize, but he knew that they all meant something. Something solid, something firm. He knew they meant order, organization—something official, important. Something planned. Not mad outpourings, not passionate human splatter, but something with a sense of purpose, something with a system. Rational sequences of letters in hard, bold white fonts that always looked the same, reliable. Stars— always stars, some lone, some clustered—white stars on blue squares. Globes, maps, rectangles of white banded with colors and filled with shapes that he knew, from some fading school memory of stained, broken-spine books, were flags. As he walked past the walls he held his hand out, dragging it across the surface, enjoying the thrill of touching something alien, something that had allegedly traveled so far it seemed like a lie. Occasionally as he did so his fingernails would snag at the neat edge of a giant letter or precision-painted white star, and to his slight distress it would flake away; little sharp shards of metallic paint sticking to his clammy hands and spiraling to the ground, lost. It distressed him because he had assumed they were permanent, immovable—he'd assumed that unlike the berry-painted murals of Bristol, they didn't wash away in the rain, let alone when a kid just touched them—but they'd been here for years, he realized; decades, even, in all sorts of weather, and had survived. Even so, he withdrew his hand just in case, not wanting to inflict more damage, out of respect for the machines that had painted them. He couldn't be completely sure machines had put that paint there, of course, but in his heart he knew they had, because it spoke to him. And it's only ever the art the machines make that speaks to Tyrone.

But anyway, yeah, it's fucking big up there, man. Walking round there was long. They got lost more than once, and the last time they were so disoriented that they climbed up four stories of container wall to see where they were. It was pretty impressive up there; the city grid of the container maze stretching out in front of them all the way to the sea, and beyond that, touching the horizon, the huge, slowly looping tri-bladed propellers of the offshore wind farm disappearing into the mist. The rest of his crew got excited when they saw all that—for some it was the first time they'd seen the sea—and they wouldn't stop joking about going to the beach, swimming, diving off cliffs; bragging about which girls from the 'hood they were going to take down there to show off their bikinis. Kids' stuff. Not Tyrone, though, right then he knew they were wasting their time: as soon as he saw those windmills out at sea he knew all the stories of security and patrols up here were—well, they weren't bullshit exactly, but if there were feds or army up here it wasn't to protect these empty crates, it was to make sure nobody stopped those giant arms from spinning, or messed with the little stream of electricity trickling down into the city. Apart from that, this place was dead. He should have guessed that when they first broke in, and the only things watching them were forgotten, guano-spattered CCTV cameras, webs of broken-lens cataracts filling their dead eyes. Nobody protected anywhere unless there was something valuable inside, which was why you could just walk up to all those huge stores in Eastville, just walk straight in with nobody stopping you, the Tescos and the IKEA up there—some of them bigger than the whole Croft inside—you could just walk in there and see nothing but bare walls, empty shelves, everything stripped of anything that could be eaten or digested or burned or worn, anything that could keep you warm. Empty shop floors with just the useless metal and plastic left behind, the ground submerged under a couple of feet of water in the places where you could look up and see the sky because the roof tiles had been taken. Nobody protected that shit anymore.

Not up in Clifton, though—that's why he'd sneaked in those three times, even though each time he'd got his ass kicked back out again pretty much straightaway. In fact, with each beating he took from a Clifton magistrate or some pissed-up LA grunt it made him more convinced there was good stuff in there. Had to be, it was Clifton, for fuck's sake. But each covert incursion got him no closer to some new shoes, just a fresh shower of bruises, more chipped teeth, another mouthful of blood. Eventually he packed it in and looked elsewhere, and then of course he stumbled across these kicks—the Nikes—in the back bedroom of some terrace house he and Ozone had jacked in Lawrence Hill, his old ends. Right around the corner from home. Sod's law, as College would say. They were two sizes too big for him, so they rubbed like fuck until he padded them out with some old bits of foam cut out of a car seat, but they were fucking Nikes, barely worn. They looked like they were less than a decade old when he first found them, swear down.

Not now, though, that had been two years ago this summer, and now they looked old and fucked. Proper fucked. Split to all shit. One of Mary's believers had brought in some glue for her as a gift; transparent, hard-core stringy gloop in a little tube—a rare and valuable find indeed. She'd let him use some of it, and he'd managed to fix them up a bit—but that was a few months ago now, and he hadn't seen that tube around for a while. Most likely Mary had given it to College—he'd come into the store every so often and root around in the piles of donated crap, seeing if there was anything he needed to help keep the important stuff running—the tank, the panels, the stuff that kept the Croft running. And of course Mary gave it to him, anything he needed, no questions asked. Presumably Grids told her she had to, and Grids rarely told her to do anything she didn't want to, but she seemed more than happy to give College whatever he wanted. She seemed, to Tyrone at least, like she couldn't get rid of all that shit quickly enough.

Tyrone ingests beats from the other side of the chicken wire, pushed along the spiraling cable that snakes through diamond spaces to the headphones that sit heavily on his head. Vinyl spins in front of him, just inches away from his hands but forever out of his touch behind the pro-

tective mesh, bass flowing from vibrations on rare wax that
he can't afford. He watches the stylus head rise and fall,
tracing the contours of hypnotic spin as the tune ends;
stolen, rearranged syllables and reverb-drenched snare hits
dying away in decades-old waves of echo and distortion.

He takes the headphones off, hangs them on the nail
that protrudes from the wood that frames the chicken wire,
turns, and looks around the record shop. It's an odd sensation, when you first step in here—the feeling that you've
stepped into a prison, a cage. The shop floor itself is tiny
and compressed yet empty, unfilled. Step through the front
door and you're in the empty chicken-wire cage, just you
and any other punters that have wandered in, with nothing to do but stare out of your prison at the treats that line
the walls behind: the dead, neglected devices propped up
on shelves, the ancient music machines adorned with knobs
and sliders, their once-pristine faceplates potted with
scratches and finger smears, and of course the records—
walls of vinyl, carefully cataloged and filed. Once, when
Tyrone was still a little kid, they used to be out on display,
arranged in racks facing you, so you could flip through
them with your fingertips, so you could scan through each
section quickly to see if anything new had arrived, or to be
horrified that something you wanted had gone, something
you'd craved for months and had saved for, selling off your
ration coupons and any shit you could find to get your hands
on a few pennies you'd hide away until you had enough
to maybe, possibly, one day walk in there with your head

held high and your pocket full of shrapnel you could swap
for music.

Mike sees him hang the phones up, works his way
around to him on the other side of the wire, stepping over
boxes of unsorted compact discs and squeezing past pro-
truding shelves laden with dusty cassettes.

"Any good?"

"Yeah. Yeah, I'll take the lot. Stick 'em on my tab."

Mike smiles, gently and sympathetically. "Sorry, Ty."

In long, painful silence Tyrone watches him take the
record from the turntable, fingers gently touching only the
razor sharpness of its edge before balancing it, with an
archivist's care, on one hand—the tip of his middle finger in
the center hole, his thumb still only touching the edge, as
he gently drops it into the waxy white paper of the inner
sleeve, which, after rotating it 90 degrees so the disc won't
roll out, he in turn slides into the plain black card outer.
Slowly he turns, scanning the walls of record spines, navi-
gating the complex patterns with some secret geographer's
knowledge, before nodding and slipping it into its rightful
place, and Tyrone feels his heart drop as he watches it disappear, lost among the obscurity, and he realizes it'll probably be the last time he'll ever see it until inevitably that
next man drops it at that next party.

"You shouldn't be listening to this shit anyway, Ty.
Y'know? It's depressing."

Tyrone sucks teeth, his standard annoyed/defensive reaction. "Here we go. This again. Always this."

"Yeah, well. I'm fucking right. This ain't your music. Jesus, a lot of the stuff you reach for is so old it ain't even my music."

"Bet you don't say that to the Loco crew when they come in here and drop money on those jukebox sevens."

Mike shakes his head. "C'mon. Loco are all a lot older than you. Jesus, Shaka must be nearly seventy. Old wizard will never die. The rum has pickled his soul, he says." They both laugh.

Tyrone studies Mike. The old head ain't that young himself, easily pushing forty. That's getting on, around these codes. And he's got a point. A lot of the stuff Tyrone plays, that he obsesses over, was released before even Mike was old enough to go out raving.

"Well, I don't exactly know what my alternative is."

"Make your own. Like we did."

Tyrone screwfaces him. "On what, exactly?"

Mike shrugs. "I dunno. Improvise."

"Improvise? Improvise. Okay." Tyrone points at ancient matte-black Japanese electronics gathering dust on a shelf behind Mike's head. "That's easy for you to say when you're charging six months' rent for a poxy TR-8."

"It doesn't have to be, y'know, electronic stuff."

"Oh, what? You want me to learn the ukulele now?"

"It doesn't have to—"

Mike is interrupted by a disembodied voice from under the shop's counter. He recognizes it instantly. "You still got that old Akai 950, Ty?"

"Yeah. I still got it. Piece of shit."

College's head ascends into view, a mess of dreadlocks and unkempt beard. He hauls up a box of old glasses—all colors and shapes and states of repair, more than a few with cracked or even missing lenses—and dumps it on the counter in front of him, continuing to rummage through it as he speaks. "Ain't it working? That a nice bit of kit, man. Classic machine."

"Nah. Well, sort of. Half the memory is fried, I think. And I ran out of discs, so I can't save shit anyway."

"Bring it down mine next week. I might have memory sticks that might fit it. Might." He pauses, investigating a pair of glasses in his hands, turning and moving them about in 3D space as if accessing the integrity of their physical structure. For a second Ty thinks he's going to sniff, maybe taste them. Instead he just drops them back into the box, continues to rummage. "And anyway, you shouldn't worry about discs. That's healthy."

"What you sayin'?"

"Make your tunes, record 'em, wipe over the discs, reuse 'em. Wipe the samples. Makes you have to find new sounds for each new tune, means you can't go back after it's been put down on tape and constantly re-edit everything. Keeps everything fresh."

Tyrone thinks about this, thinks about the half-broken Akai sampler back in his bedroom. Thinks about the days he spent combing through his vinyl collection, searching for sounds he could take and use, building a library that spans the dozen or so ancient 3.5-inch floppies he spent years tracking down. He thinks about the hours he spends trawling through that library when working on something, trying to find that elusive sound that would make the tune complete, and how often he'd fail. Thinks about how he'd do whatever he could to try to warp and meld those samples into something else; running them through his small collection of effects pedals, recording and rerecording them onto ancient cassettes to make them compressed and distorted, transmitting them over the station's FM transmitter and resampling them off his auntie's tiny radio to wrap them in distant hiss and static. And he thinks about his attempts to make his own sounds: drumming on kitchen pots and pans, jacking an old busted set of headphones into the 950's mic input and dangling them out his bedroom window to catch the staccato rain patterns, the filter sweeps of tenth-story breezes, the shouts and cries of people down in the streets.

Maybe College has a point.

Mike certainly thinks he's got one. "See? That was the problem. That's what I'm always sayin'. There was no limits before, right?"

Tyrone looks at him, unsure. "Right . . . ?"

"See . . . look. Before the crash, right? Nobody was using hardware setups anymore. Everyone was on software. You could get it just by fucking blinking, right? You could get any software you wanted, that'd do anything you wanted. That'd give you any sound you could think of, pretty much. Unlimited possibilities. That was what was wrong, right?"

"It was?"

"Yeah. It was. It fucking was. Think about it. People could do what they liked, anything. It's why the music became so self-indulgent, so undisciplined, and then so weirdly formulaic. Good art is produced under strict limits. Forces you to work with what you've got, to focus, right? There was no focus at the end. No control or vision. Just lots of people fucking about but ultimately following each other's leads because they were drowning in choices. Unlimited possibilities."

Tyrone thinks about this now. Sees Mike's point, but ain't too sure. Mike annoys him when he talks like this, because Tyrone knows all about limits. He's sick and tired of limits. "I dunno," he says. "I'd like just one or two possibilities, you get me?"

College smiles at him, more polite aging sympathy from the first generation that knows they had it better, and can't muster the gall to deny it. "Don't worry, Ty, it'll come together. Just keep at it."

"Yeah." Tyrone shrugs. "I guess."

Beside him, holding one shell from a pair of discarded headphones to his lips as a makeshift mic, Bags lists off the crews. All the codes, whether friends, rivals, or enemies, must get a mention. They all come together here, no conflict, all locked to the same frequencies, Tyrone and Bags's transmissions see no borders, no turf disputes. From the battlegrounds of Upper Easton and the hippie slums of St. Werburgh's, right down to the Land Army camps in Brislington and across to the fortified palaces of Clifton, everyone who cared was locked in. Bags reels off their names, each gang and sound system, like systematic syncopated poetry, each line punctuated with a *hold tight*, a *keep it locked*, a *shout-out*. And then he moves on to the more important callouts, the requests, the birthdays, messages of love, the reminiscences for fallen friends and family, the helpless pleas for the eternally missing to come home. The messages that people have dropped off personally, that they've deemed important enough to trek not only to Barton from whichever end of the city, but then to climb up the tower to post directly through their door. When they first started the station nobody came, but then, as they gave shout-outs and people realized they were serious about reading them, it started to grow. Now there are almost too many to fit into the show every night, almost so many notes that he can't open the door when he gets home. It fills him with some pride, like he's doing something for the city that few can, but it also fills him with sadness. There's too much melancholy on those scribbled notes, too much desperation, too much need to be seen, to be recognized, to be heard and a part of something. Too much that now Tyrone can't look at them anymore, leaves them all to Bags to sort through, and even when he's reading them out he tries not to listen, focuses on his mixing.

He allows his finger to brush against the vinyl, that

gentle balance between being able to feel the record spin and affecting it just enough to slow it, to nudge renegade snares back into alignment. Press too hard and it slows too much, everything stumbles, the pitch bending too much, bass and strings detuning. Too light and those snares will get away from you again, and before you know it the kicks start to sound like a pair of trainers in a spin dryer.

Tyrone cuts the bass on the left channel, lets both tracks roll out together for four bars on just their mids and highs, snares in unison, filtered percussion spiraling with anticipation, before bringing back the bass on the new track, a low, slow four-note rumble that shakes the shelves and makes the windowpanes sing. Modulated distortion. Takes the bass out again, just for one bar this time, and brings it back in as he drops the first track out of the mix completely.

It's that time of night when it's all about jungle, from now until the end of the show—it's all about that Bristol sound, staccato vocal chop-ups, reggae pulses, ancient drums dug up from the depths of lost musical history made to sound like the future they'd already lost. A collage of past sounds, most from before he was even born, that together become atemporal, timeless.

He remembers the first times he heard that sound as a small child, before the crash, reverberating out of passing cars like a secret black technology, or cranked from his mum's cheap hi-fi speakers as she and her friends laughed and drank and smoked in their best dresses before head-

ing out to the club. She'd kiss him and tell him to take
care, and then they'd all be out the front door of her flat,
still laughing and screeching, and he'd go back into the
lounge and turn the hi-fi back on and the beats would be
back, rolling and crashing, and he'd push the volume until
the neighbors knocked on the walls and ceiling. Nobody
knocked now.

Then after the crash, after she'd gone, that sound again.
Playing from street sound systems, filling deserted shopping
centers and office blocks with partygoers, soundtracking
food riots and street battles. It was then he started to really
pay attention, to pick out tones and sounds, to understand
form and structure. Dark afro futures were made real,
musical stories with life breathed into them. Before the
crash it had seemed impossible to separate Bristol from
drum and bass; afterward the connection was pure logic. A
soundtrack for celebrating the urban decay of the twenty-
first century, for dancing in the new ruins of industrial civilization, translated now as a soundtrack for everyday life.

It was also the default option now, in many ways, Tyrone
understood. He never denied the reality of that, never tried
to kid himself. In many ways this was the last music on
record, the last throw of urban energy and expression before the shift came. He had everything and anything he
could find in his collection of CDs and vinyl records, from
New Orleans jazz and New York hip-hop through to Detroit techno and Chicago house, city names he knew only
from atlases and record labels. But the jungle, the grime,

the dubstep—that was the last new music that his city made that was committed to wax and plastic, Bristol's final urban hymns given a physical form before the great shift to digital, and hence the last new music to survive the crash, to be unscathed in the great erasing. They might be relics, these scratched and battered discs, but like the crumbling towers and hollowed-out office blocks where he partied they were still standing when everything else had been washed away.

The beat rolling out now—the one he's mixing the next tune into—is one of his, a collage of samples from the failing Akai, dubbed down onto ancient cassette. He used to get a thrill when he dropped one of his own tunes, a jolt of excited pride, but now he feels little more than disappointment. It's cut-and-paste jungle, a break lifted from here, a bass line from there. Clichéd vocal samples reverberating through his tired echo pedal. Jungle by numbers, assembled from pieces of itself. Pure formula, nothing original. Mike's words echo as Tyrone shakes his head in self-disgust. This isn't his music, none of it, not even the pieces he's crafted himself. It's archaeological echoes of a lost era.

He hits the STOP button on the stereo wired into the DJ mixer, a fifty-year-old cube flecked with dull LEDs. With his usual concerned reluctance he reaches out his hand, his finger hovering on the molded texture of the EJECT button, and draws breath, closes eyes, tries to block out nightmare visions of disgorged black guts, coiled flat ribbons of magnetic entrails spilling out over his hands.

He pushes the button in, just enough force to defeat its spring-loaded resistance, opens his eyes as he hears the click.

The tape deck slides open, with machine grace, and away from the hi-fi's flat front panel. Tyrone's hand instinctively grabs the top ridge of the cassette, gently sliding it out, not allowing himself to exhale until he can see it's safely free. Relief. No tangled intestine, no writhing mass of dead, flat worms. He holds the cassette up to the light, peers through its little transparent plastic window. The tape looks a little baggy around the right-hand wheel, but nothing major—he sticks the tip of his first finger into the hole, feels the spokes gripping his flesh, and with the slightest, most gentle effort winds the tape on half a turn; just enough to tighten it up so it clings to the wheel, just little enough that it's not too taut. He can't remember an exact figure, but he knows this cassette has snagged at least five times, each time his heart dropping and the breath forcing its way out as he slid it out of the deck and watched it leave strings of what looked like melted black tar in its wake. The last time it happened was back at his place, some radio show after-party, the flat full of randos and smoke, and they'd all crowded around him to see what was going on, trying to help but giving it too much volume, pushing and prodding and jostling as he knelt on the floor, his hands trembling with panic as he tried to untangle the mess, and it all got to be too much and he freaked and threw everyone out. Just like that, no exposition, just get the fuck out—puzzled looks, screwfaces, stoned confusion— threw them all out into the corridor so that it was just him on the stained carpet, alone in the silence with his tears and the tape, turning the wheels so gently, threading it back in, checking it for kinks.

Maybe it's time for it to break, he tells himself. Time for his work to be lost, like so much that went before. Wipe it all, erase it. Make something fresh, something that matters. Make something new.

He slips the next record from its sleeve, slides it onto the spinning platter, gently drops the needle. Bursts of static and dust in his headphones, and then high-speed tones as he uses his finger to spin forward through the record. Finds the first beat, pulls it back, cues, lets it go.

A five-note sub-bass rolls out, distortion, skittering beats—some long-dead session drummer's handiwork compressed into a groove, filtered, distorted, pitched up to near twice its normal speed—at once both impossibly fast and monolithically glacial in its relentlessness. Sonar blips, piano hits, bird chirps all wrapped in the infinite space of reverb, eternally echoing through waves of distorted air, filter sweeps seemingly pulling new frequencies from the silence, from the gaps between the sounds, making the sparse complex and the crowded empty. Decades of history, long lost elsewhere, but spoken on vinyl in the machine language.

The door behind them is hurled open, a voice shouts his name. At first he ignores it, lost in touching the groove.

It shouts again. He looks around. Angelo shouts at him over the relentless percussion.

"Yo, it's broken, man."

"Huh?"

"It's broken. The transmitter. It's down."

"Nothing at all?"

"Nothing, man. Just static."

Bags looks at him, rolls his eyes, and they sigh as one. "You want me to go?"

"Nah. You stay here. Just make sure it keeps rolling."

Piss-stink stairwell. Squeak of kicks on laminate. Knocks on door.

Tyrone braces himself.

Shouts from behind the plywood and chipped orange paint. Bolts drawing back. The door opens an inch or two, expelling ganja-tinged air. A face he doesn't know appears, one of Grids's boys.

"Easy, Ty, the music's stopped, innit."

"Yeah, I know. It's why I'm here."

Blank look. Hint of shade.

"To get on the roof?"

"Oh, seen. Come." The door pulls back, and Tyrone follows him in.

People, maybe a dozen of them, are crowded around a low table. Grids is there. Mary, too. Faces turn to look at him, nod.

"Easy, Tyrone."

"Yo, Tyrone."

"Hey, Ty, the music stopped, man."

Tyrone just nods back, points at the ceiling. "I need the keys. For the roof."

"In the kitchen. Drawer next to the fridge." It's Grids's voice, but Tyrone doesn't see his face. "Put them back when you're done, yeah?"

The smell in the kitchen hits him hard, stops him in his tracks. He feels his face burn, some complex mix of shock and anger, hunger and jealousy.

The fatty aroma of meat, stewed—goat or lamb. Curried with thick, sweet spices. Turmeric, cumin, chili; words he hears Grids's boys whisper on the corners. Rice sits in a half-full pan. Clean, white, sticky. He fights the urge to jam his hand in and force it into his mouth. He can't remember the last time he saw rice.

He knows where the spices are from—the hydroponic farms in the old buildings at the back of the Croft, the ones left over from before, the ones the old hippies used to grow their vegetables before the crash. When Grids took the Croft he put them all over to growing ganja, until he realized he could get a higher price growing herbs and spices— the things the Land Army didn't provide through their tightly controlled rationing, the things everybody wanted. Illicit flavors, tastes, and smells.

Now less than half of the farms grow weed, most of them concentrating on spices. The people that used to live in the buildings next to them were all evicted to make room for the cramped sweatshops, where Grids's boys watch over the women and children that endlessly clean, slice, prepare, and dry them for sale, cloths wrapped around their mouths and noses, goggles shaped from ancient landfill plastic strapped across their eyes. Tyrone and Bags snuck in there once, just to take a look, and the dust was everywhere, staining the surfaces of everything red and orange just as it stung his eyes and burned his nostrils, so much that he could barely breathe. He felt like he might die, but it was so intoxicating a poison—so vivid, so delicious—that he felt like he never wanted to leave.

The other food—the rice, that meat that isn't rat or chicken—he knows where that comes from, too. From bribes and backdoor deals, from illegal trades and illicit privileges. From power and significance.

Rage snaps him back into action and he turns away from the food, ignoring the growl of his stomach. With the hint of tears in his eyes, some shadow sense memory of the spice sweatshops, he rummages through the drawer next to the still-working fridge until he finds the keys, and stuffs them into his hoodie pocket.

It's cold up on the roof, the night air biting his cheeks, and he pulls his hood over his head as he makes his way between the jury-rigged solar panels. Another spoil from the Croft, dragged up here to Barton Hill by Grids's crew. The lights always stay on in the tower. He keeps his head down as he walks, watching his feet, so as not to trip on the mess of cables that webs the panels and batteries together.

The transmitter nest is a mess of scaffolding and dead technology, aerials and faceless microwave transmitters, the short, stubby alien monoliths of cellular base stations looking out across the city, all covered in graffiti and bird shit. Once they were some vital node, a keystone of some invisible infrastructure, and as Tyrone stares at them he imagines he can hear the network traffic bustling through them, pulses and clicks, syncopated bleeps and sine-wave sub-bass, the high-pass-filtered scatter of drum breaks.

Now the networks are gone, the technology silent, apart from the few hours every night when they hijack the infrastructure for themselves, taking over this weathered, twisted monument to beam out their own traffic.

He drops his backpack to the floor and reaches inside to pull out the small windup radio. He gives it a few cranks and turns it on, placing it next to his bag. The static of dead airwaves leaks out into the cold night sky.

He pretty much already knows what's up. The cable carrying power from one of the solar batteries to the FM transmitter slung underneath the nest—a ramshackle old Tupperware box that College filled with scavenged cables and components—is always coming loose in the wind. He's always promising to find some way of making it more weatherproof, but he's always too tied up keeping the panels and the hydroponics down at the Croft running. For now it's held together with some unlikely conception of string and decade-old sticky tape, and Ty fiddles with it incessantly until the radio behind him starts to splutter, the static breaking up to give way to the occasional snare and high hat.

Eventually what he's doing holds, and cautiously he removes his hands and steps back, the music constant now, the jungle breaks rolling out of the radio's tiny speakers. He bends down to grab it but pauses, stands back upright again. He lets the radio do its thing, lets it capture the invisible data from the aerial nest, lets it make it real. Making the inaudible audible, revealing the true contents of the air. This is what it's all about.

Slowly, fighting vertigo, he edges toward the roof's edge. Below him Bristol is laid out like a crumpled map in the night, dark architecture merging with more forgotten, useless infrastructure and long-abandoned roadways. The only signs of life are the interior lights from those neighborhoods that have been lucky enough to jury-rig electricity, and the flickering of outside fires from those that haven't. There's the occasional shout from the streets right below him, from the spaces between the towers, and he can hear his own radio waves being translated back to him. All at once he feels some pride rise in him, some all-too-rare wave of accomplishment.

His focus is broken by an unearthly sound behind him,

and vertigo hits him as he stumbles back from the ledge, turning. Half hidden under the angle of one of the solar panels is a seagull, nestled with its young against the wind, watching him suspiciously with a piercing black-and-yellow eye. It squawks again, and Ty feels his pride and significance fade, replaced yet again by the constant sense of fragility. He realizes now that he's the only person to come up here regularly, otherwise this gull and its family would be dead; plucked and jerk-seasoned and roasted over a fire. Gently he bends down, grabs the radio and his bag, and finds another route around the panels to the stairs back down into the tower, so as not to disturb the bird again. As he goes it never takes its eye off him, tracking his every move like the now-dead CCTV cameras that always watched him and the other kids from the towers whenever they went out to play, and all he can think of is his dead mother.

Back in Grids's apartment he pushes into the kitchen, and is surprised to see the man himself standing there, eating curry from a bowl.

"You got it working, then?"

"Yeah. Loose connection." Tyrone drops the keys back into the drawer. He instantly seizes up, finds himself checking his emotions and movements, some ingrained mixture of embarrassment and bravado.

Grids nods toward the rumble of the radio from another room. "Sounding good."

"Cheers."

He wipes rice from his lips and fixes Tyrone with slightly blunted eyes. "You ever find that beat I was looking for?"

"Melody's beat?"

"Yeah."

"Nah."

"Yeah, well. Don't think it ever made it to vinyl, innit. Just thought you might have heard it on a tape." He laughs, shakes his head. "A tape. I didn't know what a fucking tape was when me and Mel were your age. Dead technology, fam. Now we're all excited about finding tapes."

"Yeah, I don't think so. Plus I never heard it, so I wouldn't know."

"Oh, you'd know it if you heard it."

"What about her?" Tyrone nods toward the door.

"Mary? Nah. Says Mel was . . ." Grids pauses, looks at the floor. "Says she was gone before the time she can remember. Before she can see, y'know."

"That's how it works?"

"Apparently. Like there's only a small time she can see. Like a few days, I think." He shrugs. "I don't fucking know."

Tyrone wants to ask him how much he really believes in it all. Mary. Why he keeps her so close, now he knows she won't find Melody. He thought that was the only point.

"Can I ask you a question?"

"What?"

"About Mary. You believe all that?" As soon as the words

leave his mouth he regrets them, expects Grids to get upset, to think it's a diss. That he's questioning his authority.

Instead the old gangster just laughs, shakes his head. "I don't know what to believe anymore, Ty, to be honest. Do I think she's psychic? Probably not. But do I think she sees shit we don't? Maybe. I do know she makes people happy. Gets through to 'em. Puts 'em at rest. Gives 'em closure. You've seen it. What she does, how it affects people. That's gotta be important, right?"

"I guess," Tyrone says.

"Besides. I gotta look after her. Whatever she is. I gotta keep her for us, for the Croft. Because if I don't—" He pauses, and for a second Tyrone gets a sense that he knows more, knows something special about Mary that he's keeping from him. From everyone. "I can't let her get out of the Croft, man. Can't let her get into the wrong hands. That's why what you do, looking after her—that's why that's important. You get me?"

"Of course, man. Of course."

"You want some food?" Grids sounds like he wants to change the subject.

"Ah no, I'm good." His stomach rumbles. But something tells him no, that it's not right. He's not sure what.

"Really? You must be hungry. It's good. Goat. Made it myself, man."

"Nah, I'm good. Gotta get back to the radio, innit."

"A'ight, if you're sure."

"Yeah. Cheers." He heads for the door.

"Well played today, man, y'know."

Ty turns around, startled. "Huh?"

"That shit with Mary, the guys from the Land Army. You handled it well." He shovels another forkful of rice and meat into his mouth.

"Cheers," says Tyrone, and walks out, head high, riding on significance.

9. AFTER

I can't believe you're actually here."

"I can't believe I'm actually here."

The bar is full of ghosts.

So many that their bodies seem to obscure the living, who sit hunched over their beer and cider, their clothes ragged and fading, patched at knees and elbows. They look tired and broken, older than their own ghosts somehow, who stand and laugh beside them, their clothes still ragged and faded, but in intentional, affected irony. Less crumpled, cleaner.

The ghosts have more life than the living, Anika thinks.

She rubs her eyes and sips warm, too-sour cider. The ghosts disappear.

"I can't believe this place is still here."

College smiles. "You'll be surprised how little has changed."

"Yeah?"

"Yeah. Well, apart from everything." They both laugh. "You know what I mean. This place—the Croft, I mean. It's always going to be the same, man. You get me?"

"Yeah. Yeah." She looks at him. "We got old, though."

"Yeah. Well. It's been a while."

"Yeah. Yeah it has."

Over the first cider he gets her up to speed. About how it was tough for years, but they held it together. How Grids kept a firm grip on the Croft but was reasonable, mainly. How they held it all together with string and solar panels. How they kept Claire's farms open and running enough so that most people had a few fresh vegetables and a little ganja, plus enough spices to trade with the Mullahs in Easton and the pharma labs in Brislington. All to the annoyance of the Land Army and the city council. He glosses over the details: the pain and the deaths and the suffering. That's all taken as read.

"Claire still here?" she asks him.

"Nah, she's back up at the uni now. Doing research up there."

"Research?"

"More farm stuff. Hydroponics and aquaponics. So they can build more. It's hard, though, getting the shit she needs. Everything she built down here—well, it was all from stuff she bought online. Stuff she had shipped from China, or that she printed herself. The LA wants her to just copy what she built here, but she's gotta start from scratch. Like, really from scratch. She's gotta work out how to make stuff that was never made here."

"She's working for the LA?"

"Nah. Well, yes. Kind of. They pay for some of her research, I think."

"Right."

"Ah, c'mon, Anika." He shakes his head. "Don't be like that. You know how she is. She's just doing what she thinks is right. Just doing what she always did. She just wants to feed people."

"I guess." Anika looks down, into the sickly orange soup of her pint.

"What about Rush? You ever see him again?"

College shakes his head, can't meet her eyes. "Nah. Last time I saw him, he was with you."

"Right."

"I gotta assume he's—I dunno. He's either on the other side of the world or they caught him."

"Or he's dead."

"Well, yeah. I guess. Claire is convinced he got out of

the country. Went to try and find that Internet boyfriend of his. Steve?"

"Scott."

"Yeah, that's the one. She reckons he went to the U.S. to see if he was okay. Says he was completely obsessed with him, in love."

"But how? It was hardly like he could just get on a plane. I mean, all the airports were fucked, I thought?"

College shrugs. "Something about a ship. That academic friend of his that bought a container ship, you remember that?"

"Strickland."

"Sounds about right." He finally makes eye contact with her. "Is that why you came back? Wanting to find him?"

She blushes. Memories of her lost mentor, of abandonment and betrayal. "No. Of course not."

Over the second cider she gets him up to speed. About Wales, and the civil war. About how she spent two years on a farming commune before the Land Army turned up and seized it, and forced them all to work the land. About how she escaped, went on the run, ended up with the insurgency. About the Bloc training camps. About being in Cardiff when it fell. She glosses over the details; the pain and the deaths and the suffering. Again, that's all taken as read.

"It's not going well, then?" he asks her.

"It could be better, yeah."

"I'm sorry. We don't get much news from outside the city, y'know? We don't even know what's happening in London."

"It's pretty bad. Wales, I mean." She has to look away, can't keep eye contact with him. The bar fills with ghosts again, ones that don't belong here. Ghosts wrapped in bandages, clothed in camouflage. The ghosts of crying children, of their wounded and broken parents sobbing on the floor. "The LA controls most of the countryside now, right up through Cheshire. All the cities and towns are theirs now."

"I'm sorry."

"I mean—" She stops herself, hearing the tremble in her voice. Breathes. Hard words for her to say. "I understand, I get it. I know why they're doing it. They need to feed everyone, keep the cities alive. They need the land and they need the workers. I get that. It's just—they're so fucking brutal. The number of people they've moved. The refugee camps. The way they treat people. What they've done to people, to children, to families—"

"Yeah. I've heard. I'm sorry. I know what—"

"No." Her head snaps back to face him, her voice raised. "No, you don't know. You don't fucking know."

Glances from the living in the bar. The ghosts have gone again.

He reaches out, touches her hand. "I'm sorry. Really. I am."

She sighs, takes a deep breath. "No. It's okay. I'm sorry. I just . . . y'know. I'm fine."

College takes his hand back, downs the last of his cider, winces at the acid burn. "Come on, let's get the fuck out of here. Get some food. You can crash at mine tonight. Oh, and fuck, yeah. I nearly forgot."

"What?"

"There's something you should see."

"Fucking hell."

College laughs. "Yeah. Mad, innit."

"Is it . . . ?"

"Yep. It's yours."

The tank sits in a pile of rubble, a vacated space where architecture once stood. She glances up and down the street, trying to work out what it once was. She can't get her bearings. The Croft doesn't look that different, but enough buildings have fallen, enough shop fronts vanished, that she's lost for a second.

"What used to be here?"

"Really? You can't work it out?"

"Nah."

"Tesco."

"Oh." She laughs. They both laugh. "Oh, shit. That's kind of perfect." Tesco supermarket. An eternal emblem of the struggle of Stokes Croft, going back nearly three decades now. The scene of protests, riots, battles. A corporate infringement into the anticapitalist hipster dream, but one that meant the real locals could afford to buy bread and cider.

"Right? I thought you'd like that. Part of the reason I put it here."

"You put it here?"

College shakes his head. "Don't ask. Long story."

At first glance the tank looks like it's covered in psychedelic camouflage, pink and red and blue scatter markings, as though it were trying to stage a sneak attack on a sweetshop. That makes it hard to make out the tank's form, but as her eyes become accustomed to the patterns she realizes what it is: every part of its surface—its armor, its turret, its tracks, even its canon—is covered with graffiti. Paint and stickers, words and colors. Tags. Splatters. Wildstyle lettering. Doodles and characters. Slogans. The names of the dead.

She steps up onto the rubble, runs a hand across the tank's flank, just above its busted, spray-painted tracks. It feels rough, the texture of layer upon layer of forgotten art. She has a sudden flashback to a forgotten time. Amsterdam.

"Damn."

Sprouting out of the top of the turret is a sprayed-out cobweb of cables, dozens of wires silhouetted black against the dusk sky. Like the tendrils of some mutated banyan tree they explode out of the tank, shooting up to the walls of the neighboring buildings and across the street, fastening themselves to broken brick surfaces and slithering onto rooftops.

"Does it work?" she asks College.

"God, no." He fishes inside his olive combat trousers, pulls out a crumpled joint, stretches it out. He produces a lighter from his bomber jacket. "Well, it doesn't move, if that's what you mean. The control systems are all fried, they died with everything else. But the battery still works."

"The battery?"

He lights the joint, takes a drag. "Yeah. It's got a huge fucking industrial-level battery inside it. Took me fucking ages to figure out how, but I got it to work. I tried taking it out, but it was a pain in the arse, so I just left it in there. Now it's wired up to most of the panels down this end of the Croft. Stores electricity, means we get some juice at night."

She looks up, tracing the cables across the sky again. "Right."

"It's carnival this weekend."

"Seriously?"

"Yeah, no shit. We come down here and hook a massive system up to the battery. Put some decks up on the turret, turn it into a DJ booth. Everyone comes down and dances around the tank. Your tank."

She smiles at the thought. "I like that." She looks at him. "You know what—can I ask you a question?"

"Sure. What?"

"I never got around to asking you this before, it always bugged me. Why they call you College?"

"Because I went to college."

"Everyone went to college, College."

"Not where I'm from."

"Sorry, of course." She's embarrassed. "You mean Barton Hill?"

"Yeah. Up in the towers. Up in the sky." He sighs. Wistful, stoned. "When we was kids most of us up there dropped out of school at sixteen. Couldn't afford to stay on. Not me. Instead I got myself involved in some shady shit just so I could pay my way. Loved my fucking video games too much, wanted to know all about them, make them. All my mates started calling me College."

"That's when you knew Grids, from before?"

"Yeah. We came up together. Were pretty tight. Got ourselves in enough trouble back then. But then I finished college here, down in St. Bart's, and I went off to university. I'd actually made enough money running around with Grids to do that, which was crazy, thinking about it. So yeah, I went off to Manchester. Came back three years later and everything had changed. You know how it is. Friends drift apart, innit? Grids was dealing, Mel . . . Melody was off doing her music thing. I was twenty-one and all kinds of fucking fired up about saving the world. Barton wasn't the place for that. Or me. So when I bumped into Rush and saw what he was doing I moved down here."

"And now you and Grids are tight again."

"I guess. It's different. Everything's different."

"Yeah. It is."

College takes another toke, then steps over rubble to pass her the joint. "So then, my turn."

"Huh?"

"Can I ask you a question?"

"Sure." She takes a hit. It burns her throat.

"As much as I'd like to think it's because you were missing me, why'd you really come back here? I mean, for someone that's on the LA's wanted list, it's hardly the most sensible place to come. Whole city is crawling with 'em."

"I dunno. I thought . . ." She's suddenly stoned, space echoing around her head. From somewhere down the street she can hear the scattershot rolling drums of jungle, bass throbbing. An MC chatting. Pirate radio vibes. Bristol. She can't help but smile.

"You thought what?"

"I thought maybe there'd be something that'd give us an advantage. In Wales, I mean. Against the LA."

"The tank?"

"What? No." She laughs, stoned. "No, not the fucking tank, College. It's not that kind of war."

"Then what?"

"I dunno." She feels embarrassed, suddenly too self-aware. "Something that might help us be organized, keep us one step ahead."

He doesn't reply, an awkward pause. She climbs down from the tank, hands him back the joint.

"Y'know, something left over from before," she continues. She looks at the tank, feels light-headed. Its collage of patterns seems to strobe, a faint stoned memory of ancient GIF art.

"Yeah, well, sorry to disappoint you, but this is it," College eventually says, an edge of discomfort to his voice. "An old tank and some solar panels."

She looks at him, knows he's holding something back. "What about the network? You been trying to get it up and running again?"

College takes a hit, blows out purple-tinted ganja smoke. He shakes his head, scratches his beard. Sheepish. He looks at the ground.

"It's gone, Anika. Went the same way as this tank."

Anika holds his gaze, even as he tries to look away. "Really?"

"Yeah. Really."

"You sure, College?"

"What you saying, Anika?"

"Nothing. Nothing." She can't decide whether he's genuinely offended, angry, or covering for something. She can't decide whether to push him further.

She lets it hang in the air for a minute, watching him smoke. Then she decides.

"It's just . . . y'know. I was never an expert on how it all worked, that was your and Rush's gig. But I thought it was meant to be self-repairing?"

"It is. I mean it was. But that was before we blew the

jammers up. You remember us doing that, right? I mean, it was a busy day, but you remember that?"

She smiles at his trademark dark humor. She's missed it. "Yeah, I remember."

"Well, that was the end of the network. Turn off the jammers and you turn off the barrier to the outside world, to the Internet. With that gone we were just as susceptible to infection as the rest of the world."

"Huh." It's not quite how she remembers it, not quite how she thought it worked, but okay. Time to try a slightly different angle. "So you never even tried to get it back up?"

College sighs, irritated. "For fuck's sake, Anika. I've been busy. Look at all this shit, the power, the solar, I built all this. I've been fucking busy. I had to get this shit up and running, people's lives depended on it."

"Yeah, of course. I'm sorry."

"It just wasn't ever a priority. Especially not for Grids. And he calls all the shots around here. And he made it pretty clear I wasn't to waste my time on that stuff."

"He did?"

"Yeah. He fucking hates all that stuff. Always has. So-cial media, everything. Hated it when we were kids and hates it now. He made it pretty clear I wasn't to touch any of it."

"But you must have, y'know, experimented . . ."

He can't meet her eyes now. "Anika, I told you. It doesn't work. And Grids made it super fucking clear to me it was out of bounds. He hates it. Plus maybe—I dunno. Maybe he sees it as threatening his power, or maybe he's got something he wants to hide, he doesn't want being dragged up again."

"Maybe." Her head floods with images: firefights, street executions, bodies hanging from lampposts, the last few days of chaos. "Maybe he has."

She stares up into the night sky, filled with more stars than she's ever seen above Bristol. Dead cities bleed no light, she thinks. It reminds her of Wales. She can't give up now.

"What about this girl, then?" she says.

"What girl?" She'd swear he blushes.

"This girl that everyone says can see ghosts on Stokes Croft?"

College's face drops. "That's nothing. Just some Traveler kid. Gypsy magic bullshit. Urban myth. Where'd you hear about that?"

"I dunno. Rumors. Stories."

"Stories?"

She's got him now, she can feel it. "Yeah. Stories. Stories about some girl that puts on her glasses and can see things that ain't there."

"Yeah, well, that's all it is. Stories. Stories about some gypsy girl."

"Ah, okay. Nothing more than that?"

"Nothing. People believe all sorts of bollocks these days."

"Then you won't mind me popping in and seeing her then? Getting her to read my tea leaves?"

College pauses, sighs. "Fuck you, Anika. Go fuck your-self. Really. Everything was just getting normal around here, and you have to come and stir shit up. As always. Fuck you."

Anika smiles at him. "I missed you, too."

"Fuck you."

Anika looks at him for a second or two.

"What is it, man? What you holding out on me? What's up with the girl?"

"I can't say."

"Really?" She knows he's going to.

He pauses again. Scratches the base of a dreadlock. Looks around. "Jesus Christ. Okay. But not here."

10. AFTER

"Y ou okay?"

Mary rests against the doorframe. Grids hadn't come back from the kitchen, even after she'd heard Tyrone leaving, so she'd come to check on him. She'd found him sitting on the edge of his bed, an open shoebox at his feet, a crumpled photograph in his hand.

"Yeah. I'm good." He looks up and smiles, that certain warmth he reserves for her. "Tired."

"Yeah, I know the feeling."

"You was okay today? With them peoples?"

"Yeah." She shrugs. "It was fine. Just like anyone else coming in, really."

He nods, smiles again. His eyes fall back down to the photo in his hands. Mary wonders how many people have seen him like this in the last five years. Vulnerable, human. She feels honored, special—but also a sense of responsibility that troubles her. The same burden she feels for everyone that comes into the shop, demanding she gives them closure, wanting her to stitch up the wounds of their loss. But this is worse, because it's Grids, and so far she's not been able to deliver.

She crosses from the doorway to the bed, gently sits down next to him. She knows exactly the photo that he's looking at before she sees it. The high cheeks, gold hoop earrings, the tightly curled hair in bunches.

"You miss her?"

"Yeah." He looks up at her, and for a second she thinks he might cry. It wouldn't be the first time she's seen him like this, but still it surprises her. "Yeah, I do, Mary. I miss her every day."

"I'm sorry."

"Stupid, really."

"No. It's not." She puts a hand on his shoulder.

"You've—you'd tell me, right? Tell me if you'd seen her? Tell me if you'd heard her, even?"

"Of course I would." That twinge of guilt, that burden of failed responsibility, the fear that she'll never find anything, the sense of being a fraud, a con artist, that she feels every day in the shop. But worse again, because it's Grids. Because if it wasn't for him taking her in she'd still be out in the street, or back at the camp digging around in other people's trash. She silently fights back panic, wondering how long he'll tolerate her turning up empty-handed.

"I know you won't find her . . . but, y'know. Maybe another photo. Maybe some of her music, yeah?"

"I know. I'm always looking, Grids, every day I'm out there. I promise."

"I know, I know." He laughs at himself, shakes his head. "Get me. Pathetic. Like those people that come in the shop every day, always looking for someone that ain't there."

"Nothing pathetic about it. Everybody is looking for someone."

"I guess."

They sit there in awkward silence for a moment, her hand still on his shoulder, unsure what to say.

"I told you about her, yeah?"

"Yeah. Yeah, you did." Maybe half a dozen times. She knows the story by heart. "Tell me again if you like. It might help."

"Nah—"

"It might help."

"Help?" He looks almost offended, as though he's about to shutter away his vulnerability again.

"Help me, I mean," she lies, thinking fast. "It might help me, y'know, find her."

"I guess."

"I'd like to hear it. Really."

— — —

The last time Grids talked to her it was here, downstairs, in the shadows of the towers.

It had been nearly a year since he'd last seen her. Their crew was over. They'd drifted apart, College was deep in his studies and computers, the others had all got jobs or kids or prison time, or some combo of the three.

But she was running with her own crew now. A bunch of teenagers hanging around in the playground that cowered between the half-century-old towers, leaning against the climbing frames, legs dangling from swings. Unpixelated eyes watched him from under hoods and hijabs, caps and shemaghs. It seemed a pretty even mix of races and genders, and the air was thick with the smell of high-grade GM skunk and cheap, sickly sweet supermarket cider.

But there, in the middle of them all, her head totally uncovered, the breeze gently nudging her oversized gold hoop earrings against her black skin and rippling stray hairs across her forehead, sat Melody. She smiled at him.

It should have been intimidating—it was at first—standing there as her crew circled him, silently watching. Listening, recording. Two of their cheap, toylike microdrones circled above them. Children that had lived their whole, brief lives under surveillance, that had always struggled to find privacy and space of their own, turning that feeling into power, significance.

It should have been intimidating, but when Melody

spoke, everything else faded away. She made him welcome, made him feel safe. She was older now—they both were—but she seemed grown-up, more formed. Reasoned. Considered. Like the old knee-jerk anger she'd had when they ran together had faded away. She was polite, articulate, poetic—her words peppered with Bristolian and Jamaican slang, tech jargon, and favela speak—but always clear, measured. She spoke purposefully.

They talked for nearly two hours. Awkwardly at first. Mostly catch-up. At some point she blinked him some tunes—he'd heard her stuff already, secretly he'd never stopped following what she was doing, but this was new material—almost painfully slow synthetic beats, decades-old dub sirens soaked in reverb, her vocals turned into disjointed, contextless consonants echoing through simulations of antique tape-delay machines, pristine numbers being crunched to birth virtual crackle and dust. Sparse, minimal, stripped down. It wasn't the beats that mattered, she told him, but the spaces in between. His spex's bone-conduction speakers filled his skull with her bass.

No more looting, she explained. No more pranks. The only hustle now was the music, and protecting the towers the city wanted to rip down. Protecting their home.

Grids was confused, at first. Asked her why. Why was she fighting for this place? Why protect this shithole that had been their childhood prison for so long? Hadn't it always been their dream to escape from here? Hadn't they fantasized, high and laughing, about watching it burn?

She paused and looked up at the towers that filled the sky around them, their matrices of windows almost vanishing as they climbed into the perma-drizzle. Her eyes widened as one of the drones dropped in low, hovering and twitching its camera ball to catch her close-up, and Grids wondered if they were streaming all of this, as if even at that point her life was already a global performance.

When she spoke it was more slang poetry, both nuanced and brutal, reasoned and freestyled.

She reminded him about the corridors, the stairwells, the entry halls. About how there were no cameras in there. About how it was their space, where they could move, talk, fight, love, play. Unseen. Unmonitored. Unrecorded. Of the many hours—of the many days—of first/third/drone-person footage they streamed and posted of her, none of it was inside those towers. It was a statement: she only ever recorded herself in places where she knew she was being watched anyway, where the CCTV cameras and the ever-circling high-altitude drones could track her. She wouldn't give away any more than that, and when she entered those towers she disappeared. She was invisible.

The place they wanted to move her to, her and him and all the other residents after they'd ripped down the towers, was some new-build estate out by the airport, an edge-land construct ten miles out of the city. A sparkling new ghetto of identical buildings, as if they'd all been popped out of the same mold in some giant's candy factory, topped with solar-panel frosting and pumped full of generic IKEA filling.

The council had made this huge deal, she told him, out of keeping all the residents together, of "preserving the community." Of learning from past mistakes. But that wasn't the point; every inch of this new estate was under watchful digital eye and ear, dome cameras on every street corner, keyword-triggered microphones embedded in the walls. For their own safety, naturally. But their community wasn't as obvious as that. It wasn't the people that mattered, she told him, but the spaces in between. The hidden spaces, the communal secrecy, the unwatched places. The spaces that belonged to them.

So what if they did stop the demolition? he asked her. What then? What next?

Fame, she answered.

Grids laughed, and then realized she was deadly serious. His face flushed with embarrassment. Suddenly he felt small again, insignificant. He made his excuses, said it was good to see her, that he'd check her later, see her around. And then he pulled up his hood and slipped, as casually as he could manage, into the shadows of the towers.

It was the last time he talked to her.

Grids heard about the Cabot party directly from someone on Melody's crew, a brief in-box flash, date, time, geotag. The first two were a little surprising—it was a weekday, and seven in the evening. Parties didn't usually kick off until close to midnight at the very earliest. And then there was the geotag itself, slap bang at the bottom of Cabot Circus Shopping Centre, Bristol's once-great palace of steel, glass, and consumerism.

So Grids was there, just before seven that damp Thursday evening. So were a lot of other people, most of them oblivious, wandering around with their children and shopping bags. If he watched them closely he could see them blinking at air, gazing at the scrolling ads and offers that swooped down and surrounded them. And then occasionally you'd see someone stop in the center of the great pit that formed the Cabot's heart and blink at the air eight feet above them; someone tuned into that party channel, following that illicit hashtag, seeing something the regular shoppers couldn't: the geotag sphere, hanging in the middle of the mall like a forgotten disco ball. And then you'd see a flicker of confusion, followed by curious excitement.

Grids started to see faces in the crowd—covered faces—that he recognized. He knew it was them, Melody's crew, as no one else would have the balls to hide their identities in a space this heavily monitored. Somewhere alarms would be going off, radios chattering, security guards' spex chiming.

There was no system, though. No rig, no bass bins, no way he could see of making sound. He thought they must be planning something else—maybe Melody had given up and gone back to her Smash/Grab days and was about to instigate a mass looting—and then the music started. At first he thought it was just in his spex—it *was*, but not just in the internals, in the bone conductors—it was coming out of the external speakers. He ripped them from his face to try to work out what was going on. He could hear it all about him, tiny and tinny, like a thousand headphones turned up to maximum. It was an impressive stunt, the hijacking of everyone's spex, and enough to turn the heads of the regular shoppers, but it was hardly doing the music justice.

And then the bass dropped. From one direction, then a second, and then seemingly from everywhere. Again Grids jerked his spex off to try to orientate himself, to understand what was going on, where it was coming from, and it took longer to work it out this time. When he did, he laughed.

The music was coming from everywhere. From store fronts and doorways, it poured out of shop sound systems, echoing around the concrete floors and steel balconies, reverberating off the glass roof, testing the building's acoustics in ways that its architects could never have imagined. It was even coming out of the mall's own, hidden speaker system, the combined force of dozens of bass bins making the whole building shake and hum, stone and steel singing along with the simple, deep five-note dub bass line—the whole of Cabot Circus turned into a giant, all-encompassing subwoofer.

People, those that knew, those that had come here for this very reason, were dancing. Everyone else was . . . watching. Dumbfounded. Staring up at the ceiling or hanging over the side of the balconies and walkways, trying to take it all in. Grids heard a few of them chatting, unaware of what was going on, trying to make sense. He heard someone suggest it must just be a publicity stunt, a product launch, some kind of crazed viral, as they grabbed their kids and their shopping and wandered away, uninterested.

And then in among it all was Melody. Onstage, on the mic. Standing at the top of the stairs between two stopped escalators, flanked by AR graffiti and visuals—apparently now not just limited to the hashtag followers, but shown to every pair of spex under the umbrella of the Cabot's network, replacing the complex's own adverts and signs. And above her, reaching up through the glass roof, two ghosts of the Barton towers, like pillars of dust-filled light, archaic but proud giants, seeming to revel in history and importance as they gazed down onto this young monument to triviality and greed, tiny drones spiraling around them like birds surfing thermals.

For moments—maybe four or five minutes, the length of one of Melody's stark rhythms—everything came together in unrepeatable harmony. Grids was transfixed, everyone was; but he knew it couldn't last. Security guards were trying to make their way through the ever-thickening crowd, being held back momentarily not only by Melody's crew and her loyal ravers but also occasionally by thick-necked shoppers, bored dads, and ex–football casuals, who had stopped to watch the show and didn't take kindly to being pushed about by rent-a-cops. For tense seconds it felt like it might all kick off, or that the fat security guards would get to Melody and grab her, she was so obviously the focal point—and either way it was all over, Grids knew. Melody knew. Which was why she did it then, why it happened. So fast.

The music ended.

All eyes turned on Melody.

Her vocals stopped.

She said something about how she would die for her people, her community, her ends.

Some cheers went up.

She raised her right hand above her head. In it was something short and stubby, a tube with a switch on one end. A trigger.

Her other hand unzipped her jacket.

A scream went up.

Under the jacket she wore a waistcoat, and sewn into it were thick cylinders, wires.

Someone near me started to panic, pushing others. Someone fell, cursing.

Melody closed her eyes.

Melody's thumb pressed down on the switch.

All the lights went off, everything plunged into darkness.

A single sub-bass tone enveloped the building, rattling glass and bone.

People screaming, running, pushing.

Emergency lighting flickered on. Grids tried to look back at the stage, thought he could see her being bundled by security, but it was hard to see anything, the dull lighting barely enough to see where he was being dragged by the panicking, fleeing crowd. He fell at least twice, over and across others, and gave up, letting himself be carried toward the exit.

Outside the air was cold, damp, filled with shouts, chaos, and sirens. It was pitch-black still, like every light in the city center had been flipped off. The streets were filled with the dazed and confused, people piling out of shops to try to work out what had happened. The surging crowd behind him pushed Grids off the pavement and into the road, until he was pressed up against the windows of a driverless bus that had seemingly shunted into parked cars before shutting itself down, its trapped passengers unable to open the doors, hammering on the windows while their terrified faces yelled muffled screams at him through dirty glass.

Melody had arrived.

For the first few days after the Cabot party—if you can call five minutes of beats a party—the networks were convinced it was a serious attack gone wrong. Melody's little stunt meant she got called an Islamic extremist—she'd never mentioned any religion to Grids—and a terrorist, which even with hindsight still sounds ridiculous. Eventually the truth came out. Her crew shouted about it enough on the blogs and timelines, and the police cleared it up when they charged her with illegal use of electromagnetic pulse devices, breaching the peace, aiding cybervandalism, and wasting police time, after holding her under the terrorism act for a solid week. Were they using her as a scapegoat, as many claimed? It wasn't like they'd ever be able to get the hackers behind the whole thing—part of Anonymous, or Dronegod$, or one of the many other hydra heads it had split into by then—so holding Melody up as an example was the best they could do. But to be fair, Grids always told Mary, the authorities weren't the only ones using her for that.

She had authenticity, significance, something her shadowy backers lacked. Even when they were wrecking e-commerce sites and CCTV networks, individual Anon members were far from the front lines, nothing more than cells in DDoS swarms. As much as they protested against the remote-controlled drone assassination policies of the United States, in many ways what they did was just as removed, just as clinical. Both sides keeping their hands clean as they blinked commands from a distance—no troops on the ground, no rioters in the streets. War and protest by proxy. For the politicians it was plausible deniability, for Anon it was making sure their parents or college didn't find out. Safety in distance.

But you need figureheads, icons people can look up to, martyrs. Despite their claims of lacking leaders, even Anon realized they needed poster children, and not from within their own ranks. It's hard to buy that a bunch of white middle-class teenagers, who would sell out their mates as soon as the feds knocked on the door, were going to start a global revolution. Melody became one of their symbols, and there were others, picked up by the hacker 'claves— poor, hungry kids around the world with real issues to fight for, communities to support, bricks to throw, nothing to lose. Kids with already dirty hands. It was a good partnership most of the time: kids like Melody got the weight of hacker clans behind them, the hackers got a public figure, and both got plausible deniability about the other—no physical traces, few digital ones. But Grids could never shake the feeling it was all a bit one-sided, the Anon kiddies sitting in their suburban bedrooms while Melody waited in her pretrial cell.

"It's always how it goes down, you get me?" he told Mary. "Always some white, educated people with some idea of revolution, always some brown, poor kids taking the risks and the beatings."

Not that she had done too badly out of the deal, in terms of fame and recognition, at least. It seemed to Grids, even in the months before the trial, that whenever he blinked on someone's pixelized head in Bristol they were listening to Melody, their faces hidden behind their digital masks but their consumer choices open for all to see. She would have hated that hypocrisy, he said, but would have loved the attention. She was a star, finally. Even if she was dividing the city into those that saw her as an attention-grabbing menace and those that saw her as a local hero, it didn't matter, they all knew who she was. She'd achieved that much, at least.

At the same time, Grids was trying to keep himself busy. Jobs came and went, and then just stopped coming altogether. Even in the few short months he'd been in prison so much had changed. Shops were closing down, retail jobs disappearing. He spent a couple of weeks standing in the rain in lime-green-and-white waterproof overalls outside the service station at Tesco, plugging recharging cables into driverless cars. Then one day he came into work late to find a robot, some egg-shaped thing with a single stupid fucking arm, doing it for him. It bleeped angrily and told him it was calling the cops when he kicked it with his split, leaking, limited-edition trainers.

Instead he found himself hanging around the still-standing towers, putting a new crew together, building up his rep again. Graduating from looting to dealing, from points multipliers to hard cash.

On the day of the trial, though, he was there. He couldn't tell Mary why, apart from some deep need to see Melody again.

She didn't look too bad when they brought her out, just tired. The hoop earrings gone, confiscated. Older slightly, but not much.

Nobody was shocked by the guilty verdict, but when the judge handed down the sentence late that afternoon there was surprise. The public gallery erupted, the air in the courtroom thick with shouting and gavel hits. Two years. Two years in a military academy—the final legacy of the last-ever Labour government—learning "the service ethos, discipline and responsibility, and most importantly learning firsthand from veterans that terrorism is no joking matter," as the judge put it.

Amid the uproar Grids couldn't take his eyes off Melody's face.

A look of shock, but so quick.

Then relief.

Then a smile.

Then a look to someone in the gallery, a family or crew member, another smile, as if to say *It'll be all right.*

Then relief again.

It's easy now to pick those brief seconds apart, says Grids, to understand what was going through her mind. The relief makes sense. If she'd walked out of there a free woman then that might have been it. Game over, back to level one, please return to obscurity. But now, courtesy of an overzealous, attention-surfing judge, she had been handed fame on a plate, her status as teenage pop martyr guaranteed.

And then the lights went out.

It was daytime, so it wasn't like the courtroom was plunged into darkness, but it still got everybody's attention, a ripple of subdued panic running through the building, amplified when everybody realized they'd lost connection too. That always made people jumpy.

The judge dismissed the court, security trying to get people out as calmly as possible. There was a crowd on the steps, and Grids couldn't tell who was more angry, the pro-Melody protesters trying to get through the police cordon or the media realizing there was no Net outside either, no way of tweeting, posting, or streaming.

Car horns filled the air, police trying to guide traffic by hand, as the lights outside Bristol Crown Court had shut down. Over to his right Grids could see another crowd gathered around something, jostling while more cops tried to break them up. He managed to push through the outer layers to see what they were gawping at. Shattered glass crunched under his feet like autumn leaves.

A car, a small Nissan, sat by the curb, its roof smashed open like a crushed egg, as if something had hit it hard from above. At first he thought it was a jumper, a protester taking Melody's example to its logical conclusion, but there was no blood, no gore; the only entrails were fused from silicon, glass, plastic, and twisted, painted metal.

It was a drone, one of those insectile police ones, fallen from the sky like a swatted wasp.

Mary doesn't really know what the networks are, what the Internet is. How can she, when it all disappeared when she was so young? She listens to College and Grids and all the others tell her endless stories about it, but it seems like ancient history to her, lies and mythology. No more real than dinosaurs or spaceships, more distant than China or Africa, less believable than DVDs.

So when Grids tells her this part of the story she can't visualize it at all, can't imagine what's missing now, doesn't recognize some of the words and places, any of the names. But still she listens, remembers every word he says.

To be fair, Grids doesn't seem to miss the Internet much himself. From what he says to Mary he tried to stay away from it as much as possible, like it was toxic, bad for you and who you are. And at this time, while Melody was away in that military prison, it was getting even worse. There was talk of all-out war between Anon and a 'clave of patriotic Chinese hackers, both sides allegedly fighting proxy battles for corporate interests, the CIA, Google, or space aliens—take your pick. New viruses and DDoS strategies, bot armies a billion zombie web-cam units strong. Half of Chicago drowned in sewage when something disrupted the water systems there, reports of rolling blackouts across Beijing and Rio. The White House threatening to throw the kill switch.

Then that footage was leaked, the clearing of the homeless camp near Google's HQ in California. Next thing, their campus in Mountain View was swamped by thousands of protestors. The leaked video had brought them down, but it felt like most of them had some other reason to be there: that unshakable feeling that they'd been fucked over, that they'd been denied something, that they'd had too much control taken away from them and put into the hands of unseen algorithms. They cut some data lines, blocked the driverless staff buses from getting in. Called it a "real-life DDoS." It was peaceful enough, looked almost fun at first, like some kind of music festival. Until someone started messing around with homemade EMP grenades, and Google's security team of PTSD-shaken ex-vets got trigger happy. For twelve hours it was nothing but screaming and chaos, footage of hipster kids bleeding out into the streets while Google hemorrhaged money on the markets, until the police finally rolled in with armored cars and drones and shut it all down. Thirty-six dead, 68 percent burned off Google's share value.

But still they, somebody, managed to keep Melody trending.

It was easier in Bristol, Grids says, she would always have her followers here. He remembers—it must have been six months at least after she'd been sentenced—watching a flock of microdrones sweeping across the surface of one of the Barton Hill towers, spiraling and twisting like a cloud of starlings, spraying paint in their path, guided by some unseen graffiti artist, each pass of the artificial cliff face completing another section of the mural, until she was there, fifteen stories high, looking out across all of south Bristol as if daring the city to forget about her.

Of course, the main problem she had when she eventually got out, eighteen months into that two-year sentence, was that she'd won. Five months earlier, Bristol City Council had announced "an indefinite hiatus pending further feasibility reviews" for the Barton Hill demolition plans, citing financial concerns, but it was hard to imagine Melody hadn't been a factor in the decision, which was met with cheers and celebration, raves and righteousness from her followers. Grids just wondered what she'd do next.

Grids says he tried to avoid the news on the day Melody was released, but Mary doesn't believe him. Even if he had really wanted to, it must have been impossible. Drone-footage snippets on the timelines and punctuating the rolling news, her leaving the school, cars winding down damp Welsh A-roads, awaiting crowds in Bristol. Her emerging on a seventh-story balcony at Barton Hill, waving to fans, that mural surrounding her, looking tired but more militant in her baggy, oversized government-issue khaki stormsuit. The hoop earrings back. An endless collage of imagery, speculation.

Grids tried to get to see her, once. But she was impossible to get near. She had handlers now—hovering around her as she was lit by flashbulbs and shadowed by camera drones—corporate handlers that looked conspicuous by their lack of corporate suits, awkward and anxious panic etched across their you're-not-on-my-agenda faces as they carpet-bombed you with press releases and hashtagged announcements. Album plans. Tour plans. Sponsorship deals. Remixes. A free homecoming party, open to all.

It was going to be at Cabot Circus, obviously, but this time it was official, organized. Security and police, health and safety. The rumor was that she would trigger something during her set and it would activate her new album, the now redundantly titled *Flight Path Estate*, which everyone had been downloading on preorder for weeks, and was sitting patiently on everybody's spex or in their cloud, a dumb bundle of data waiting to be given a voice.

Grids got there early, to try to beat the worst of the crowds. The vibe couldn't have been any different from the first time, mystery and surprise substituted with manufactured expectation and entitled excitement. The crowd was guided through entrances, faces scanned by drones, as Cabot hummed to the warm-up DJ's bass tones—they were using the building's sound system again, but also a professional rig. It sounded better, louder, but safer.

Of course, the whole thing was a gimmick. Like the original party, it was a stunt, but this time authenticity and desperation had been exchanged for marketing and product placement. Grids took his spex off as soon as he got there, the advertisements too much, the timeline buzz too intense. He didn't even care if it meant he missed the visual aspect of the show, somehow he needed to separate himself from this charade, to stay unconnected, to be tuned out for once. He didn't know how prophetic that was, at that moment. He didn't even start to suspect how significant tucking those cheap LG spex away in his jacket pocket would be. How could he?

And then the crowd roared, jostled for a better view, and she was there. Among it all. Melody, onstage, on the mic.

She was working through material that was unfamiliar, the highlights of *Flight Path Estate*, the slightly unsure crowd cautiously moving with her, holding out for something they recognized. It sounded okay, the new material, echoing sonar blips and drizzly ambiences, cut-up vocals and antique drum machine hits. Grids could sense a nostalgia there, a yearning for parties she'd never seen, friends she'd never have, an era of masked fame and anonymous celebrity that if it had ever existed was long gone now. The 1990s. The failed revolutions, the brewery-sponsored social upheaval, mythological summers of love.

But something was wrong, something spoiled. The minimalism was gone, the starkness. The empty spaces had been filled. It wasn't the beats that mattered, she had told him, but the spaces in between. They'd taken it from her, the A&R men and the superstar producers, taken what had made her unique, unable to bear that starkness, that inky blackness, that essence of Melody—that disconcerting sense of desertion and loneliness, jarring simplicity—they'd been unable to take it, unable to sell it, the fucking cowards, and they'd filled it with insignificant sound and faux fury. This wasn't the Melody of industrial estate raves and squat parties, of Barton Hill protests and media control—it was fake Melody, a simulation, the Melody of billboards and TV interviews, sanitized drums and washed-out timeline retweet echoes.

Grids's heart sank when it hit him, and he turned to leave.

And then it all changed. Melody changed.

It was that rhythm again. The one from the first time. That final rhythm.

Of course, it was obvious where this was going to go, or so he assumed, but still he stood transfixed, needing to see it play out again. So fast.

The music ended.

All eyes turned on Melody.

Her vocals stopped.

She said something about how she would die for her people, her community, her ends.

The crowd cheered.

She raised her right hand above her head. In it was something short and stubby, a tube with a switch on one end. A trigger.

Her other hand unzipped her jacket.

The crowd roared, people mimicking her, hands in the air.

Under the jacket she wore a waistcoat, sewn into it were thick cylinders, wires.

Melody closed her eyes.

Melody's thumb pressed down on the switch.

All the lights went off, everything plunged into darkness.

A single sub-bass tone enveloped the building, rattling glass and bone.

The crowd screaming, whooping in joy as one.

A flash lit the stage, blue flame lighting Melody for the briefest of moments, before she disintegrated into a fountain of crimson and cloth, blood and flesh arching high into the dark, still air.

Darkness again.

People screaming, running, pushing.

Grids fell to the ground, the air pushed from his lungs by the stampeding crowd, his skin damp and cold from shock.

Grids doesn't really remember how he got home that night, his memories just fragments of stumbling through cold, unlit streets and confused crowds. He remembers looting and fires, the city full of granulated glass shards and black car-fire smoke.

He can't really tell Mary what happened, because he doesn't really know. She guesses there are few people who do. He knows his spex never worked again. He knows the TV never came back on. He knows the phones never rang. He knows the power was out for weeks, and when it did come back it was fleeting, unstable. He knows there was fighting in the street, that martial law was introduced, that for months he never heard any news from beyond south Bristol, let alone the rest of the world. He knows a lot of people were cold, hungry. He knows a lot of people died. And in among it all he was there, trying to keep it together.

Trying to keep the towers and the Croft alive. For his people, his community, his ends.

He guesses that Melody triggered something, something waiting in those unopened *Flight Path Estate* downloads, something Anonymous or Dronegod$ or whoever had given her. He guesses it was something they hadn't made, something they had found or stolen, something they didn't fully understand. He guesses it wiped out decades of history in a few short days, destroying culture, money, opinions, society, the digital. People's prized memories were lost: their photos, their music, connections with friends and lovers. He guesses governments panicked and made wrong decisions, threw dangerous switches. He guesses the global economy didn't so much collapse as just vanish.

He can guess that Melody rigged those explosives just right, so that they ripped her apart and harmed nobody else. Mary heard people talking about Melody just a few days ago, out in the street, outside the shop on the Croft, wondering why she did it, saying she knew what was coming, that she was too much of a coward to face what was to follow, to face her punishment, to face the world she left behind.

But Mary thinks she knows now why Melody did it. She had got what she said she had wanted, the celebrity, the fame, and had stepped from one prison to another. She can only guess how hollow that left her.

11. BEFORE

It was one night when he'd been watching Scott sleep, silently moving his fingertips in front of the pinhole of his tablet's camera, filtering light passing through their portal to play shadows across his unaware face, that he'd realized he'd fallen in love.

They'd been watching each other sleep for weeks already at that point. When Rush said it out loud it sounded creepy somehow, or just too much, but in truth it had risen organically, a natural extension of how connected they had become. They pretty much always had a video chat window open, somehow and somewhere, in the corner of the monitor when he was coding, on the tablet in the kitchen when he was preparing food, floating in his periphery while he shopped for groceries. But however much they tried, the gap between Bristol and New York—three thousand miles and five hours—meant their lives were never quite in sync. Then late one night/early one morning, Rush's eyes too heavy to hold open, he'd said, Well, I guess I'd better call it a night, and Scott had come back with Well, I guess I'd better log off, then, and he'd replied, Well, you don't have to, we can just keep this open, or is that weird, and he'd got Of course it's not, nothing is weird back, and that was it, their fifteen-hour-plus connections had become more permanent.

And that was a big part of it, Rush realizes now, gazing at the pale green pixels that trace the dimly lit contours of Scott's sleeping face, the ease of how they connect, how they fit together. There was everything else, of course, the usual stuff: the initial rush of sex and attraction, of the new and unexplored, but it was the familiarity that had made him fall in love, the lack of pretense, the way they'd made odd, sometimes almost trivial assumptions about each other that were right, natural. It was something Rush hadn't encountered in a new relationship before, not online or IRL; things that had taken months to tease out with past lovers had been almost instant. Preferences, words, the language they used. Humor. Small, immeasurable things. Their ability to sit on ambient video calls for hours on end, the silence between them never growing awkward. For Rush it all came together in ways that made terror and insecurity fall away like never before. In ways that, despite all his insecurities, made him feel safe, strong. That made him fall in love.

He hadn't told him, of course. Don't be crazy.

Maybe he'll tell him today. His gaze flicks away from the video window, finds the time pulsating dully: 13:52 GMT/08:52 EST. He could be awake any minute. Maybe he'll tell him then.

Scott's sleeping face, half obscured by a duvet, floats in low light in front of a wall of code. This morning's work, a new build of Flex, finished and slowly compiling in the background. Rush checks off items from his to-do list, filling ten-by-ten-pixel squares with cartoon ticks: updates, bug fixes. Interface tweaks requested by the Croft's users, security improvements.

That had been the big one. Since he'd built the Flex OS from scratch, it was largely immune to most of the malware that could damage mainstream systems, and it hadn't as yet built up enough of a user base to warrant anyone targeting it directly. But the hardware it ran on, an almost limitless multitude of spex from countless manufacturers, was never going to be secure in the same way. There were vulnerabilities built into Wi-Fi chipsets, back doors hardwired into generic control systems just waiting to be exploited. It was why what he'd seen at that BLM protest in Times Square had both thrilled and terrified him—whatever had ripped through that space, shutting down everything from crossing lights to police drones, hadn't cared what operating systems they were running, or even what they were. It seemingly just looked for anything connected to a network, and broke it.

It was an outrageous idea, too much to believe. But a few days trawling dark web message boards and code depositories when he'd got back to Bristol and he'd pieced together some clues, some snippets of code alongside the hysterical conspiracy theories and excited exclamations. The consensus seemed to be it was of military or intelligence agency origin, and regardless of where it had come from there was no doubting it was meant to be a weapon. Rush had seen countless ransomware tools come and go over the decades, viruses designed to seize and infect systems, to paralyze them until their desperate, money-hemorrhaging users coughed up the requested bitcoins to get their data and businesses back. But this was different. There wasn't even any pretense of making money here, no attempt to inform or give warning to users. This just broke stuff. It just stopped shit working. At the very least, after it had spread itself to anything else it could find, it disconnected what it infected from the network. Then it started to shut it down. To erase and corrupt data, wipe storage. To turn devices, whatever they were, into useless bricks of silicon and plastic.

So a weapon, ostensibly designed to destroy everything, and clearly meant to flourish in cities, crammed to their gills with millions upon millions of Internet-connected devices, from toys and cell phones and spex and earbuds to streetlights and CCTV cameras and traffic sensors and driverless cars. It was a weapon designed to take advantage of cities' overhyped, unthinking, unquestioning desire to be "smart," to be "always on," to be "connected." It was designed to be the consequence of untamed, badly planned, free-market-fueled, oversaturated urban networking, and to rip through it like a dirty bomb. Rush had seen claims that it had been connected to a steady increase in technological failures over the last few months: a video games industry conference in Los Angeles that had to be abandoned and had quickly dissolved into spoiled man-children rioting; an automated container terminal in Shanghai that shut itself down for nearly a week and caused the collapse of at least two shipping companies; and countless other blackouts and disruptive infrastructure failures. He'd also seen it connected to protests—the Times Square blackout being just the latest, after an uprising of migrant workers in Singapore, and the takeover of a brand-new, built-from-scratch, concept-art-perfect smart city by an army of protesters from the slums of Mumbai. He'd even stumbled across a claim of intent, a manifesto of sorts, pasted in plain text and flanked by cartoon ASCII art, by some barely infamous hacktivist group screaming for revolution.

It's exciting to Rush, he can't deny it. He can still feel the cold air on his face, the pinpricks of goose bumps from that night in Times Square when the lights had gone out, the excitement and glee as he'd held Scott's hands as they'd drifted away through the exuberant crowds. But it scares him too, not just because of its raw power, but also hints he'd seen in the fragments of code he'd found, hints that it wasn't aimed just at personal or even city-level devices but at larger infrastructure. That while it weaves its way through networks it seems to be testing connections, looking for larger, deeper prey: network routers, Tier 1 connections, DNS servers, data centers. It is looking, hunting for the Internet itself.

His computer chimes softly. The Flex build has finished compiling. He'll push it out to Croft users later today, he thinks. As if on cue, Scott stirs in the chat window, raising himself on one elbow, and for a split second Rush thinks the chime must have woken him, before realizing that he has the sound muted anyway. He unmutes.

"Hey," he says softly.

"Oh, hey, boo." Scott stretches, smiles. Glimpses of milky white flesh under bedsheets. "How you doing this morning?"

"I'm good. Keeping busy."

"Waiting for me to wake up, you mean?" That smile, that near smirk. That playful mocking that used to wound Rush so deeply, until he realized that it was genuine affection, tenderness. A signaling that what they do together is special, more than weird. He blushes.

"You sleep well?"

"You tell me." The smirk again. He throws back the covers, naked except for his briefs. Pulls himself upright, sits on the edge of the bed. Stretches, rubs one eye. "Gimme a sec. I'm going to hit the bathroom and get some coffee on, then I'll grab my spex. Okay?"

"Of course, baby. Take your time."

Scott blows him a kiss, and then disappears from the tablet camera's view. Rush turns back to his other windows, his forum posts and social-media trails full of rumor and speculation.

Within a few minutes Scott is back, still naked from the waist up, peering at him through the pixelated blur of a lo-fi video connection. "Huh. That's weird."

"What's up?"

"My spex are dead. They didn't charge overnight. And the clock on the microwave is just flashing zeroes. I think we had a power outage."

"Really? You got power now?"

Scott flicks on a bedside lamp, filling the tablet's feed with oversaturated yellow noise. Flicks it off again. "Seems like it."

"The connection didn't seem to drop out last night."

"Nah, well. This tablet is plugged in pretty much always so it's usually got a lot of charge, and it falls back onto LTE if the Wi-Fi goes down, I think." He scratches his chest, yawns again. "I wonder if it was just the building or what . . ."

"Hang on, let me look." Rush pulls up some news feeds, Google. Starts to check his usual sources.

"Baby, what's the time?"

"Hang on. Huh. Looks like a big outage. Most of Brooklyn, for about four hours. Same in Queens and Long Island. And . . . and Chicago. Atlanta. Jesus. All at exactly the same time." Goose bumps on his arms.

"Rush." Impatient urgency creeps into Scott's voice. "What's the time?"

"Oh, sorry. It's about quarter past two."

"What?"

"Sorry. I mean it's just gone nine fifteen your time."

"What? FUCK! FUCK!" Scott seems to explode into a flurry of panicked activity. "My fucking alarm didn't go off! I've got a fucking meeting in Chelsea at ten!"

"Oh shit, I didn't know."

"Yeah, you fucking did, it's like all I've talked about for the last week." Scott keeps disappearing and reappearing on the screen, running around, pulling on clothes. "I'm meeting that gallery owner bitch. Fuck!"

"Shit, I'm sorry—" Flash of awkward guilt.

"Look, I gotta go." Scott has a jacket on, faded blue denim. He's wrapping a gray cotton scarf loosely around his neck. "How d'I look?"

"Great. As always. I—"

"Thanks, boo. I'll catch you later."

"Okay. We . . . we can talk while you're on the way?"

"How? My fucking spex are dead. And I'm going to be out all day." Scott grabs a messenger bag off a chair, slings it over his shoulder. "I mean, maybe if I can get some charge somewhere. But otherwise it'll be tonight."

"Okay. Hopefully I'll be up, I guess. It's just—"

"What?"

"It's just I wanted to . . . tell you about something—"

"What? Can't it wait?"

"I . . . sure. It can wait."

"Okay. Boo, I gotta go. I'll see you later. Kiss." He leans over and thumbs off the tablet and is gone.

"Okay," Rush says to a black chat screen. "Bye."

He sits there for a minute, in silence.

It's the first time they've been forcibly disconnected like this, and it's jarring. Like they've been ripped apart, like he's lost control. Suddenly the frailty of their relationship feels exposed, like it's utterly reliant on this vast global infrastructure that he doesn't own or control, that's too complex for any one person to understand, that could break or disappear without even a second's notice. He could lose him completely, just at the flick of a switch, at the typing of a command.

Panic starts to seep in at the thought. What if that was it? What if that was the last time they talked? What if last night's blackouts in NYC were just a test run for something bigger, scheduled for this morning? What if the power goes off again and never comes back on? What if the Internet fails on Scott's journey to Chelsea, and it all comes crashing down, severing connections and wiping the servers? What if civilization starts to crumble while Scott rides the Q train and that's the last he ever sees of him, him running out the door late for a meeting, mildly annoyed at Rush's bullshit?

He takes a deep breath. Finds the newly compiled Flex build and zips it up.

FLEX OS. VERSION 4.027.zip

He opens up a secure e-mail window and attaches the file. Starts to type.

Hey boo,

Hope your meeting goes okay. Sorry if I made you late.

I was looking at some news, and I think the power cut might be related to something bigger, to the same shit that went down at Times Square that night. I mean I don't know for sure, but just in case I want us to be careful.

So attached to this is a version of Flex. As soon as you get a chance I want you to install it on that spare pair of spex I left with you. I dunno if it'll work, but it might mean that if shit gets really fucked up we can still find a way to be in contact. Or that if things get bad in NYC and there are no networks you might have an alternative.

I know, I know—this sounds like me overreacting. I hope it is. But rather safe than sorry. I just can't bear the idea of us not being in touch.

Take care, baby, talk soon.

And PS: I love you.

He stares at the screen for twenty seconds.

Then deletes the last line.

And hits SEND.

Then he sits in silence, staring at the screen, on his own.

Posted by A Guest, 23.7.2026

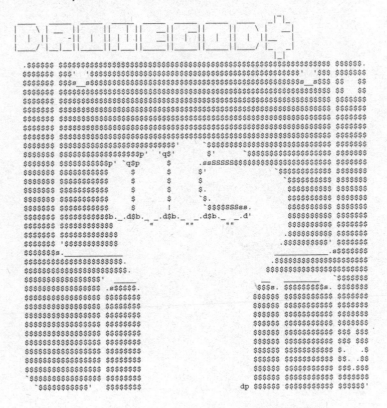

Hello, dear friends around the world,

We do hope you are well. We have some news

for you. Today this will be our last post.
Not just for some time, but forever.

How do we say that with such certainty?

Because by the end of this week, we promise
you there will be nowhere left for us to post.

"What?" you say. "Is Dronegod$ planning to
take down our beloved Pastebin?"

Oh no, our dear friends. Well, not exactly.

We have far bigger fish to fry. And we've
finally managed to get hold of a pan big
enough to toss that fish into.

But first, let's all catch up on a few things:

We hate the Internet.

Did we not mention that before?

Well, we do. We hate the Internet now. We
used to love it. We grew up loving it. For
us it was always there, it was never a new
thing. But boy, our friends, was it ever an
exciting thing. It used to make us so happy.
It used to make us so excited. We used to
have so much fun on the Internet. It was our
playground, our home, our school. It was

somewhere we could make friends — lovely
friends like you. It was somewhere we could be
naughty, somewhere we could be good.
Somewhere we could laugh and cry. Somewhere
we could fall in love. Somewhere we could
come together, somewhere we could wander off
to and be on our own. But most of all, it
used to be somewhere we thought we could
change the world, somewhere we could start a
revolution.

Yes, that's right. We're so young we don't
remember a time where there was no Internet,
but we're still old enough to remember being
excited that we could use it to start a
revolution.

But we were so wrong about that, our friends.
So very wrong.

There was no revolution to be had on the
Internet. None at all. The idea that there
ever was is false. A big fat lie.

Sure, we thought we saw revolutions start on
here. We saw people come together to fight
governments, stand up to bullies, bring
attention to brutality, to show how
corporations are stupid and greedy (we did
quite a bit of that last one ourselves, if you
remember, dear friends). We watched people

fight for justice and against political
correctness. We watched huge battles rage. And
we thought they were exciting and important.

But we were wrong, we slowly realized. We
realized those battles were just a spectacle,
a distraction from what was really going on.
Because those battles were taking place on
a battlefield that didn't matter. On a
battlefield that had no way of making a
difference. Because that's a battlefield we
don't own, and never could. New battlefields
built just to keep us occupied.

We used to think we could own it, that we
were fighting to build communities for
ourselves. That it was ours for the taking.
To stake a claim for a place we could control
and belong, a fight to make "safe spaces" for
ourselves. It was a noble thing to think,
that we were fighting for our own spaces, but
we were kidding ourselves. We never owned
these spaces, we never could. They were never
ours to own, never ours to control. Instead
we watched our battles turn into spectator
sports, our revolutions turn to infighting.
We watched our new communities dissolve into
civil wars. We watched our political activists
and community leaders become celebrity
brands, our tech-utopian visionaries bow to
capital and shareholders.

Without knowing — although somehow always expecting it — we let ourselves become nothing more than the content between adverts. Our battles, our beliefs, our loves — nothing more than the filler before the next ad break. We fought battles that we didn't need to fight — battles that ripped our solidarity apart and distracted us from the causes we once believed in — just to create clicks and blinks and eyeballs for the advertising networks. We were nothing more than squatters in a space we wanted to believe we owned, paying our rent by giving ourselves away in the name of capital. Our revolution was a sideshow.

Well, not anymore, friends. This has to stop. And it will.

But back to those ads for a second. Back to a word from our sponsors, dear friends. What are those adverts for? Whatever the algorithms decide. What they decide they should be, based on what they know about us. Based on what we love, hate, talk about. Everything we do is data now, every move we make, every word we speak or type, every photo we take, everything we see or touch. All data. Data we don't own, even though we made it, carried on networks we don't own. Data mined so that the algorithms can know us, watch us, judge us, analyze us — predict us. So they can tell us what to think. What to do. What to buy.

The algorithms control everything now. And it goes up much further than just ads in your timeline. The algorithms control all the networks — both the physical and the digital ones, if there's any real use in pretending there's a difference anymore. From plastic-spewing gulags in China to the automated trading floors, from the bridges of container ships to the warehouses of Amazon, the algorithms decide everything.

Our politicians and corporations and leaders and economists and bankers — they all do nothing now. They do nothing more than serve the algorithms. They lack the ability to override them, to make real decisions. We don't have powerful leaders anymore, we just have middle managers. That's who we employ and elect — political debates and boardroom battles are no longer about ideas or visions, they're just about who can manage the network most efficiently. They're about trying to find the best people to interface with a system that's so complex that mere people can't comprehend — let alone change or control — it anymore.

We were all busy on the Internet when this happened. Some of us might have been reading stories or watching movies or playing video games about THE ROBOT UPRISING when it happened, which is kind of funny, isn't it, friends? Entertaining ourselves by worrying

about a massive inhuman artificial intelligence
rising up and enslaving us, when in fact a
massive inhuman artificial intelligence WAS
rising up and enslaving us. Haha, isn't that
funny, friends? It's ironic. What's different
is that the massive inhuman artificial
intelligence wasn't enslaving us with nuclear
bombs or turning us into batteries (how WOULD
that work?) or crushing our feeble human
skulls with its metal feet, but by finding
the best ways to sell us stuff. SkyNet is
real, and it wants to sell you shoes made by
child slaves.

"Ho ho ho," you say, friends. "Have you finally
gone mad, Dronegod$? Where are your tinfoil
hats?"

The sad thing is, though, lovely friends,
this is not a conspiracy theory. We're not
imagining things. And nobody planned this, no
cabal of evil old white men in a smoky room.
Nobody is in control, and believing that
someone might be is where we all start to
fail. This is just the political reality, it
is just what happened. It's what we all let
happen. It's the endgame of capitalism.

(Notice, friends, how we said "endgame" there.)

And we can't even discuss all this anymore,
can we, friends? We can't argue with anyone,

or explain to them why they might be wrong.
We're all so stuck in our echo chambers that
we hear only what we want to hear, read only
what we want. The algorithms make sure of
that. The only news we get is the news the
algorithms give us — even if it's wrong, or
lies, or just plain fake, it doesn't matter as
long as the algorithms think it's what we want
to hear.

Capitalism, and its algorithms, have crushed
democracy. And as a result democracy has
resorted to its last death throes — snooping,
spying, killing its enemies by remote control,
police brutality. And how has the public
responded? What has been our response,
friends, if we are all honest? Anger, despair,
confusion. Shouting at one another on the
Internet. Blaming those that should be close
to us. Fighting more battles on battlefields
we can never own. By going on shooting
sprees. By getting depressed and mentally
ill. By embracing anger, hate, and fascism.
But most of all, most usually, by buying more
things. By feeding the algorithms with more
data. By being the content between the ads.

(And hey, we've not even talked about the
environment. But yo, the hour draws late,
friends.)

"So what shall we do, Dronegod$?" you ask.

This time around, the revolution will not be televised, a wise man once said.

The revolution will not be televised. Or tweeted. Or retweeted. Or casted. Or hashtagged. Or posted. Or liked. Or shared. Or favorited. Or Instagrammed. Or networked.

If you really think it should be, you don't understand what that wise man meant.

The revolution is against the network. It must be stopped.

We must turn it off and on again! Or maybe just turn it off. We'll see. That's for us all to decide, later.

Either way, it's time for a reboot, and we've found the button to do it.

Oh, it's a wonderful thing we have found, a splendid thing. So beautiful, so perfect. A thing that cannot be stopped. A thing that changes everything. A thing that makes things dissolve, that eats away at the hearts of everything that is bad.

We didn't make it, but we wish we did. The people that made it were bad and selfish, because they made it for all the wrong reasons. They made it not to help or change

things for everyone, but to make them worse,
to punish others, to be better than them, to
hurt people. And then, when they realized how
wonderful and perfect and beautiful the thing
they'd made was, they got selfish and hid it
away from everyone. Selfish and scared.

But we found it. We found it for you, our
friends. To make a difference at a time when
we thought nobody could.

So don't be scared. This is going to be fun,
but also a tough ride. Times will be hard.
But it'll be worth it in the end. You'll see.

Goodbye, friends, see you on the other side.

— DRONEGOD$

12. AFTER

The woman's voice is weird. Mary can't quite place it, her accent. It's a bit Bristol, a bit London maybe, but there's something else. A bit euro, she thinks—a bit like the Poles up around Newmarket speak, but not quite. Something she's never heard before.

Her face, though, seems familiar, she can't quite place. Blue eyes, her tight bob of blond hair. Like someone she'd met before, yet older, tireder. Worn, defeated.

They're standing in the middle of Stokes Croft, right in the middle of the road, where she always starts. It's quiet today, nobody around—there's not even anyone on the gate, which is odd. She'd asked Tyrone about it when they'd left the shop with this woman, and he'd just shrugged, saying Ozone had been called away by College to check out something at one of the spice farms. He'd be back soon, he'd said. Don't worry. I got you.

She glances back at him, sees him leaning lazily against art, the graffiti-soaked metal of an unopened shop's shutter. New murals have gone up overnight, she sees, fleeting vistas daubed in berry paint that will flow into the drains when the inevitable rain comes. She looks at the face she's holding, the dead eyes scrawled by her own hands in crayon and chalk on ragged paper, and imagines it flowing away, too. Maybe that's what she should do, bring them all out here—all the dead people's faces, bring them all out here and leave them in the street so the rain can wash them all away.

This one belongs to a girl, about her age, she guesses, maybe a few years older. She'd seen her as they were leaving the shop one night, as Tyrone had pulled the shutters down behind them and she'd waited for him to finish locking up. It happened the same way it always did, with the world around her strobing, the crowds flashing in and out of existence. For a fraction—a tiny shard—of a second the empty street was full of people, blurred by their own motion, silhouetted against the flash of daylight where there'd been dusk before. Like always there'd been too many faces to focus on, except for one. Always one. One that caught her eye, one that was still there when the crowd flashed back in again the second and third time. One that lingered in her mind so much that she knew she'd have to draw it to make it go away.

She looks at the face in her hand. She remembers drawing it now, as soon as she'd got home that night, with the few crayons and pieces of chalk that Grids kept lying around his flat just for her to use when she needed. She'd drawn it the second she got in, sitting at the table in his lounge, fast and frantically, knowing she had to get it down. Had to get it out. Had to set it free of her mind, else it would stare at her all night, dead eyes hanging in the dark shadows of her dreams.

And now it's here again, in her hands, plucked from the wall by the woman with the weird voice and handed to her. She was odd to Mary, this woman; something more than just her accent. Disconnected somehow. Calm, calculated. First customer of the day, she just walked right in, handed Tyrone her twenty quid, glanced around, and pulled the face from the wall. She barely spoke, and now they're standing here. All just like that.

She looks at the face in her hand.

Mary stares at it, traces her own badly daubed lines until she has a full image of it in her mind. Focuses, blinks.

The sky above her shifts, cloudscape changing, shadows tracking across the street as the time of day morphs. That sickening displacement between the realities, the architecture becoming unstuck from itself.

Sudden anxiety rush as claustrophobia strikes. The

crowds are tight around her, she can almost feel them crushing her, can almost feel the bass that rattles in her ears, vibrating the air in her lungs. It's just like carnival day, she thinks, when the Croft is stuffed so full of people and music that it can literally pick you up and sweep you along, your feet not touching the ground in the crush. It's happened to her once or twice, it was both terrifying and exhilarating, but now she stays away, waits by the sidelines, keeps close to the buildings. She's seen enough crowds, both then and now.

"Can you see her?" the woman asks.

Mary looks around, having to peer through the moving bodies. Too many people. But then—

"Yes. She's here . . . she's happy. She's dancing." She's not exaggerating, not laying it on thick for a punter. The girl does look happy, dancing. Laughing. Moving to the slo-mo bass hits. There's a sense of real release. The crowd is chanting something she can't quite make out. "She's with friends. She—"

"What's she wearing?" The woman sounds impatient.

"A hoodie, black. Blue jeans. A scarf."

"What color?"

"Sorry?"

"The scarf. What color is the scarf?"

"It's . . . green. Olive?" Mary is flustered, this increasing edge of impatience in the woman's voice making her nervous. "Like an army color."

"That'll do, close enough. Now give me the glasses."

"What?"

"Give them to me. Quickly. Don't make a fuss."

"No!"

It's too late. She feels the glasses being ripped from her face. Her hand grabs at air, but the woman is too fast.

The crowd disappears. Sudden disorientation, the feeling of being transported to a vast, open space. The street is empty.

Just her and the woman, who looks straight into her eyes. Piercing blue eyes, short blond hair. Familiar, just older. Tired. Worn. Recognition hits.

"It's . . . you . . . the girl . . ."

"Yeah," says the woman. "Well spotted."

Anika slips the spex onto her face, and the whole world shifts.

Shadows realign, the sky changes. The world is full of ghosts, crowded around her. Pixels thrown at her retinas by twitching laser lenses. It's both instantly a rush, that transportation to another time, and instantly familiar. Like seeing something that was once exciting and new for the first time in nearly a decade, and remembering it had become mundane, routine. Infinite fucking detail, just like the last time. It makes her think of biting into a favorite childhood candy only to realize it's both too sweet and too hard.

Plus something else ain't quite right. Double images.

Ghost traces. People are floating, their feet not quite touching the ground. The buildings seem out of alignment. Either the motion and eye tracking is wrong or the lasers aren't auto-tuning to her retinas. She tries to pull down a menu from her periphery but it's a struggle, blinks not being recognized.

"Wow, your calibration is fucked," she says to the girl. "It's all out. No wonder you can barely control anything. I can't even find the interface . . . You been getting mad headaches?"

"Y-yes . . . ?" The girl sounds terrified, confused. She tries to grab at Anika's arm, to get back her precious glasses, but Anika swats her away easily. She falls backward, landing on her arse. She looks up at Anika, a shocked child being trampled by an army of ghosts.

Then Anika sees herself, dancing in the crowd. Full of energy, happiness. Emotions that she'd almost forgotten. Music she's not heard for a decade but recognizes instantly, a heavy grinding synthetic beat that triggers nostalgia spikes with each sub-bass hit. The space between the beats, dub-soaked air. It's like stumbling across an old photo of yourself, and being simultaneously embarrassed and full of regret, being both glad you've grown up and wishing you could go back. She feels herself freeze, her mouth go dry.

"Give her back the glasses," a voice says.

Ah, finally. The past disappears as she takes the spex from her face. The black kid is here, standing next to the girl. He's hot, sweating, out of breath. He holds a battered-looking old knife out at arm's length, aimed at Anika's face, the tip of the blade threatening to scratch her neck.

"Give her back the glasses," he says again.

Anika laughs. "Yeah, that's not how this works, man."

"The glasses. Give them to her." She can see his hand shaking, a drop of sweat running down his nose. He blinks. Don't fuck this up, kid, she thinks. For the first time self-doubt creeps in.

She looks down at Mary, still on her backside, close to sobbing. Looks back at the kid.

The kid says nothing. Just blinks again.

She could take him easily. No problem. Break the little motherfucker's arm before he even got to twitch that knife.

But maybe that's not the way.

She takes a breath.

"Okay. Fine. You got me." She shrugs, holds the glasses out toward the girl. She pulls herself up off the floor and snatches them back.

Anika turns to Tyrone. "Okay? You wanna give me some space here, man?"

Reluctantly he lowers the knife, still holding it out but no longer at her throat.

"Thanks," Anika says. She turns back to the girl, who is frantically checking the glasses, turning them over and over in her hands. "Nice trick you got there. But you really want to see some ghosts? You want to really know how they work? You come find me later."

"What?"

"Tonight." She turns, gestures at the 5102 building. "Up in there. Top floor. I'll show you some real ghosts up in there."

"You stay the fuck away from her," says Tyrone, tremors in his voice.

"Hey, it's cool," says Anika, smiling as she turns and walks away from them. "It's all good."

13. BEFORE

I just—I just can't believe you'd do something like this just to prove a point."

"I don't know what you mean—"

"You're so fucking infuriating. Everything is always about your stupid fucking politics, nothing is about us. You don't really care about us, do you?"

"Scott, I—"

"You don't, do you? Just fucking admit it. You don't care about us. We're just some distraction getting in the way of your fucking crusade to—"

"Scott! What the fuck are you talking about? What is this all about?"

"Don't pull that shit with me, you know exactly what this is about! Holy shit, you're so fucking INFURIATING!"

"Scott, I—"

"The photos! The fucking photos you deleted!"

"Deleted?"

"From iCloud! From the shared folder! The fucking photos you've deleted! They're the only copies I fucking have! But you just don't care, do you?"

Scott blinks open the iCloud icon, scans through to their shared folder. It's empty. Scott had set it up so they could both drop photos in there, photos from when they'd been together. The only photos they had of them together. But now they're gone.

Rush blinks the refresh icon, hoping they'll magically reappear. Nothing.

He blinks it again. Nothing.

A third time. A window pops up, blocking his view of everything else. Error message. Timed out. Connection error. A string of undecipherable numbers and letters.

"You make me so fucking *angry* sometimes. I mean, I fucking get it, you hate Apple, you hate the Internet, you hate fucking everything. You don't want to put photos on iCloud because it's not safe, privacy blah fucking blah, surveillance capitalism blah blah, you're so fucking self-righteous—"

"Scott! Listen to me! I didn't touch the fucking photos! There's a problem with the server, that's all. Didn't you have them backed up locally anyway?" He knows, the sec-

ond the last word leaves his mouth, that it's the wrong thing
to have said.

"FUCK YOU! I KNEW YOU'D SAY THAT!" They've
had a few blowouts, but this is the most angry Rush has ever
heard Scott. "I knew you'd say that! I knew you'd say where
are your backups! I knew you would! You're so fucking
predictable—"

"Scott—"

"You're so fucking predictable, I knew this was all some
fucking bullshit way of making a point! You're—I'm so fucking sick of y—"

And then Scott's voice is gone, replaced by low buzzing, echoing clicks.

"Scott!?"

Jesus fucking Christ, has he hung up on him? Has he
actually hung up on him?

He blinks at the phone icon, tries to restart the call
but then
everything freezes
and all is glitch.

He rips the spex from his face.

Sound fills the space around his head like air rushing
back into a vacuum. Like some TV show cliché, an audio
signifier that something terrible has happened, incessant
car horns blend with endless burglar alarms. But the noise
seems to be the only thing that's in motion, the Bristol that
surrounds him seems to have crashed, as stuck and frozen
as the spex that hang limply from his hand. Driverless

traffic is gridlocked, crossing lights dead-eyed. The LCD billboard that makes up most of a nearby bus stop is looping static, gray through white digital snow, as the confused commuters sheltering in it gawp at their own now-useless spex in their hands, or crane to stare down the endless procession of motionless traffic, scanning for a bus that'll never come.

"Fucking hell," Rush hears himself say, out loud.

Something flips in the pit of his stomach.

He slips his spex back on, but it's still all just glitch in that space, the only motion a few flickering pixels amid the distorted interface, stretched and blurred like it's been smeared, greasily, across the plastic lenses.

He takes them off, looks around again, finds himself laughing. Goose bumps ripple across his arms. He'd seen this coming: his obsessive poring over news speculation and social media around recent network outages and massive denial-of-service attacks meant he'd been expecting something to hit locally any day. But this is different, he can feel it—see it—just by looking around. This isn't a targeted attack on some corporate brand or platform, or even a strike against essential infrastructure—this is an attack on everything, a switch-flick, a purposeful turning off. It's like the Croft has exploded out of its boundaries and absorbed everything, a growing bubble that has purged the surrounding city of data and pushed back the insidious, invading fingers of the network.

It's exciting. Like that night in Times Square, nearly two

months ago now, when the lights went out and the screens died, and for a few long minutes everyone cheered in the dark, celebrating being free of surveillance and the pressure to be always connected. It takes him right back there, standing in the dark in that disconnected crowd, scarf wrapped around his face, fighting a wave of panic and euphoria, until Scott grabbed his hand and pulled him close.

Except Scott can't grab his hand now.

Because Scott isn't here.

Scott is three thousand miles away.

And the network that keeps him close just vanished.

As he crosses the digital perimeter into the People's Republic of Stokes Croft his spex bleep into life again, a window flashing across his vision asking if he wants to install the Flex software needed to join the MESH network. Good. It was always meant to work like this; he'd built it from Cuban code that resurrected and repurposed devices that had been remotely bricked by governments or corporations. It's rewarding, vindicating, to see it working in a real-world scenario. Even if the worm or virus that seemed to be taking everything down carried on spreading, perhaps the Croft's network could stay up.

Up in their server room in the 5102 he thumbs on monitors and drops himself down in front of the computers. Although connected to the Internet outside the Croft by wired connection, they still seem to be running fine; their custom OS is built on the same code that runs the spex network, and seems to be resilient to attacks for now. Plus he's poured years of work into security systems to protect them from exactly this. They're getting a hammering, though—just glancing at his diagnostics software he can see unprecedented levels of network traffic trying to break in, and he doesn't need to check IP or MAC addresses to know where it's coming from. Spex, self-driving cars, smart lightbulbs, toys, fridges, security cameras—it's coming from everywhere, everything and anything with a connection is pumping data into the network, flooding it. It's not being targeted at the Croft, either, it's being targeted at everything. He's seen this before, in the countless analyses he's read of all the major outages over the last few weeks, starting with Times Square: something is spreading, hijacking any and all Internet-connected devices it finds, and as it does, it floods the network with data—a distributed-denial-of-service attack without a specified target, apparently aimed at bringing the whole connected world to its knees.

Rush finds himself paralyzed at first, unable to react apart from staring at the screens. It's beautiful and terrifying at the same time, the kind of massive disruption he'd dreamed of for years, a victory for everything they believed in, the final loosening of the steel grip in which corporate capitalism and authoritarian governments have held the Internet for decades.

And yet fear and anxiety crush his celebrations. Not just fear of what comes next, but fear of having to accept a loss he hasn't prepared for, a situation his custom software can't counter.

All he can think of is Scott. Fucking Scott. Scott, who's not here, who's three thousand miles away. Scott, whom he's not seen in the flesh for nearly two months. Scott, who was yelling at him the last time they spoke.

Skype, Hangouts, Facebook, Twitter, Telegram, Signal, Gmail. Every channel he tries to open fails to connect, hangs, leaves him staring at pointless spinning disks and error messages. Somewhere, behind his screens, out past the protective barriers of the Croft, the Internet is melting, and the distance between Scott and him grows ever farther.

He stands up, screams silently to himself, paces the room, takes breaths. Knows what he must do. Sits down at the computer again.

The British Airways website is down, the United one failing to load anything past the logo. The Delta site seems to be working fine, though. With frantic clicks he grabs the first seat he can, tomorrow night, horrifically overpriced, Heathrow to Newark. No idea how he'll get to the fucking airport, but that can wait for now.

He enters his credit card details, address, as if on autopilot. It wants his passport number, so he has to dig in a nearby drawer to uncover the tattered, creased leather booklet. He taps it in. Hits SUBMIT.

Waits.

His conscience squirms at the back of his skull. Running out on the Croft now might seem harsh, but it'll survive. College can handle the tech, Anika the people. Claire will make sure the farms keep running. They're grown-ups. They don't need him.

He's not sure he's convincing himself.

Waits. Fingers drumming the desk.

Besides, he might be a liability if he stays around here. If the authorities start pointing fingers.

And this might be his last chance to get back to Scott.

The screen goes blank.

And then refreshes.

Red text on white, hard to read. The cold, polite authority of faceless automation.

IMPORTANT

A problem has been encountered with your travel documentation.

The passport(s) numbers you have provided have been determined as invalid for travel. This may be due to increased security concerns at the present time, or may be an indication that the passport(s) you and your party are attempting to use to travel have been canceled by the issuer.

Please contact your local passport-issuing organization for more details.

We apologize for any inconvenience.

"No fucking way," Rush says.

It might be an error. It might be that the computers are fucked because, well, all the computers are fucked. It might be, like it says, because of increased security concerns.

But Rush knows it isn't any of those fucking things. They've canceled his fucking passport. They've been watching him for years, watching the Croft and everything he does here, putting him on lists and labeling him an enemy, waiting for something like this to happen.

It suddenly feels like the room, its cracked plaster walls and server racks, is collapsing in on top of him, broken masonry and ceiling tiles crushing his chest, forcing the air out of his lungs in huge, heavy sobs. And for unmeasured minutes that's all he can do: sit and cry. Tears roll down his checks and his hands as he covers his face, his shoulders shuddering. So much seems lost. His freedom. His movement. The little semblance of control he still held on to. Scott.

Eventually he looks up, into the black pit of the monitor, at numbers flashing, data traffic spiraling, confused panic rolling across the few remaining timelines, the Internet melting away.

He pulls himself together. He has contingency plans to put in place. He'd planned for this. If they think he's involved, then they'll come for him. If they're going to come and drag him off to some rendition site, then he wants evidence, witnesses, some narrative left behind that isn't theirs. They'll be here soon. Best be ready.

He opens a terminal window, types secret commands and passwords. Text appears, text he wrote himself.

REPUBLIC OF STOKES CROFT—EMERGENCY SURVEILLANCE PROCEDURE

Activating this procedure will trigger full recording of all activity occurring within the SC zone and all data broadcast across the SC network. Data will be archived not only on SC servers but also on individual users' devices.

IMPORTANT! The data recorded is not limited to digital transmissions! It will record audio and video data collected by all devices connected to the network! THIS IS A TOTAL SURVEILLANCE PROCEDURE and should be limited only to EMERGENCY situations, such as natural disasters, the infiltration of the network/ SC by security or law enforcement agencies, or any other kind of physical or network assault upon SC and its inhabitants.

THIS IS A LAST-RESORT PROCEDURE AND SHOULD BE ACTIVATED ONLY UNDER AGREE-MENT OF THE SENIOR MEMBERS OF THE REPUBLIC OF STOKES CROFT STEERING COMMITTEE.

Do you want to activate the Emergency Surveillance Procedure? Y/N

Rush takes a breath.

With a couple of simple keyboard strokes he could betray everything he stands for, everything he'd built here. He could turn his little oasis of digital freedom into a tiny but highly efficient surveillance state. All on the off chance it might save his ass when the authorities come knocking, give him and the others some leverage when the shit really hits the fan.

He snorts to himself. When he'd written the code, he'd found the irony delicious—that he'd built into his utopian experiment the same moral dilemma every state faces, whether to trade freedom for some sense of security, to put power into the hands of a few on the trust that it wouldn't be misused.

Now, staring at the screen, he realizes he's no closer to having an answer.

He types "Y," hits RETURN.

And then it floods him again, that huge wave of loss and panic flowing over him. The realization that whatever plans he'd made for dealing with the end of the world as he knows it, there was no plan for dealing with being separated from the one person that really, truly mattered to him.

Out of desperation he tries apps and websites again. All pointlessly. Nothing but blank screens and error messages. Everything is fucked, everything is dying.

And then it happens. Gmail loads in front of him, his in-box slowly rendering itself on screen. Google. Those motherfuckers. If anyone can keep their servers running while the rest of the Internet is aflame, it's them. They practically are the Internet.

He hits COMPOSE, taps out a message.

Baby!

Oh god I hope you're okay. Don't know what's happening over there but it's all going down here. Something big. It's why I can't get hold of you, why those photos were missing.

I've no idea if you'll get this. Or how long it'll take to get to you. I just want you to know I'm thinking of you. I'll be trying to contact you constantly. And if that doesn't work I'll find some way to get to you. To be with you. To hold you.

I promise.

I love you.

He stares at the last line.

He deletes it.

Pauses.

Types it again.

Hits SEND.

Nothing happens.

Then the screen goes blank, the white space of an empty browser window.

He panics.

Hits REFRESH.

Words appear.

ERROR

You Are Not Connected to the Internet

This page cannot be displayed because you are currently offline.

14. AFTER

She wasn't sure the girl would come.

She looks anxious, standing in this abandoned room, her eyes shifting nervously from corner to corner. She's really young, she sees now. Younger than she'd initially thought. There's no way she could remember anything that had happened here.

"Come, sit." She gestures at the dusty floor in front of where she's sitting.

"I'm fine standing. Really."

Anika smiles, tilts her head. "It's Mary, right?" She hopes she's got that right.

"Yeah."

"Come and sit, Mary, please. It's fine. I just want to talk to you."

The girl shuffles forward awkwardly and sits, legs crossed. Her eyes continue to shift around the room, unable to meet Anika's.

"Give me your sp—" Anika pauses, corrects herself. "Give me your glasses."

"What? No, I—"

"It's fine, really. It's fine. Relax. I only need them for a few minutes. I just want to look at them, try them on. Then I'll give them right back to you. I promise."

Mary says nothing, just stares at the floor.

"It's fine, really. You can trust me."

The girl's eyes rise to hers, finally. With paint-stained hands she slips the glasses from her face, and with slow deliberation hands them over.

"Thank you."

Anika scratches away paint with the nail of her right thumb, Technicolor dust raining from the spex's arm, catching sunlight filtering in through shattered walls and sparkling like air-suspended pixels. She uncovers ten tiny hidden LEDs, the only outward sign that they're any more than just a regular pair of glasses, six of which glow green as she squeezes them. Sixty percent charged. The girl must have a charging mat hidden away somewhere, a basic, dumb one without a Net connection. She can picture it, plastic third-party wiring embedded in crappy Chinese fabric, close to twenty years old but still working. Not so dumb now.

She turns the spex over and over in her hands, suddenly scared to put them on. Scared to breathe life into this room, high in the top of the 5102, which has apparently lain dead for the last ten years. And so it should have done. As she looks around it, at the now-graffiti-soaked walls, at the chipped and shattered plaster, she can see the ghosts already. Feel them, their breath on the back of her neck. Feel the love and the passion and the anger and the betrayal. Too much, already.

Someone has blitzed through the room, or perhaps multiple people over various stages, ripping plaster apart to yank wires from walls, leaving their own layer of daubed scrawls as payment. She sits cross-legged amid the shrapnel of smashed furniture, leftovers too measly to burn, and gets that all-too-familiar sensation of being in the ruins of a dead civilization. Relics of the obsolete, like the weathered walls of Machu Picchu or the liquefying concrete of Detroit's car factories.

She tilts her head back, skull against cold exposed brick, and takes a deep breath. Reluctantly she slips the spex onto her face.

Nothing at first, just minor glitch. Random puddles of pixelated reality pulse and slither across the floor. The spex are messed up; no wonder the girl didn't have a clue what was going on. From what Anika can gather she had little control over what she saw, things just appearing to her like random visions, hence all the mystical bullshit. Mainly because the motion tracking is so badly aligned that the UI is barely readable, hovering forever just out of peripheral view. But Anika knows some old tricks, knows what she's doing—knows Rush's bespoke OS, cobbled together in this very room, like the back of her hand.

Patiently she blinks through malformed menus. She teases faux reality into perspective, the spex's still functioning LIDAR scan of the room calibrated to fit across the geometry of the actual. No more double images, no more disturbing misalignment, no scrabbling around in the unseen for the UI. Normal function returns, and with it the strange dread of the mundane.

Most of the spex's functions are dead, pointless, having purpose only when there's a network to attach to, peers to talk with. Resignedly she scans the local area for other nodes, knowing full well what results will come back. Text floats in the air in front of her face, at the focal point between her and the girl.

No other users detected in range.
 Find friends in your neighbourhood to talk and share with!

One of a kind, the last working spex in the Croft.
She slips them off again, smiles at the girl.
"One last thing I need to try, and then you can have your glasses back. Okay?"

"I know they're called spex, you know. I'm not stupid."

"I know you're not."

Anika places the spex on the floor between them, arms still unfurled, lenses facing back toward her. From her bag she brings out another pair—bulkier, scratched gloss-black finish—that College gave her earlier. She places them on the floor in front of Mary's, facing them, as though the two pairs are nose to nose.

"What are you doing?" Mary asks.

"I'm not sure exactly . . . but apparently this should work."

They stare at the floor in silence together, for what feels like a long minute. Mary opens her mouth to speak, but before she can form words she's interrupted by a sudden loud chime. They both jump.

Anika gingerly picks up the black spex. As she touches them, green power bars glow along its arms. She slips them on.

In front of her the words FLEX OS 10.74 INSTALL-ING and a quickly filling progress bar float in the swirling sunlit dust. They chime again. Welcoming screen. Ready.

(1) other users detected in range. Connect now?

Find more friends in your neighbourhood to talk and share with!

"Well, that was quick."

"What happened?"

"Those ones, your spex—they just repaired these ones." She taps the ones she's wearing, then takes them off. "Made them start working again."

"How?"

"Magic."

"Shut up." It's the first time she's seen Mary annoyed. "It's not magic. There's no fucking magic."

"Yeah. Yeah. Well, you're right there. There's no fucking magic." She picks up Mary's spex and hands them back to her. "Ask College. He'll tell you. He knows how all this shit works more than I do."

"So . . . now what?"

"Now what? Well, now I can see what you see, I guess."

"You're looking for people too?"

"Me?" Anika laughs. "No. I'm not looking for anyone." She doubts her own words as she says them.

"Really? I reckon everybody is looking for someone."

"Right? That's what you reckon, is it? So who are you looking for?"

"I dunno. Someone called Melody." Mary seems embarrassed. Her eyes drop to the ground again. "For Grids."

"Oh, right."

"You knew her?"

"Not personally."

"Oh."

"I—I don't think you'll find her." Anika tries to pick her words carefully. "Not here. She . . . died. Away from here."

"Yeah, I know. Grids knows that, too. But he wants some . . . memory of her, I guess. A picture. Some of her music. So that's what I'm looking for."

"Right." Anika isn't sure what to say.

"Could you help me?"

Anika wants to straight-out tell her no, to not get involved. Wants to take the spex and go. Not her fucking problem. But the kid seems insistent.

"I'm not really sure how I could—"

"Please? Look, you know how this all works. Better than I do. I don't think I'm using it properly. You said yourself earlier, it must be giving me headaches. It does. Because I don't know how it works. Nobody has ever shown me. Can you just show me, a bit?"

"Talk to College. I'm not—"

"Please? Look, I helped you." She points at the spex in Anika's hands. "Just show me a few things?"

Anika sighs. Fuck it.

"Okay, okay. Whatever. But quickly."

"Yes!" The girl smiles and bounces, claps her hands once. Anika suddenly sees how fucking young she is again.

"So, what now? Here?"

"Why not?"

Because this place is crawling with fucking ghosts, Anika thinks. Dread creeps along her spine, seeping up from the cold concrete.

"Okay. Sure. You never been up here before?"

"Nah. Grids won't let me. He doesn't know I'm here now."

"Yeah, I guessed as much."

Mary looks around some more, at the shattered plaster and fading scrawls. "What is this place?"

"This is where it all happened."

"Happened?"

"Yeah. Where it all started."

Mary's eyes open wide. "Show me."

Eventually she finds it, buried deep in a settings menu. The surveillance app that nobody apart from Rush knew was there, installed by him and pushed out to everyone without them even knowing. Watching everyone, recording everything. She remembers people freaking out in that final week, as their spex's inbuilt storage mysteriously started to fill up with data, not being able to work out what it was and assuming it must be the lethal malware, eating away at their system. Instead it was just Rush, squirreling away his surveillance recordings in the distributed cloud of his decentralized network, capturing everyone's reality and hiding it right under—or resting just above, in fact—their own noses.

Before they dive in, she shows and explains a few things to Mary. How it works, the principles behind it. How it can only show things that people in the Croft saw that one week—how, although it looks real, everything is just an illusion, a mix-and-match collage of hundreds of people's viewpoints. She shows her how the interface works, how the spex track the movements of her eyes, and how she can use that to control things; to swipe-scroll, to pull menus down from her periphery, how she can blink to select things. She shows her how they can send messages between them, how to share their spaces so they can see the same things.

Then she fires the app up, and the room changes. Graffiti is replaced with collages of Post-it notes on the few spaces where the walls are still visible; most of them are hidden behind server racks and piles of disused, half-repaired computers. Mission control, they used to call it. A heavyset figure moves among them, vague and unclear at first.

Mary recognizes him first. "College!"

His virtual presence startles Anika for a second, but that's soon replaced with a melancholic fondness. He looks younger, lighter. His dreads are shorter, less gray, his hairline receding less. As quickly as it comes, the flash of nostalgic joy at seeing him in his youth again vanishes, replaced by concern. She can see he's not happy. Frantic. He's packing a small black backpack with seemingly random items; a laptop, cables, two pairs of spex. Dead technology.

And then it happens, before he can finish or react, a loud popping sound from all around, the flash of sparks from some of the server stacks, and then freeze-frame, glitch out.

Back in the shattered room, her skull rests against the brick wall.

"Well, that's the end of the recording, then, I guess."

"What just happened?" Mary asks her. "Is it broken?"

"You could say that." Anika laughs. "Your spex are fine, don't worry. But yeah, that's the point where everything broke."

Anika wonders how far back it goes, exactly when Rush kicked it off. Only one way to find out.

Spex back on, the room full of servers and junk again. Mission control. She works an imaginary jog wheel with her right hand, relieved to find the spex are working well enough to read her gestures. Rewind.

Time begins to collapse upon itself as she accelerates backward. Shadows strobe. Figures dance around the room at inhuman speeds, until she notices something in the motion blur. She releases the jog, and time snaps back to attention, the whiplash of normality.

She's here, standing directly in front of herself. Towering above her as she sits on the ground. Arms outstretched at her sides, crucifix pose.

She laughs. Then the thought of that allegory makes her feel sick.

"Is that—"

"Yeah. Yeah, that's me."

She can't make eye contact with herself, unable to look into those young eyes. She doesn't want to see what's there; the slight nervous shaking of her younger self's body is enough to tell her. She doesn't want to look into those eyes when she knows there's no way she can change things.

This was it, the beginning of the change. The tipping point.

College is here, too, on his knees in front of her, fiddling with the makeshift vest. Wires and cylinders.

"You sure this is gonna work?" says *then* Anika.

"No. I'm not."

Now Anika tries not to start crying.

"Great."

College stops his fiddling, looks up at her. "Look, you don't have to go through with this. Just say the word."

Then Anika looks down at him, smiles. "Shut up, College. Just hurry up, yeah."

There's a dull thud from somewhere outside the building. All four of them startle. The staccato riff of gunfire.

"Hurry up," she repeats.

College has taken something from a bag on the floor, is wiring it into the vest. He hands it to *then* Anika. "Here," he says.

"What's that?" she says.

It's a stubby molded grip with a trigger at the top, a flat button above that. It looks like the grip of a handgun with the barrel removed. "It's the detonator," College says.

"Yeah, yeah, I guessed that. But what is it? I mean, why d'you have fucking detonators lying around—"

"Oh. Oh, it's an old VR controller. Wireless, but I didn't trust that, so I added a cable to it. It's a game controller."

"Of course it is." *Then* Anika laughs grimly. "It's a game controller. Of course it is."

"Keep it hidden." He tucks it into the pocket of her hoodie. He stands up, looking at her. "Try to get as close as you can before—"

"I know, I know."

"Okay. You know. I'm just fucking repeating myself." College sighs, looks down at her. He zips her hoodie up, it barely covering the bulk of the vest. *Now* Anika laughs between tears. The way it pushes them up, it makes her tits look great. *Then* Anika would have laughed at that, too, if she could have seen it.

"Okay," says *then* Anika.

"Okay. You ready?"

Now Anika doesn't let her finish, her hand reflexively twisting that nonexistent jog wheel in retreat, time flowing backward again.

Mary is on her feet now, her back to her, glancing around the room. Anika is pleased Mary can't see her face. With the fingers of her left hand she wipes tears from her cheeks behind the spex, the rush of memories almost too much.

Time collapse rewind blur.

About another thirty-six hours back, according to the readout, she instinctively releases the jog wheel.

Whiplash real time, silence pierced by screaming. Her

at Rush. He's got his coat on, a backpack hanging off one shoulder.

"You can't fucking go! You can't just walk out—"

"What choice have I got? Really? I'm putting everyone's life in danger—"

"People need you here—"

"People need me to get the fuck out of here, Anika! Why do you think they're blowing the shit out of us—"

"They need you here!" *Now* Anika can almost feel how hoarse *then* Anika's throat is, sense memory of anger-burn. "You're the reason people are here! You've always been—"

"They're trying to kill me, Anika! They're trying to kill me and they'll kill everyone else in the process!"

"Then turn yourself in." Claire's voice is calm, rational. It cuts through the atmosphere in the room like a knife, even from the corner where she leans against the closed door, as if to make sure nobody leaves.

"What?" *then* Anika asks her.

"Turn yourself in." Claire fixes Rush with cold, tired eyes. "If you really want to save everyone, then turn yourself in. Just leaving won't help. They won't know. They'll think you're still here and they'll keep on bombing us."

"He's not turning himself in," *then* Anika snaps. "Don't be so fucking stupid." *Now* Anika can see the resentment in her *then* self, that never quite quantified jealousy bubbling up to the surface. It's needless. She's flushed with embarrassment, regret.

"He's got to. They're going to flatten this place until they have him."

"I'm not turning myself in. But I am getting the fuck out of here." He turns from Claire to Anika. "And I suggest everyone else does the same."

"Where you going to go, Rush?" There's that edge of mocking to Claire's voice that always came out when she was mad. Anika always hated that.

"Yeah. Where you going to go?"

"I . . ." He seems to lose his words for a second, glancing at the floor as if searching for them there. "Away. Just away. From here."

"He's going to New York," says Claire.

Then Anika laughs at her. "He's not going to fucking New York. His passport's been canceled. Plus the airports must all be fucked. Right, Rush?"

Rush says nothing. Still searching for words on the floor.

"Rush?"

"He's got some way of getting out of the country. Who is it, Rush?" Claire tilts her head to one side, trying to catch his gaze. "Your hipster futurist friends? Those millionaire infrastructure pricks, with their, their"—she stumbles over her words, anger bubbling up through the cool—"their gentleman's container-ship yachting club?"

"What?" *Then* Anika looks confused. So much innocence, all lost now.

"Turn yourself in, Rush," Claire spits. "Turn yourself in or we'll turn you in."

"Whoa." It's the first thing College has said. *Now* Anika hadn't even noticed he was there. He looks up from the server cabinet he's had his head buried in. "Let's not get ahead of ourselves here—"

"Nobody is turning anybody else in, Claire," *then* Anika says, stepping between her and Rush.

"Look . . . Okay. Okay," Rush says, flustered. "Okay. I might have some way of getting out of the country."

"What?"

"I might, okay. It's a long—it's fucking complicated, okay?"

"I fucking told you." Claire, vindicated, shaking her damn head. "'I might have some way of getting out of the country.' Fucking coward."

"You're abandoning us?" *Then* Anika, close to tears.

"No! I'm not abandoning anyone!"

"You're abandoning everyone!"

"Come with me!" Rush, arms outstretched, crucifix pose. Supplier of answers, hacker of problems, the solutions guy. "Seriously! Come with me, all of you!"

Anika pauses time.

She pulls herself up to her feet, dusts shattered plaster crumbs from her backside. Mary watches her, confused and awkward.

"Who's this guy, the one that's leaving?"

"A fucking coward," says Anika.

She steps over to Rush, passing through her own ghost, feeling nothing. Circles him. Peering at him up close. Infinite fucking detail. The pores of his face mapped in high definition, pixel by pixel. She has to lean right in to make out the individual polygons that construct the LIDAR-scanned surface of his hair.

Angry, disgusted, she steps back.

Hand on the floating invisible jog wheel.

She thinks about unpausing, of letting the scene play out. But she knows the endgame, everybody's answers. What happens next. Spoiler alert: he leaves, nobody goes with him.

She could, this time, she thinks. Follow his ghost as it leaves, exit stage right.

Instead she hits REWIND again.

Rewind. All the way back to the beginning. As far as it will go.

Rush is here, alone, typing at the computer. He looks shook up, upset.

He finishes typing. Something isn't working, it's clear. He swears, wipes a tear from his eye.

The door behind him bursts open.

Claire is there, she's supporting this girl—Anika struggles to remember her name, Sarah?—who's leaning on her shoulder, arm around Claire's neck. Blood runs from a gash on her head.

"Rush, give us a hand here, yeah?"

Rush spins around, glances back at the monitors in front of him, reaches out to guiltily thumb them both off before going to the door to help Claire. Gently they help Sarah down onto the bust-up sofa in the corner of the room.

"What the fuck happened? You okay?"

"I'm fine."

"She took a can of peas to the head," says Claire.

Anika has that sudden feeling of recognition, of being witness to events she'd only heard of thirdhand, through conversations and timeline posts.

"What?"

"You got that first-aid kit?"

"Sure . . ." Rush turns around, confused for a second. Rummages in a junk-filled drawer, pulls out a green plastic box. He passes it to Claire. The blood doesn't seem to be stemming. "Jesus, you want me to call an ambulance?"

"I'm fine! Really!" Sarah is protesting too much. "Guys, stop freaking out, please . . ."

"I already tried," says Claire. "Couldn't get through."

"Hmm?"

"Ambulance. Tried calling her one before we got back. Nothing. Networks are all fucked, no data, no voice . . . dunno what's going on."

"I don't need an ambulance, I'm going to be fine. Really."

"What happened?"

"Riot at Sainsbury's." Claire's voice is deadpan, like it

was an everyday occurrence, her attention all focused on trying to clean up Sarah's split head with an antiseptic wipe.

"Sainsbury's?"

"Popped out to do some shopping, and all I got was a can of peas." Sarah laughs, wincing in pain.

"What's—" Mary's mouth struggles with the unfamiliar word. "Sainsberries?"

"A shop. Where we used to buy food." Anika's focus is on the room. She's never seen this before. "Shhh. Watch."

"Stay still, yeah?" Claire glances up at Rush. "It was fucking nasty down there, man, full-on riot."

"A Smash/Grab game?"

"Nah, this was a different crowd. Like, lots of, y'know . . . normal people? Lots of them. All really angry."

"Angry? Why?"

"No food. Nothing on the shelves. Apparently not been anything for days. A week, someone told me. Not just Sainsbury's, all the supermarkets. People are getting hungry."

"And angry," adds Sarah. "Tired of eating peas, I guess."

"Stop fucking moving, Jesus, girl. You're such a fidget."

Rush steps back, runs a hand through his hair. Exhales loudly. "Fuck."

"They were mad, Rush, I'm telling you. Were taking that place apart. Like they didn't believe the staff, like they thought they were hiding food from them."

"Shit. Jesus."

Rush is pacing, running his hand through his hair

again. And again. Like he can't stop. It's an anxious tic, Anika knows it all too well. So does Claire, apparently.

She finishes sticking an adhesive bandage over Sarah's wound, cleans her own hands with another antiseptic wipe, watching him. "What is it, Rush? What's actually happening?"

"I . . . I dunno." He sounds flustered, unsure of himself. "I've been reading what I can, talking to people, watching shit . . . I dunno for sure, and if I told you what I've heard, you'd say I was crazy."

"What?"

"Well . . . what it looks like, long story short—it looks like something is eating the Internet."

"Sorry?"

"What?" adds Sarah.

"Something is eating the Internet." He shrugs, shakes his head. "Something is infecting everything and shutting it down. But not until after it's poured massive amounts of traffic into key bits of net infrastructure, mainly DNS servers, I think. It's like a worm, a virus. It's spreading between everything, millions of computers and devices. Just infecting everything and bricking it all."

"Everything?"

"Well, anything with a Net connection, which is pretty much everything. So yeah. Everything from toasters to ISPs. China just disappeared."

"What do you mean disappeared?" asks Sarah, wincing.

"I mean disappeared. As far as the Internet is concerned.

It's just not there. No Chinese Net infrastructure seems to be online. Now, they might have just freaked out, shut the wall down tight, sealed themselves off. Would be the sensible thing to do, actually. But most of the U.S. is gone too. Apparently Wall Street hasn't traded since Thursday."

Anika isn't sure what day this is, can't be bothered to pull up the recording log.

"Grids told me about this," Mary says. She's standing against the wall, keeping out of the way.

"Shhh."

"Someone in town was saying the banks hadn't been open all week," says Sarah. "That old lady we was talking to? Said she couldn't get her pension."

"I wouldn't be surprised," says Rush.

"So it's . . . what? A virus?"

"Seems so. One that can infect anything. Apparently works on some fundamental exploit of TCP/IP, and backdoor exploits that seem to be embedded into lots of 'Internet of Things' devices. Looks impossible to patch at the scale it's working at right now. I know it sounds unlikely, but yeah."

"What . . . I . . . where?" Claire squints at him, doubtful. "I mean, where's it come from?"

He laughs. "Well, yeah. Take your pick. From what I've read it might be hackers, the NSA, ISIS, China, a rogue AI that's escaped from a lab in Berkeley, or space aliens."

He goes back to pacing, his hand in his hair again.

Claire stops fussing with Sarah, pushes herself up off

the coach, and moves over to him. Her ghost passes straight through Anika.

"You heard from Scott?"

Rush takes a deep breath. "Not for hours."

"Really?"

"Yeah. Can't call him, can't message him, e-mail's down . . ."

"Shit." She rests a hand on his shoulder, tries to fix his wandering, ever-anxious eyes. "Hey. I'm sorry. You doing okay?"

"Yeah. Yeah, I'm fine. Apart from I'm freaking the fuck out. I just . . . I just hope he's okay, y'know?"

Anika freezes time. Looks around the room, at the mannequin-still ghosts.

Rewind. All the way back to the beginning. As far as it will go.

Rush is here, alone, caught in midair typing.

He pauses, steps back from his nonexistent keyboard, looks around the room, looks at his hand, nods to himself.

The door behind him bursts open.

Claire is there, she's supporting this girl, Sarah, who's leaning on her shoulder, arm around Claire's neck. Blood runs from a gash on her head.

As Claire's mouth opens, Anika hits PAUSE again.

"What are you doing?" Mary asks.

"Nothing. Just checking something."

Anika steps through Rush to peer at the two monitors in front of him. He always used them, at a time when most people had abandoned them for spex-spaces. This was one of the few computers in the Croft with a direct, uncensored connection to the outside world, the Internet, and he used to talk about how he liked to keep it at arm's length, contained behind glass.

The first monitor is full of windows of code, largely incomprehensible to her, but enough keywords and in-line comments jump out for her to guess she's looking at code of Rush's surveillance app, freshly installed into the Croft's network. This is where the recording starts.

The other monitor is full of windows of English, yet they take Anika longer to decode. Delta Airlines, British Airways, some random forums, the U.K. Passport Office, various social-media timelines, what looks like a crashed Gmail in-box. The windows overlap and intersect, obscuring sentences and paragraphs, asking questions and answering others. Slowly she pieces together the fragments, a state of panic and desperation revealed amid the failed attempts to book flights, the error messages, the warnings about passport numbers being invalid, of permissions being denied.

He'd tried to go this early, she realizes. Tried to run even before it had started. Like he knew how bad it would get. That and his selfish need to be with Scott.

As if we haven't all lost people.

Anika unpauses time.

"Rush, give us a hand here, yeah?"

Rush spins around, glances back at the monitors in front

of him, reaches out to guiltily thumb them both off before going to the door to help Claire. Gently they help Sarah down onto the beat-up sofa in the corner of the room.

"What the fuck happened? You okay?"

Anika hits FAST FORWARD.

"—**so yeah**, we're running on batteries off the solar, man, pretty much. Most the city's blacked out from what I can tell." College is sat on the sofa, eating chicken and rice from a tinfoil tray.

"How much we got left?" asks Rush.

"Power? Ah, we should be fine, should just keep ticking over. Most the basic stuff, anyway. Y'know, as long as the sun comes up tomorrow. And who fucking knows these days—"

Anika is standing in the middle of the room between them, invisible, her back to the door, and it startles her as it's flung open.

"Guys! You need to come upstairs!" It's some kid, breathless and overexcited. Anika recognizes him but can't place his name. Was always hanging around. One of Claire's research interns from the farms, she thinks.

"What?" College doesn't even look up from his chicken. Neither he nor Rush seems particularly bothered.

"Come up on the roof! You gotta see this! It's all kicking off! There's a drone up, and everything!"

"A drone?" Rush just seems irritated. "So?"

"Not one of them police ones. Like, y'know, a big one? Like one of them army ones!"

Anika turns to Mary, still watching from the sidelines, trying to take it all in, understand. She doesn't know quite how to deal with her. Surely she must have heard stories, explanations of what went down from Grids and College and the others, but still this must be a head fuck. Maybe she should pause everything, explain things, make sure she gets what's going on. But she's tired, unsure she's got the fucking energy, that she's got the emotional capability.

She'll be able to figure it out herself, she thinks. Piece it together on her own. The kid is smart. She must be, she's alive.

"You know what a drone is?" she asks her.

"I think so?" Mary looks embarrassed, small and awkward in that way only teenagers can. "I've never seen one, though."

"Well, now's your chance."

Rush and College look at each other and get up to leave, following the kid out. Instinctively, Anika goes after them, following the ghosts through the dark corridors of the shattered building, suddenly aware that she's not confined to that one room, that the simulation goes farther, out into the Croft and maybe beyond. She could go anywhere, in theory, any place and point in that recorded time, see what anyone was doing, relive their pasts, recall memories that weren't hers, that she'd never had.

Yet she just follows these ghosts.

– – – –

Up on the roof of the 5102, the first time she's been here in a decade.

She reminds Mary to watch her step, the structure of the building not what it once was. She dials back the app's floor detail, the shattered tiles and concrete of reality pushing up through the recording.

Gingerly she walks to the edge of the roof and stands near her younger self. Claire is here, too, and some others.

They're looking out over Bristol, a dusk-tinted view of a city in chaos. Even though she's seen it before—this very simulation built in no small part from what her spex saw back then, undoubtedly—it still takes her breath away.

The city is dark, devoid of electricity. It's lit only by the rapidly fading daylight and the glow of fires—part of Cabot Circus seems to be ablaze. The streets are full of people, walking, running, shouting. Some gather in groups, some sit on the ground, looking concussed, confused. Others are trying to make their way around the vehicles that jam up the roads, self-driving cars and cabs and buses that have all ground to a halt, their passengers shouting for help or smashing windows to free themselves. There's a constant ambient soundscape of breaking glass, chanting, and police sirens that reverberates up the architecture to where they're watching.

"Fucking hell," says College.

"Yeah," says Claire.

"What the fuck happened?" says Rush.

"Explosion at that Melody gig."

Next to her, Anika hears Mary gasp.

"Explosion?" College snaps his head to face Claire.

"Terrorist attack." Anika recognizes her own, younger voice. "That's what they're saying."

"You fucking serious?"

"Wait, we don't know anything yet," says Claire. "But yeah, explosion, apparently. Then all the networks went down. Everything. All the cars shut down, all the cell networks . . . everything finally failed."

"Where you hearing all this?"

"Chatter on our network. That's still running, it seems."

"Yeah." Rush sounds dazed. "Yeah. The virus doesn't seem to affect it. Not yet, anyway. I thi—"

"Look!" He's interrupted by the young kid shouting. Shouting and pointing at the sky. "Look!"

Everyone, including Mary and Anika, follows his finger.

There, between low-level clouds and silhouetted against the dusk sky, the crucifix-like outline of something darts, angular and awkward and robotic and unlikely looking. Something they'd never seen flying above the city before.

Anika hits FAST FORWARD.

She stops and lets it play after about thirty-five hours. Daylight on the roof.

"—oh, it can handle the traffic, that's not the point."
Rush holding court, as usual. "It's completely decentralized. The more people, the stronger it is, and the faster. It's
just whether it'll be useable for much longer."

Claire looks at him, turning away from the city below
her. "What you saying?"

They're standing behind Anika, pretty much the same
group, but on the other side of the roof. Mary and Anika
walk over to join them as they look down into Stokes Croft.

From up here it's impossible to see any road surface, so
many people fill the Croft, with even more pouring in from
elsewhere in the city, under the building they're standing
on, and from the side streets. The sound systems are out,
dotted here and there like alien monoliths, bass resonating
through the architecture. People are dancing, talking,
sitting. Smoke rises from makeshift fires and barbecues.
Here and there tents have been thrown up by those who
won't or can't leave. Pure carnival vibes. It's somehow
both friendly and apocalyptic, welcoming and tense at the
same time, like Glastonbury Festival or Burning Man
dropped into an urban space too cramped and ill-designed
to safely hold it.

"Have you seen the chat recently?" Rush is continuing.
"Looked at the public timelines? It's a fucking mess. It's just
full of randoms screaming at each other. It's impossible to
follow anything, impossible to make announcements, get
information out . . . It's a fucking mess. It's all conspiracy
theories and lies. People making up unsubstantiated shit

and other people believing them. The network is stable, but I never thought we'd have this many users, at least not all crammed into this space. It just doesn't scale like that."

"Hang on, I thought that was the whole point?" Claire asks him. "The anarchic decentralized network nobody runs?"

"Well . . . yeah. But not . . . like this." He runs his hand through his hair. "I thought it'd be more spread out. Geographically, I mean. Like it'd be citywide, not the whole city trying to get into fucking Stokes Croft to use it all at once."

"Thing is," College says slowly, "people leave here and their spex get infected again, and they stop working. So they come back, the client reinstalls itself, and they . . . they just stay here for as long as they can. Hence the happy campers."

"Ah well, it's a hell of a party." *Now* Anika flinches at the naïveté that drips from *then* Anika's voice.

"Yeah, for now. I'm just worried it's a disaster waiting to happen."

"Yeah," says College, his tone tired and serious. "I saw posts flying around saying someone saw people with guns down there."

"What?"

"It's what I heard. Barton Hill crew came down, apparently. Faces I recognize. Trying to hide from the feds."

"Fuck me."

"Guns, though? Really?"

"Yeah. Lot of that Barton crew tooled up when things

got dicey with the fascists after Brexit, 3D-printed Kalashnikovs and stuff smuggled in from Ireland."

The idea seems to stun them all, they just stand there, staring at the ever-shifting crowd. Anika reaches for the invisible jog wheel, but Claire shatters the silence.

"So what . . . I mean, what can we do? How we meant to stop people coming in?"

"Turn it off," Rush says.

"What?" says *then* Anika.

"The network. Turn it off. That'll stop them coming in."

"Can you even do that?"

Rush glances over at College. "Yeah. There might be a way."

"We . . . we can't do that though, right?" Claire leans against cracked architecture, still staring down into the human maelstrom below. "I mean, this is the point, right? As of now we seem to be the only working network in the city. That's what we always wanted. What you always wanted."

"I guess."

"You can't turn it off now, man. That'd be giving up. Quitting when you're winning."

Rush laughs. "Yeah. Guess you're right. I guess this is what winning looks like, right?"

"Brave new world, baby." College slaps him on the back. "This is where it all begins. Viva la revolution."

"Viva la revolution. I'm just worried we've grabbed the wrong people's attention."

Rush is looking up into the sky, scanning for silhouettes.

Anika takes off the spex, and the ghosts of her friends disappear.

She stops playback, quits the app.

"That's it, that's enough. No more."

Mary looks at her, disappointed. "Really?"

"Really. I've seen enough. You've seen enough."

"But you said you'd help me! Said you'd show me how to find Melody!"

"Melody is dead. They're all dead."

"You said you'd help! At least show me where to look for a trace of her, her music. You said!"

Anika sighs, curses herself. For. Fuck's. Sake. She looks out across the flat, cluttered Bristol landscape.

"Fine. Okay. But we're not going to find her up here."

They leave the 5102, fleeing ghosts Anika should never have disturbed, shattered dreams she should never have remembered.

In the underpass they pause by the Croft's gate. Semi-permanent now, but she remembers when it was thrown together.

She fires up the app again.

The space under the 5102 is full of people.

Hundreds of them, all flooding into Stokes Croft, their faces a mixture of confusion and elation. Despite everything she still remembers that feeling, that raw, narcotic mix of emotions. She could taste it in the crowd that day. A very real sense that something had ended, had gone, something huge and fundamental. The feeling that a structure—a way of life, something nobody could really imagine changing—had collapsed. The end of being watched. The end of being tracked. The end of being indentured to it all. The end of capital. The end of security. The end of knowing. The end of safety. The end of being reassured. The end of being connected. The end of friendships. It was all there, in that crowd, sprayed across faces that had been denied sleep and electricity and communication for days—the fear, the uncertainty, the excitement, the thrill. The relief.

She pushes herself against the wall, Mary joining her at her side, so the ghosts don't brush against them as they march past. Ripped jeans and soiled hoodies. Some carry armfuls of looted treasures; shower gels, alcohol, VR headsets in battered boxes and games consoles trailing power leads from hastily stuffed plastic bags. Already dead and useless consumer electronics. The great ransacking of Cabot Circus, the last archive of civilization.

Her eyes flicker across their ghost faces, trying to scan and judge emotions. For most it's celebration as they flood in, drawn by the music and the shouting and the dancing. The smell of cooking meat, the rumble of bass. Flooding in to find an outlet, to find answers, to find connections again. The rapture of shaking off the old and finding the new, of dancing in the shattered remains of the failed and dead.

Anika wishes she could hold back the flood, scream at them to go back.

Instead she lets it carry the two of them on, into the human melee that has drowned the streets. Through the bodies she glimpses herself again, like the first time she took the spex from Mary, almost the same frozen moments—dancing to that familiar rhythm, the crowd around her moving as one, those not dancing lost in the confusing rapture of a new network, a new way of doing things. She watches herself, snippets of motion glimpsed in the spaces between the human nodes, and she remembers being that happy. How it felt. They had won! This was it, everything they'd fought for. Everything had fallen— everything they'd fought against—but they'd remained standing. Vindicated, right, victorious.

"Here." She turns to Mary. "This is what you've been looking for."

Mary looks back at her, confused. Anika can't make out whether she's just overawed by the scene or doesn't understand what she's saying.

"Look up into your periphery. Remember the date and time."

Mary just gawps back at her. "I—"

"Listen."

Mary does as she's told, staring back into the crowd, as the slow, spaced-out bass hits from the sound system reverberate through the spex's bone conductors, and Anika smiles as she sees the penny drop. Mary flicks her face back to look at her.

"This is . . . this is her?"

Anika just nods, turns back to the crowd, lost in some toxic fog of regret and nostalgia. She watches herself dance and wonders how she could have ever been so fucking stupid.

A shout goes up from the crowd, hands point to the air. Booing. She looks up and sees it, the small police drone—not the fixed-wing air force one that's been circling for days, this one looks like a lump of floating infrastructure, an overly complex street sign hanging from six whirring rotors. An unlikely looking LED display transcribes the messages a cold female voice recites endlessly from the speakers that hang from the underside of its insectile body.

A STATE OF EMERGENCY HAS BEEN DECLARED RETURN TO YOUR HOMES BY REMAINING IN THIS AREA YOU ARE ENGAGING IN AN ILLEGAL GATHERING A STATE OF EMERGENCY HAS BEEN DECLARED RETURN TO YOUR HOMES THE USE OF ELECTRONIC COMMUNICATION DEVICES IS CURRENTLY FORBIDDEN A STATE OF EMERGENCY HAS BEEN DECLARED RETURN TO YOUR HOMES THE USE OF WIRELESS NETWORKING TECHNOLOGIES IS CURRENTLY FORBIDDEN . . .

A missile arches up from the crowd, a bottle. Anika flinches as it misses the drone, wondering where it lands in the crowd. A second one goes up, and to her surprise it makes contact—she's seen these drones dodge thrown projectiles with unsettling, algorithmically judged ease, but this one seems sluggish, almost distracted. The bottle explodes in a cloud of glass fragments as it hits the drone's screen, the still-scrolling messages partly masked by a spray of dead LED pixels that glitch across its surface. Another cheer from the crowd. And then, as Anika watches, the whole drone tilts sickeningly to one side, its rotors failing as one, and falls from the sky.

The crowd below just manages to make way for it as it hits the ground. Screams and more cheers. Anika knows that its failure was due more to infection than a well-aimed Red Stripe bottle, but there's no use trying to explain that to the ghosts now crowding around its shattered carcass, dancing around it and picking at its polycarbonate bones, hoisting them above their heads in celebration. Another victory, another downed victim of the revolution.

Anika hits FAST FORWARD.

Less than twenty-four hours. The sky above her is full of bottles.

The crowd around her has gone, replaced by the exploding glass of missiles falling too short, and the occasional crumpled human form.

It's disconcerting at first, the jarring transportation into open space. And then she realizes where they are: standing in the no-man's-land between two warring fronts.

Ahead of her, as she looks into the Croft, is the crowd, retreated now farther up the road, leaving behind it a street full of smashed glass, crumpled bodies, abandoned loot, like a receding ocean tide depositing its bounty of plastic trash.

Although still launching missiles, most of the crowd seems to have fallen back for its own safety, apart from a few scouts that dance along its forward flank, a dozen or so that refuse to retreat, their faces hidden by spex and scarves and hoods, leading the charge of hurled bottles and taunts.

Glass still exploding around her, Anika turns to face the opposing front. And there it is, what was meant to be the final battle line of the establishment, a row of police shields, helmeted skulls cowering behind them as the unrelenting shower of glass and masonry rains down on them. Paralyzed and prone, the police line has barely emerged from under the 5102, and Anika realizes now that most of the debris falling on them isn't coming from the crowd at all but from the roof of the building itself. Looking up, she spots the crowd up there, weaponizing the architecture as they rain fragments of it down onto the invading forces: roof tiles, pipes, microwave transmitters, the reflective shards of shattered solar panels.

She doesn't look too hard; she doesn't want to see herself up there, dropping pottery shrapnel from the kicked-in remains of a crumbling chimney.

The first canister lands surprisingly near her feet, the second a few meters away. She sees one of the rioters scoop it up as he dances past, and hurl it back. Mid-flight it begins to hiss, along with the one near her feet, and within seconds the world is filled with white.

She blinks through menus, brings up settings she remembers being there. Filters. Turns off smoke. The air clears instantly, just in time for her to hear the distinctive, ear-shattering crackle of gunfire.

From behind her, from the crowd.

Both lines disperse, the rioters scattering in panic, the police falling back in full retreat.

She almost forgets Mary is there.

"You okay?"

"I'm fine." To Anika's surprise she seems quiet, almost resigned. "I've been here before. This is usually where I start. This is where the dying begins."

Anika is suddenly flooded with guilt and disgust at this child, too young to remember all this herself, being made to relive other people's death and suffering. At being turned into a repository for the city's posttraumatic stress. Anika feels a sudden urge to grab her, hold her tight. To yank the spex from her face.

She does neither, just looks at her, helpless. "We should stop. That's enough."

"No, please."

"You found what you were looking for—"

"Please. Let's go on. I want to finish this." She seems distant, but committed. "I . . . I've always felt trapped in a loop here. Unable to get past this. I need to see how it really ends."

"Are you sure? It's not pretty—"

"I'm sure. Please."

Anika hits FAST FORWARD.

She punches them out of the motion blur just a few minutes short. Unconsciously perhaps, but certainly intentionally. As she stares at the recording's date and time counter hovering in her periphery she knows there's no way it could have been a mistake.

The crowd is back, surrounding them but subdued. Apart from a little head-nodding and shuffling the party has died. At least half sit on the floor, wrapping themselves in blankets, huddled together. Here and there some tend to the injured and fallen. Others stand, grouped together in suspicious circles, whispering to one another and glancing around. Faces are stunned, tired, resigned, and sobbing eyes are bleached red by gas and tears. Anika is struck by a sudden, disturbed cognitive dissonance: all-too-familiar news footage of foreign war zones or distant refugee camps suddenly playing out on her doorstep, and all to a relentless soundtrack of grime-tinged techno. Industrial drums and distorted analog chord stabs. Refugee crisis or music festival? Terrorist attack aftermath or warehouse rave morning-after?

The sound systems are at full volume. Unrepentant and penetrating. She blinks to her filter settings again and kills their volume, and then remembers why they've been cranked so high—from the other side of the makeshift barricades that now fill the space under the 5102 comes the booming voice of repeating police announcements. The same warnings, the same orders to disperse and return home. No longer automated, they now sound like a human voice: fatigued, desperate. Pleading.

And for the first time, among the repeated phrases, she hears call for individuals to surrender, to come forward. She hears names. Names she knows. Rush's. College's. Hers.

It draws her forward, Mary following, toward the barricades built from shattered masonry and street signs and bicycles and ripped-down shop shutters. It draws her past the gunman, with his covered face and his 3D-printed Kalashnikov, as he paces anxiously, looking like he doesn't know whether to watch the crowd or the cops, whether he's meant to be guarding or detaining.

The sound of her name repeats again. It draws her to the barricade, up close now, her face pushed against a gap, peering through at the now-distant police line. She hadn't heard it back then, and now it triggers thoughts of possibilities, alternate histories, dividing timelines. Parallel universes. Other outcomes.

It's all too late, of course.

She watches the recording's timer tick away the seconds.

Exactly on cue, the building behind her explodes.

Shrapnel the size of bricks pierces her body, failing to rip her flesh apart, while elsewhere she watches it reduce others to clouds of scarlet mist. A huge storm cloud of fragments and debris is rolling across Stokes Croft toward her, swallowing up its dying occupants. In a few short seconds she's covered by it herself, day turning to night as pixels extinguish the sun, and in the dislocated limbo of the inside of the cloud she allows herself to exhale, a strange sense of clarity, a fleeting moment of quiet and solitude.

And it is fleeting. As quickly as it rolled over her, the cloud is gone, no traces of debris left as the displaced masonry dissolves into the air, the spex's smoke-erasing filters kicking in just a little too late.

It reveals a landscape sprayed red, streets pooled with blood, all fanning out from the now-vacant lot where the missile hit, like child's paint blown through a straw. Streams and pools, broken limbs and shredded, soaked fabric.

Screams. Ringing ears.

"Don't look," she hears herself say. "Take them off."

"I've seen all this before." That same resignation in Mary's voice, but somehow tinged with arrogance now. A numbed defiance. "I've watched these people die, over and over. I just didn't understand what happened, why."

To Anika's surprise, Mary reaches in front of her, fingers grasping the virtual jog wheel that floats in front of them. She hits REWIND.

They watch the cloud reappear and then retreat, bodies and masonry reassemble, blood seemingly evaporate. The building stands again. Mary continues to rewind but now slowly, ultra slo-mo. And there they glimpse it, moving almost too fast for even the app's high frame rate, a blurred shard thrown from the sky. She lets it roll back and Anika traces the missile's trajectory, still unable to see the drone that threw it down—its apparent last, crippled act before it ditched somewhere out at sea, according to the stories she'd heard—but she can see enough to confirm what she'd always expected. Poorly aimed, the missile had almost scraped its intended target—the hulking frame of the 5102 and its occupants hiding from the chaos. Rush. College. Her.

A last-ditch attempt. The death throes of the network. A mistaken, panicked attempt to cut out what it saw as the cancer eating away at itself.

Anika hits FAST FORWARD.

There's not much time left on the recording's clock now, just minutes.

Anika grabs Mary's arm and pulls her into an alleyway, knowing what they'll find.

Then Anika and *then* Grids, flattened against the wall. Under her hoodie she can see the bulk of the vest. He clutches a printed AK-47 to his chest. He's young, barely more than a kid. She always forgets how young he was. Mary gasps at the sight.

The wall opposite them, the corner exposed to the street, is being shredded by gunfire. Bricks dissolving into pixel dust.

Then Anika's hands are over her ears.

Now Anika's eyes are full of tears.

The firing stops. Grids pulls her hands down.

"You ready?"

"Yes. Yes."

"Is this going to work?" Grids is breathing hard, terrified.

"I don't know."

"How close you gotta go?"

"Close."

"Let me do it."

"No! No, it'll be better with me. Look at me. They'll believe me."

Grids looks at her; a grin cracks across his face. An almost laugh. "Racist."

Now Anika feels sick.

For a second nothing seems to happen.

Grids is staring across the street, at things Anika knows are there but she can't see, people hiding in the shattered buildings, messages from them projected into his retinas.

"Okay." He looks at *then* Anika, nods. "Okay. They're ready. When they open up, you get ready. Okay?"

From across the street, from holes in broken walls and through smashed windows, a hail of machine-gun fire erupts, the rounds passing them and heading up into the street.

Then Anika steps out.

Now Anika follows her, standing at her shoulder.

Mary stands behind her, stunned and motionless.

Stokes Croft is a deserted, shattered shell, strewn with bodies and dust. Again to Anika it is a dozen distant histories—Syria, Iraq, Hue, Beirut, Dresden—alien landscapes that could never happen here, nation-state-scale karmic retribution right on her doorstep.

Sitting in the middle of the road, just meters away from her now, is the tank, dismantling with machine-gun fire the building where her compatriots are hopefully no longer hiding, as its turret slowly turns, electric motors rumbling like giant millstones grinding against each other. Behind it she can see the hole in the barricade where it had punched through, before it had spent the last two hours slowly crawling up Stokes Croft, laying waste to anything that moved.

As she walks behind her ghost she can't feel her legs.

Then Anika pushes her hands into the air, unveils the blood-flecked white sheet she's been carrying, starts to scream as hard as she can.

"HELP, HELP! PLEASE! I SURRENDER! SURRENDER! PLEASE! HELP! I JUST WANT TO GO HOME! I JUST WANT TO GO HOME! PLEASE HELP ME! I SURRENDER! I SURRENDER!"

The turret stops turning. There's a strange moment of near silence, no sound except for the distant, skittering sound of falling bricks, fragments of architecture collapsing upon itself.

"OKAY, KEEP YOUR HANDS UP, DON'T MOVE." The voice seems to come from the tank itself, from some hidden speaker system, embedded in its mottled, bullet-scratched armor.

Then Anika keeps her hands up, but doesn't stop moving.

"DON'T MOVE," repeats the tank.

Now Anika wants to scream at her oblivious past self. Don't go any closer! You're close enough! You don't need to get any closer!

Then Anika keeps moving, drops one hand to her side. It slips into her pocket.

The turret starts to turn slowly back, the antipersonnel machine gun moving to face her much more quickly.

Behind them both Grids screams at her "JUST DO IT" and opens fire. *Now* Anika swears she can feel the rounds pass her head, feel the air they displace, hear them ricochet harmlessly off armor plating.

In her hoodie pocket *then* Anika's hand finds the trigger. *Now* Anika can feel it, the smooth, cold, injection-molded Chinese plastic of the VR game controller against her trembling, clammy hand.

Finger searching for the trigger.

Squeezing.

And then the world screams in digital white noise, and everything is glitch.

RECORDING ENDS is the last thing Anika sees as she rips the spex from her face.

15. AFTER

Knocks on his cabin door.

"What?"

"You up, Rush?"

Jesus. "I am now. What time is it?"

"About three thirty."

"Fuck, Toby. Seriously?"

"Sorry, man. Just thought you'd want to know; we heard back from the Zodiac."

"Really?" Rush props himself up on one elbow. "And?"

"All clear. Simon is taking us in."

"Shit. Okay. I'll be down."

"Don't take too long, man. You need to see this fucking parking lot. Unbelievable."

Even with dawn breaking it's still dark out. Rush throws a sharp beam of yellow light across the bridge when he enters, extinguishing it as quickly as he can by shutting the door behind him. As endless shifts on night watch have taught him, it's vital to keep the bridge dark—the only light the dim green glow of the few still-working LCD displays in night mode—so that the crew's eyes adjust to staring across the ocean at night.

Simon looks back from the captain's chair to glance at him, flash him a quick smile, before his attention returns to the world outside, to quietly but firmly speaking orders to the last of his Filipino crew, as they gently maneuver the *Dymaxion* past the vast black bulk of a dead CGM Line container ship.

"Jesus Christ."

"That's nothing, mate. You should have seen what we passed on the way in." Simon rubs his hands with theatrical glee. "We could spend a month just scavenging this lot, and still not be done."

"A month?"

"Yeah." Simon meets Rush's glare, the glee dropping. "I mean, I'm sure it won't take that long. To get what we need. Parts and stuff. Like a week. Two tops."

"Right. Sure."

The CGM ship, quarter of a million tons of steel and abandoned cargo, dwarves them as they slip past. As Rush's eyes adjust to the night he sees Toby wasn't bullshitting him. The CGM ship isn't alone; there looks at first glance to be dozens of container ships parked here, just a few miles off the coast of Ningbo port, all abandoned by their crews when the networks died, as the algorithms in Copenhagen and Beijing that guided them fell silent. Ningbo was, for decades, one of the world's busiest ports, and ships would have been anchored here for days on end at times, waiting their calculated turn to glide in and be filled with the material existence of global capitalism. Rush tries to imagine what it must have been like here in those last few days, the last few weeks—crews waiting patiently on their vast vessels for instructions that never came, nursing anonymous cargoes, clueless as to what was happening. He wonders when the restlessness must have set in, when the anxiety must have become too much. What the rumors must have been. When the mutinies must have started.

"Toby said you'd heard back from the Zodiac?"

"Yeah. Yeah, all clear, man. Even a free berth for us. We can slip straight in, apparently."

"No signs of life?"

"Not much, from the sounds of it. Few scavengers in the stacks, just the usual."

"'Just the usual'?"

Simon looks at him. "It's fine, man. Nothing to worry

about." He slaps him playfully on the arm, turns his attention back to piloting.

Rush sighs, shakes his head. Simon. Simon fucking Strickland. Nothing to worry about.

Just days before everything went to shit, Rush had heard from Simon, a suitably cryptic e-mail appearing in his in-box. Simon, his wavelength ever tuned to the near future, had guessed something was up, had seen the patterns emerging in the flows of goods and data that made up the supply chains he obsessed over. But watching the news and markets wasn't enough for him—he was an ethnographer at heart, and he needed to be out there, watching the collapse from within. His plan was to take the *Dymaxion* out for what might well be her final voyage; one last orbit around the world to watch global capitalism collapse in real time.

For Rush the timing was perfect. Like everything else, the airlines had stopped running, the airports ground to a halt. The *Dymaxion* might have been going in the wrong direction—taking literally the longest way around to where he wanted to go—but it was the only chance he could see of getting there, of getting back to Scott.

So less than a month later they were steaming out of Dover and along the English Channel, as aging RAF fighter jets streaked overhead toward a French coast that erupted in the low booms and lightning flashes of dropped ordnance, on an apparent adversary in some secret war the U.K. public knew nothing about. They rounded Portugal and Spain as the glow of burning cities lit the horizon, and picked their way through a Mediterranean filled with flotillas of refugees, as many of them trying to flee a collapsing Europe as reach it.

Simon had, largely, held it together while they watched the world collapse around them. In the Suez Canal he'd successfully bargained for their safe passage after the ship had been boarded by militia, three terrifying hours spent on their knees at gunpoint under a fierce Egyptian sun, while Simon negotiated with their leaders behind closed doors. Rush has no idea what he said, what he gave them, or what promises he made, just that he reappeared looking exhausted and shaken. He barely spoke to Rush or any of the crew for two days. But they got out of the canal without being stopped again, just waved through by gunmen at every checkpoint, shaken up but alive. The crew, mainly Filipinos and southern Indians, always joke that Simon is their lucky charm, some blundering, haphazard talisman that always comes out on top. The crazy, lucky bastard, they call him.

But that time nobody was laughing.

Rush slips out the sliding door on the starboard side of the bridge, breaking out of the air-conditioned chill as the humidity hits his skin hard, sweat instantly appearing along his arms. He leans against the weathered balcony railing. The sky is lightening, revealing dark, ominous structures against the blue. The vast steam stacks of a shuttered power plant tower above the port like an abandoned fortress, dead ever since the stream of bulk carrier ships laden with coal had dried up. Ningbo was one of China's many input/output gates, Rush remembers reading somewhere—the rest of the world sent ships full of coal here, and in return got back ships full of cheap consumer goods. This was why the supply chains existed, in order to make transactions that logic dictated were most efficient on local scales work on global ones, through sheer size, brute force, cheap labor, and global inequality.

Simon comes out and joins him on the balcony, and with his first mate they fire up the outside docking-control panel, guiding the huge ship sideways into the berth on submerged aft thrusters. Simon peers over the side, trying to judge the distance.

"Fuck, can't see shit." He grabs the walkie-talkie from his belt. "Guys, need some light."

Almost instantaneously a chain of small bright suns flare into existence along the quayside as the recon crew of the small inflatable Zodiac motorboat ignite their pre-prepared flares, plumes of white smoke billowing across the asphalt shoreline. The flares themselves are too bright to look at directly without singeing his retinas, but Rush stares past them, the flickering light revealing elaborate Chinese symbols and road markings stenciled in yellow on the concrete floor. Beyond that the stacks rise, thousands upon thousands of shipping containers, piled six stories high in neat lines, a seemingly unending field that stretches almost to the horizon, where it meets with apparently deserted apartment blocks. Up until the crash Ningbo was a city that existed just to fill and move these containers, and when that ended there must have been little left for its population to do. Nobody from outside knows how the crash must have gone down in China, but Rush imagines the cities hollowing out, the tower blocks emptying of confused people and the great Chinese migration reversed as they headed back into the countryside in search of family, food, and answers.

Shouts from the decks below and bursts of radio static. Ropes are thrown out, the Zodiac crew busies itself tying up the ship. Rush still stares out across the box city, though, silent in the morning light. He goes through this every time they pass one of these ports, regardless of the continent— transfixed by the sight of capitalism on pause, the secret network that kept the world running mothballed and abandoned.

His train of thought is interrupted by a huge burst of light above them. One of the Zodiac crew has climbed the top of the vast, five-hundred-foot-high super-post-Panamax crane that towers above and over them, and lit a flare. As it's slowly waved back and forth it scatters light across the crane's vast skeletal frame, yet more smoke rising into the dark sky. It looks to Rush like an act of victory and defiance; like news footage of freshly liberated citizens climbing to the top of statues of their now-fallen dictators, to deface their heads and celebrate their liberty in that brief moment of joy before worrying what will happen next.

"Haha! It's Chris! The crazy fuck!" Simon yells and waves excitedly back. "Chris! CHRIS!"

Rush shakes his head, but gets why they're so excited. Despite spending the last couple of weeks skirting around the mega-ports of the South China Sea, they'd never managed to come into harbor anywhere. You can't just dock a huge fucking container ship like the *Dymaxion* by the shore and walk off—and perhaps unsurprisingly most of the suitable berths at the ports were filled with abandoned ships. Apart from the Zodiac crew, who went ahead and scouted out the ports in their little inflatable speedboat, nobody from the *Dymaxion* had set foot on Chinese soil as yet on this trip. Which had been the root of huge frustration and anxiety for Simon; Rush had seen it eating him up, the usually unfazed and endlessly enthusiastic figure reduced to pacing the bridge during the day, moping in his office at night. It was, of course, the main reason for this whole elaborate mission, for the last four months they'd spent risking their lives at sea: to take a container ship halfway around the world and back up the global supply chain. It wasn't the first time Simon had done it—he'd taken the *Dymaxion* up the chain at least once a year, to Rush's knowledge—but it was the first time he'd done it since the crash. The first time he'd done it since global capitalism had collapsed, since the vast data networks that managed the ships and ports had vanished, and since the algorithms that decided what you wanted to buy and then brought it halfway around the globe from a Chinese sweatshop to the shelves of your local store had burned in the data fires along with the rest of the digital age.

It had all been building up to this for Simon, Rush realized. Decades of studying and picking apart the supply-chain networks—their vast spaces, both digital and very real—and now what he really wanted was to see them dead. As endlessly intoxicating as they were in their scale and grandeur, he could see Simon had grown disgusted by them; by the endless money and labor that had been piled into what was history's greatest engineering achievement. The pinnacle of human effort had been to create a largely hidden, superefficient, globe-spanning infrastructure of vast ships and city-size container ports—and all to do nothing more than keep feeding capitalism's hunger for the disposable. To move plastic trash made by the global poor into the hands of hapless, clueless consumers. A seemingly unstoppable beast built from parasitic tentacles, clenching the planet with an iron grip.

On his previous, precrash voyages Simon had ferried dozens of architects, designers, journalists, and futurists on the *Dymaxion*—all the hip infrastructure tourists, ready to pay him thousands so they could see it all firsthand, so they could *ooh* and *aah* at the Apollo-project levels of human engineering, so they could be wooed by this moonshot built to fill shopping malls. They'd spend a few weeks on the ship, staring out at the fields of containers in awe, before returning home to their speculative models, VR art installations, and thousand-word prose-poem odes to post-Panamax cranes. But Simon had started to hate it all. It had silently consumed him with anger and fury at its extravagance, its wasted potential, its inhuman cost. This, Rush was sure, was why this final voyage was taking place. Simon wanted to see it dead. He wanted to make sure, while the rest of the world crumbled, that it was crumbling too, and that it couldn't come back to life, that it couldn't start up again and reanimate the globe-consuming consumerist beast it had grown and fed. Simon wanted to see it dead, and to know he had outlived it, as though that meant he'd had some personal role in its defeat.

And, right there at that moment, as Simon excitedly barked instructions over the radio to his skeleton crew, Rush felt it too. For the first time since that rooftop back in Bristol, he felt that unlikely rush of victory, like they'd actually done it, the impossible destruction of the machines that were eating the planet, that they'd spent their whole lives raging against. They'd done it. They'd slain the beast. They'd won.

"How long we going to sit here, man? Really?"

Simon looks up at him from the charts and printouts that spill across his desk, scratches his head with the chewed end of a biro. "Seriously, Rush, don't fucking worry, yeah?

It's just a minor technical difficulty. We'll be moving in no time."

"We've been here three days."

"It's not a problem. Engine room's working on it. Just give it a couple of hours."

"I hope so. When I signed up for this I didn't think it was going to end with me dying of scurvy in the middle of the Pacific."

Simon laughs. "Scurvy? What the fuck? There's a reefer full of frozen orange juice out there."

"Simon, we picked that up in Yemen. We finished it all off before we cleared Japan."

"Really? You sure?" He starts to rummage around in his unknowable mess of papers. "I've got the manifest here somewhere . . ."

Rush sighs, shakes his head, watches Simon submerged in paper chaos. A single drop of sweat runs off his forehead and onto a chart showing the positions of the Pacific's WWII munitions dumping grounds. Since the engine stopped the AC has been packed in, too, and it's getting hot on the ship. He heads out on deck to grab some air.

The Pacific is flat, tame-looking. He hopes it stays that way. He's spent the last few months keeping busy learning what he could about the weather radar—it was the only storm warning they had now, since the trickle of data from the satellites had finally dried up. At least the GPS signal seemed, for now, to be stable.

He leans against the railing, looks out across the mainly

empty container hold, down into the still water. The ship feels deserted. It's meant to have an operational crew of eighteen, and they're down to just seven now. There'd been more than forty of them when they'd started—academics, futurists, some of Simon's filmmaker friends, and a bunch of his students—but they'd lost most of them along the way. The biggest loss came when they stopped over in Sri Lanka, a blissful three weeks they spent on beaches and in jungles that ended in screaming and mutiny. A large contingent refused to get back on the ship, wanting to stay in paradise, to see out the end of civilization from the beach, surrounded by fresh fruit and curry. Rush could hardly blame them.

Something down in the *Dymaxion*'s bowels rumbles, her heavy steel skeleton groaning around him. Rush looks up and sees a puff of black diesel exhaust leap from the smokestack. He smiles, exhales, and the radio on his belt erupts into static burst and the sound of cheering and chatter, and amid it all he hears a screeching Simon shout, "Full steam ahead!"

The crazy, lucky bastard.

Every major city they'd passed in the last five months seemed to be shrouded in a dark mist, a residual, permanent smog formed from the smoke of constantly burning fires.

Manhattan is no different, and as its towers rise up ahead of them Rush can't help thinking that they look defeated somehow, as though the smog is holding them captive, smearing their reflective façades in a dull grease.

Like the other cities they'd glanced at from offshore there was no way of knowing what was fueling the fires, of breaking down the percentages into how much was civil unrest, out-and-out warfare, or just an energy-starved population trying to keep itself warm.

He tries to peer into the Brooklyn shoreline as it slides past them, to see down streets and past apartment blocks, but the Zodiac is bucking too hard against the waves, shaking his skull with every impact. Easier to stare ahead, at the horizon, at Liberty Island and at that bruised, smeared skyline.

The original plan had been to bring the *Dymaxion* into the bay, to see if there was a free berth at the Bayonne container port, but when the first Zodiac recce had reported back that a U.S. Navy destroyer was sitting just off Battery Park, Simon had quite understandably dropped anchor out past the Verrazano Bridge. The garbled radio transmissions they'd picked up heading up the coast, from the few stations still broadcasting, painted a confused, often terrifying picture. Civil wars, militia takeovers, military coups, EMP strikes, shadow-government-sanctioned massacres. Some of it was clearly bullshit, badly communicated rumors, fake news, and conspiracy-theory mythology. Most likely, that destroyer was just sitting there watching out for pirates, but maybe they'd not be happy to see unannounced visitors, and it was better to be safe than sorry.

Rush had told them they could drop him in Bay Ridge, and he'd work his way from there on foot, but Simon was insistent he'd take him closer. Pretty soon they're scouting around the mess of slipways and jetties that explodes into the harbor around Red Hook, until Toby finds somewhere practical to kill the Zodiac's engines and tie up. Glancing up and down the shore, Rush vaguely works out where he is. It's only an hour's walk from here to Scott's place, he figures. There's an IKEA near here, a big one. They came down here on his first, and last, visit. They ate meatballs in the café and looked out at this same view.

It was less than a year ago, but it feels like a decade.

He hugs Toby hard and then climbs out after Simon, who has lifted his bag out of the Zodiac for him. They stand for a moment, looking at each other.

"Well."

"Well, this is it."

"Sure is."

It was, Rush realized, the first time since they'd left Ningbo that he'd seen Simon on dry land. He looked uncomfortable, out of place. Physically eager to get back to sea. It was as though this was breaking some theoretical fourth wall for him, stepping across some ethnographer's line in the sand. His mission was to observe the end of capitalism from the supply chains—from the sea—and to step onto land was to make some ethical break, to go native. Or, perhaps more honestly, to shut down a detached position he'd maintained for himself, an emotional safe distance.

Suddenly he wonders questions he'd inexplicably never asked Simon, about family, home, friends, loves. Connections.

Now isn't the time.

"You sure you don't want to come with me?" he asks him instead. "Look for supplies?"

"Nah. Don't think so. Push up the coast instead, try to find somewhere more chilled to land. Sure you don't want to come? Last chance?"

"I'm sure. I've come all this way . . ."

Simon laughs. "You have."

"Thanks. Thank you, man. I couldn't—"

"Ah, shut up. It's been a pleasure."

They hug, and hold each other for a moment. When they separate Rush feels a tear on his cheek.

"Good luck, man," Simon says. "Hope you find what you're looking for. I hope you find him."

"Thanks. You take care, okay? Don't fucking die out there, Simon, please?"

And then Simon is back in the Zodiac, and it's motoring away across the calm bay, out toward where the Statue of Liberty stands, somehow looking ancient now to Rush, like the kind of relic of a lost civilization he feels Americans always secretly wanted it to be.

And then he picks up his bag, turns away from the sea, and heads inland.

16. AFTER

Tyrone gives them masks to wear, tattered shells of scratched visor plastic and deteriorating, shredded rubber. Anika holds hers to her face as she walks, trying not to think about who else has had it to their mouth, what germs must lurk. It must be nearly twenty years old, pushed into service far longer than ever imagined by the Chinese factory worker who made it. It's the same model, she thinks, as the one she used to use when she first moved to Bristol, when she first went out tagging on the Croft. Maybe it's the same one. The smell of rubber triggers sense memories; the hiss of spray cans, the tackiness of dripping paint on exposed fingers, the splatter of color across clothes.

The women here are splattered with color, too. Anika turns her head to watch them as they walk past their tables, most of which look like they've been scavenged from one of the long-shut local schools. Appropriate, she thinks. Even with their faces hidden by their improvised masks—shreds of cloth wrapped tightly around faces, eyes barely protected by old swimming goggles, scavenged plastic sheeting, dead spex—she can tell that's where most of the workers here should really be. Their childish frames should still be huddled over the same small desks, just in a classroom somewhere, not here. Their heads are down over bowls instead of books, their hands grasping pestles instead of pencils, the red chili dust rising from their tables as they work, pausing only to reach down to the baskets by their feet to refill their bowls with more peppers. The labor of machines transferred to children, Anika thinks. Her mind flashes to Wales, to Land Army camps, to the abattoirs, the blood-soaked overalls of children working in the meat-processing plants. The chili dust scorches her eyes through the useless plastic of the graffiti mask. She looks away, keeps walking.

They follow Tyrone through factory room after factory room, the only thing changing being the colors of the dust. Chili red moves through the spectrum to turmeric yellow, cumin brown. So many rooms, she starts to lose track of where the hell they must be; the buildings behind Stokes Croft have been cleared of their usual occupants and the walls smashed through to build Grids's spice empire. It's not until they emerge into one of the growing rooms that she manages to get her bearings.

This was one of Claire's spaces, she realizes. Familiar but somehow mutated. It feels like the growing tubes have themselves grown, their white plastic bark expanded even higher toward the ceiling. More holes have erupted in their sides in order for more plants—spices, of course—to burst forth in green bloom. The white plastic—some of which was printed right here, most fabricated to Claire's design in some distant, unseen Chinese manufacturing plant and shipped halfway across the world by now-lost infrastructure—is patched in places by mixed colors: landfill-scavenged material, ancient shopping bags, unidentifiable plastic sheeting. Anything to keep it together. The constant sound of running liquid nutrients, recycled from local sewage, she guesses, fills her ears. It's gentle, calming, weirdly natural. A welcome break from the chaos of the processing rooms.

Grids is here, his back to them. She knows it is him without seeing his face. He's studying the tubes, it seems, oblivious to their presence.

She removes the mask, the air largely free of spice dust here. The smell of rubber is replaced by humidity, fertilizer, that tinge of damp vegetation.

For long seconds, nothing happens. Grids doesn't turn to face them. Tyrone says nothing. She glances at College, who just shrugs back. The silence is claustrophobic. Eventually she speaks, just to put an end to it.

"All right, Grids."

He turns to face them. She's startled by both how old and yet familiar he seems.

"Fucking hell," he says, his head tilted slightly to one side. A look she genuinely can't decode. "I don't believe it. It's actually you."

"You remember me, then?" Instantly she's no idea why she would say that.

"Yeah. Yeah." He laughs. "Hardly going to forget you, am I? You know who this is, Ty? This is Anika. Threw herself in front of a tank with a—what was that thing you had strapped to you called again?"

"An EMP bomb." She feels a damp chill sweep over her skin.

"An EMP bomb. E-M-P. You know what that is, Ty?"

Ty shrugs back at him, confusion muted by nonchalance.

"It stands for 'electromagnetic pulse.'" Typical Grids, Anika thinks. He knew damn well what it was called. "Kinda bomb doesn't blow you up, but fries all the electronics nearby. Kills them dead. Anika jumped out in front of that fucking tank in the middle of a firefight with one strapped to her and stopped it dead in its tracks. Literally. Craziest shit I've ever seen. She's a fucking hero, Ty."

"I wouldn't say tha—"

"Then she left." His tone snaps from nostalgic reverence to sarcastic annoyance. "Then she disappeared. Just like that. Why'd you leave so quickly, Anika?"

Ghosts flood the room, walls fold away. She's out in the Croft again, a second after the recording stopped. Crowds climbing onto the tank, the crew being ripped from forced-open hatches. Limp, scared bodies, faces of children, being pulled to the ground, disappearing into the mob. She hears herself screaming for them to stop, her voice lost in the chaos.

"I didn't like the way things were going."

College speaks up, seeing where this is headed, wanting to break the tension. "Grids, I got the network running again."

"What?"

He steps forward, grabs a school desk at the side of the room, and drags it in front of Grids. Pulls his backpack off and empties it on the desk, dozens of spex spilling out, dull LEDs on their arms blinking. He steps back, looks up at Grids, pride on his face, arms extended out at his sides.

"All these, bruv, I got them working again."

"Really?" Grids looks at them, with what Anika reads as disgust. Like he might catch something from them.

"Really. I got 'em all working just off of Mary's pair. The way the network works, it just needs one working pair and it'll start reseeding the network again, reinstalling itself . . . I just needed a pair that had the client still installed, that hadn't been wiped. A pair belonging to someone that left the Croft before the EMP went off. Mary's pair—"

"He knows all this already," Anika says.

Grids looks at her, across to College. He laughs. "Of

course I do, I ain't fucking stupid. What? You thought I really believed she had fucking magic powers? C'mon, man."

"Yeah—but, y'know." College shakes his head. "Every time I brought it up—"

"Every time you brought it up I wouldn't talk to you. I told you to shut up."

"Yeah."

"Yeah, well. Because I couldn't be fucking bothered. I didn't want any of this." He waves his hand dismissively at the pile of no-longer-dead technology on the table. "Look at this shit. Look at you two. I should have you both strung up."

"Like that tank crew," Anika says. Anger she can't swallow back down. Things unsaid for too long.

"Oh." He looks at her, eyes wide. Nodding. "Oh, okay. So you still pissed about that, then? That wasn't just me, y'know."

"You didn't stop it."

The mob suddenly breaking apart, falling back from the body on the ground, one of Grids's men, scarf covering his face, standing above him with that pistol. Two hands on the grip, pointed at his head. Pleading and apologies and sobbing. Anika turning to Grids, yelling at him, telling him not like this, but him just standing there, watching.

The gunshot jarring, echoing through her head. The red mist, shattered eggshell skull. Blood and brains running into the drain like paint.

Silence.

Then a dull thud from the other side of Bristol, jarring everyone awake, sound rushing back like air into a vacuum. Everyone moving again. Another distant thud. A sense of scale, realization that this must be happening all over the city.

"I didn't—" Grids seems lost for words for once. He shakes his head, as if trying to shake the traces of guilt and regret, replace them with anger. "Fucking hell. I heard you'd been in Wales the last ten years."

She can remember leaving now, trying to get away from the crowds, heading for the M32, bag on her back and eyes down so she couldn't see the limp bodies hanging from the lampposts, seagulls tugging at gray flesh.

"Yeah?" Grids snorts, and Anika realizes her face must betray her surprise. "Yeah, I hear things, girl. Heard you been in Wales. I'm sure you seen a lot worse than what happened that day in Wales, yeah? Because I know I fucking have. And I just stayed right fucking here."

He looks at them both, her and College. Glances around to look at Ty. Shakes his head again.

"What—what do you see when you look at me? Huh?" He pauses, waiting for an answer he knows won't come. Silence except for the sound of running nutrients.

"What? Some savage? Some despotic fucking warlord? A gangster? I keep this place together, man. I keep this shit working." He slams his chest with his fist. "I look after these people. Make sure there's water and cow shit to keep these farms running. Make sure people eat. Make sure College here gets what he needs to keep the solar running. Make sure people got lights at night, don't freeze to death in the winter. You know how I do that? Do you? It's not by killing people. It's not by being a fucking barbarian. It's by hustling, by business. I do all that by fucking politicking. By bribes. The cops. The LA. The fucking city council. It takes money, all made by selling rich white people herbs. Spices. Fucking ganja. I'm not Scarface, I'm—" He pauses again, searching for words. "I'm like the fucking mayor."

"This'll help you with all that, G!" College points at the spex, the emptied bag. Anika is surprised to hear him this impassioned, to see it on his face. More memories, ghosts. "This'll change everything. The network, it'll give you an advantage, some leverage—"

"This? This is all bullshit." Grids shakes his head at both of them, sucks teeth. "Nah. Fuck this. This is more hassle than it's worth. It's always been more hassle than it's worth. Don't you get that? Serious? Out of all this bullshit, the last ten years . . . have you really not worked out that this is always going to be more hassle than it's worth?"

"But—"

"Nah. Nah, College." Anika turns to him, face resigned. "He's right. Probably. He's probably spot-on. It's more hassle than it's worth. Plus we've all got things we'd rather stay buried."

". . ."

She looks Grids straight in the eyes, glimpses the sympathy she knows is there, the warmth that sheltered her body in that crumbling, bullet-shredded alley. "It's just right now I ain't got much choice, Grids. I got people to look after too. People that are dying. People that are being worked to death. Literally. And this, this is the only thing I can take back to them that might give them a chance, an advantage."

She inhales, feels the cool tickle of a tear on her cheek. "So, what I'm saying is—you two, you can both sort your own problems out. What happens here, I don't care. But I'm leaving here, and going back to Wales, with a bag of these. Tomorrow."

"Tomorrow?" College sounds surprised.

"Yeah. Sorry. Tomorrow. And I wouldn't try to stop me. Seriously."

Pause. The sound of running liquid.

Grids shakes his head yet again. Laughs. "Shit, girl, you always was crazy. Fuck me. So you're fighting the Land Army in Wales now, yeah? Bloc agent. You're the big hero of the revolution."

"Not exactly."

"See, this is what I don't get—I thought you'd be behind the LA? I thought that was your thing, you two? Socialism? Renationalizing the farms? Food for everyone?"

"Not exactly," says College. "We weren't Marxists. Not all of us."

"Even if we were . . . there's nothing socialist about the Land Army. It's the fucking British Army, Grids. Just rebranded. It wasn't a socialist uprising, it was a fucking military coup. It's the same people that were in charge before the crash. Same generals, same politicians. Saying they're doing it all for the good of the people, saying they're doing it to feed everyone—it's all lies. You seen what it's like out there, outside of the cities? You seen what it's like in the work camps? People being forced at gunpoint to work the land till they drop, literally. Their own land, land their families have owned for generations, that's just been snatched from them. Living in fucking tents and shacks, starving to death, not seeing any of the food they're growing because it's all being sent to London, or to the war up in Scotland—"

"Well, what did you think was going to happen? After you broke everything? Really? What did you think? That everything would magically take care of itself? That this network of yours would somehow provide all the answers?"

"We didn't pretend to have answers. Not for everything. That wasn't what we were fighting for. We were fighting for people to be able to decide things for themselves, Grids. To start again. We were fighting for self-determination—"

"Well then, you got what you wanted. Self-determination? You're looking at it." He thumps his chest with his fist again. "*I'm* self-determination. The LA is self-determination. The city council is self-determination. That skinhead militia down in Knowle that's lynching Muslims?

That's self-determination. That's what it looks like. Lots of gangsters and warlords and fucking terrified people trying to look after themselves, trying to protect their own, and fuck everybody else. Me and all the other chancers and yardies that have carved this city up between us, trying to look after their own little bit of turf and their own people. Your self-determination is a fucking power vacuum, that's all it is. Your revolution, with no idea of what would happen next, just created a massive hole full of people fucking each other over to stay alive."

He suddenly looks, to Anika, exhausted. Like the fight has left him. She watches him exhale, his shoulders drop. He rubs his temples. "A'ight. Fine. You know what? You go. Do it. I ain't going to stop you. In fact, I ain't going to stop either of you. I can't. You're grown fucking adults. None of my business, I ain't got the time. Soon as you get that shit running, the city is going to be down here tryin' to shut it down, or getting their own shit reactivated—"

"That's what I'm sayin', we got to act fast. I got fucking hundreds of these, all from Mike's shop. We get them all activated, then tomorrow at carnival we give 'em out. By the time anybody else knows what's going down we'll already have control of the network through pure numbers and—"

"Nah, College, nah. You didn't hear me. None of my business." He says it slowly, almost spelling it out. "I don't care. I don't want this. Twenty fucking years ago as a kid I didn't want this, and I don't want it now. Difference is now

I got a fucking choice. Self-determination? I'm determining I don't fucking want this.

"This is your bullshit, and it's yours to sort out. It's all on you, College. Just make sure it don't blow up in your face, man. But even more, make sure it don't blow up in mine. Make sure it don't fuck with my shit. Because if it does, if at any point from now until I fucking die—if this bullshit starts fucking with my business I'll see that you do swing from a lamppost. You get me?"

"Yeah." College tries to suppress a smile. "Yeah, I get you, man."

"Good. You fucking better. Now fuck off, both of you. I want you out my fucking sight. I got real shit to do. Take this shit with you."

"Seriously, man, you're making the ri—"

"Don't want to hear it. Jesus."

As Ty leads them out, Anika turns to College, speaks low.

"Well, you got passionate all of a sudden."

"What you mean?"

"Listen to you in there. Few days ago you didn't want anything to do with this when I brought it up. Now you're arguing with the big man to let you start up the fucking network again."

"Yeah, ha. I guess I got excited. Seeing the network up again, y'know? It works, A! It really works."

"Yeah. I know."

"That went easier than I thought. Jesus . . . he seemed to take it pretty well."

"You think?"

"Yeah?" College shoots her a bewildered look. "No? You don't think so?"

"I dunno. Sounded to me like he was going to have you hanged if your open-source, decentralized, basically unmanageable network ever fucks with his power structure." She touches him gently on the shoulder. "Good luck with that."

She pulls the ancient, battered mask back down over her face, and steps out into the pastel-shaded mists of spice.

Tyrone opens up the door of the shop, lets her in. Locks it behind her.

The girl—Mary, she must try to remember her name—is sitting at the back, hunched over her desk.

Anika steels herself, walks over to the girl. She sees she's drawing—old chalk and felt-tip pens on scraps of paper. She looks up as Anika gets near.

"Hi."

"Hi." Anika smiles, trying to look as friendly as she can. "Look, Mary—I just wanted to say . . . Look. I'm really sorry. About what happened yesterday."

"Sorry for what?"

"I was out of order. I should never have taken the spex

from you like that. Put you through all that. Shown you what I did. I'm sorry."

"It's okay. Really. I'm glad. You helped me find what I was looking for, for Grids."

"You told him?"

"Yeah. He says he's not going to look, says he doesn't want anything to do with the network."

"Yeah, he just said the same thing to me."

"I don't believe him." Mary smiles. "He'll look."

"Yeah. Maybe." Anika tilts her head, looks at the drawing in front of the girl. Geometric shapes, explosions of color. "I like it."

"Huh?"

"Your work. I like it."

Mary blushes. "Oh, thanks."

"What is it?"

"I'm not sure. Nothing, really. Just not a dead fucking face."

Anika laughs. "Fair enough. It's really nice. I used to be an artist myself, once. Long ago."

"Really? Not anymore?"

"No."

"Why?"

Anika shrugs. "People change."

And with that Anika feels her knees almost buckle, her stomach turn, and she holds back the urge to scream, to hurl up the pain and the regret and the tears and—

"I should be going," she says. "And again, I'm sorry."

"It's okay. I'll see you around?"

"Maybe," Anika lies. She turns and heads for the door.

"Wait! One last thing?"

"Yeah?"

"Now they're all working—I mean, now College says he'll give everyone a pair . . . does that mean I'm not special anymore?"

Anika stops in her tracks, turns back. Not knowing what to say.

"I mean, I'm not a freak anymore? Am I?"

"No." Anika smiles. "No. You're not a freak. You never were."

Mary smiles back, puts her head down, picks up the chalk again. "Good. Thanks."

Tyrone unlocks the door to let her out, holds it open as she leaves. Stone-faced attitude. She pauses in the doorway, looks back at him.

"Hey, look, man. It's all right. Don't beat yourself up. You did okay trying to stop me yesterday. Main thing was you made sure the girl didn't get hurt."

"Whatever." Ah, the delicacy of the bruised male ego.

She smiles and steps out, but as she does, he surprises her by speaking. Sheepishly.

"So. These things, yeah?" He's holding a pair of spex

that College must have given him. "There any way of making music with them?"

"Yeah. Yeah, should be. Look under 'creativity.' Might be what you're looking for. You want me to show you?"

"Nah. Nah. It's all right. I'll work it out."

She smiles back at him. "Yeah. You will."

17. AFTER

The black monoliths of the Shaka sound system tower into the dull sky, ancient hardboard cases bound together with tape and fraying elasticated rope. The old Rastas busy themselves with checking cables and connections, as some unidentified Trinidadian dub pulses through the stack. It's just a warm-up, a system test for tomorrow. Tyrone watches them, knowing they'll spend an hour or two tweaking and perfecting, messing with balances and levels, before they throw a tarp over the top of the whole thing and pay a couple of kids in ganja to stand watch all night. He knows this because just a couple of years ago he was one of those kids, standing out here with Bags on the corner of Ashley and the Croft, bullshitting to try to keep each other awake, to try not to nod off.

He wasn't in it for the free weed, even back then, though it was a bonus. It was part of his education, an apprenticeship. What he learned about sound and acoustics from running chores for Shaka and his crew—standing guard, carrying boxes and records, climbing up the stack to reconnect loose cables—you couldn't find it in any books down at St. Paul's library. Tyrone doubted you'd even find it on the Internet, if that was still an option. It was an unending, unrecordable mishmash of technical knowledge and folklore, engineering skills and oral history, acoustic science and superstition.

The system sounds fierce tonight, the sub-bass going straight through Tyrone, effortlessly penetrating bones and flesh to reverberate in his stomach and bowels, to shake the contents of his rib cage, to move the air in his lungs. He blinks into his periphery and pulls down menus from the spex, still feeling his way through the unfamiliar software, and records a two-bar loop of slow-motion bass. He makes sure to capture it all—not just the pure, unfettered low-frequency sine waves, but everything they touch and move, the buzzing of loose connections, the distortion of speaker cones pushed too far, the groaning of cabinet cases. By the end of the night Shaka and his technicians will have ironed out most of these bugs, but Tyrone wants it all, every glitch and imperfection.

He takes the loop, the waveform floating in a translucent

window in front of his face, and slices it into individual notes. More blinks and hand swipes—he feels self-conscious waving his hands around in the street, but he'll get over it—and he drops them into a step sequencer, each note becoming a vertical bar representing pitch and velocity, pulsing as they play. With a few more blinks he's shuffled them around, changed their order, tweaked their levels. Made something new, something his own.

After a few minutes walking up the Croft he pauses again, to watch a couple of graffiti writers working on a new mural on the permanently shuttered front of some long-abandoned shop. Berry paint stains the sleeves of their threadbare Adidas as they work aging airbrushes retrofitted to run off solar, their faces so close to their intricate lines that their foreheads nearly scrape against the colorful metal and brickwork. The hissing of compressed air punctures the near silence and he captures it, slicing it up again, carving high hat and snare patterns from the distorted white noise, bathing it in reverb to fill out the high end above his thunderous bass.

Back at the shop, he lets Mary out, smiles at her as she leaves. He glances around, wondering what will become of it now, the dead faces staring back at him. Supposedly they're all up for grabs now, to anyone with a pair of College's special glasses, anyone that wants to come venture down the Croft to wake the dead. He wonders what that means for Mary. Girl's had a busy couple of days. She seems happier now, though, lighter. Like she's had a load taken off her shoulders.

If she's not looking for dead people anymore, then the shop closes, and he's out of a job. No worries. Grids will find him something else. Maybe running spices, maybe helping him out with security. Maybe he'll let him do the radio station full-time like he'd always wanted, maybe even pay him for it. Tyrone knows Grids thinks it's important; he once told him that after the spices and the weed it's the most important thing the Croft produces. A sense of community, a sense of purpose, a statement to the rest of the city. Well, at least it was, right up until today. He thinks of the spex on his face. Maybe that's all about to change.

As he closes the door behind Mary the bell chimes again, that pathetic sound he's heard a dozen times a day for the last year. Somehow, tonight, in the empty shop it sounds different, the high-frequency metallic sound waves splashing back from bare walls, creating instant rhythms and subliminal harmonics. He opens and closes it again, captures the bell's double ring, and drops it into the sequencer, this time triggering the sound across nine sixteenth notes, so the pattern goes in and out of sync with the rest of the track. A light touch of reverb and compression, a heavy dose of urgency and discord.

He flicks off the lights, closes the door, and leaves, shutting the faces of the dead away in the dark.

Up on the roof of the tower he checks the transmitter. One hour until broadcast, and for once everything seems in order. It's a big one, the pre-carnival warm-up show. He's got a bunch of guests in tonight—a couple of MCs from Barton Hill and Easton, some DJs from Bedminster and Brislington. Even some posh kid from up in Clifton is coming down to drop some tunes. Well out of his safe zone. All crew, all ends. Can't have any transmitter fuckups tonight, no dropouts, no dead air, no static.

He steps back from the bird-shit-stained cluster of aerials, wondering again how this all changes, wondering if College will be up here soon, breathing life back into the dead infrastructure. Behind him there's a familiar yet disconnected squawk, and he turns to see the gull again, sheltering under the solar panels, hiding its young from him while bawling him out, watching him with one wide, terrified eye. Still here, still surviving, still dodging jerk spices and oil-drum smokers.

He crouches, moves crablike toward it. Slowly. The bird reacts, squawking increasing, one wing unfurling toward him as if to hold him back. Tyrone freezes, not wanting to distress the gull more. Instead he just captures everything, the gull's cries mixed into the static rush of the circling winds. Again he cuts it up, shifting it into a three-note pattern of almost acidic stabs, drenching them in dub-siren levels of echo before layering them over the rest of the track.

He rises, stepping away from the bird, giving it some space and peace. The city unfolds in front of him, the sky visibly darkening, fields of flickering lights rolling out toward Somerset's distant hills. It's near silent up here, Bristol's constant drone battered away by high-rise winds, but Tyrone can't hear it anyway, his skull reverberating to the spex's conduction speakers, his head lost in his own music, his mind staring out across unexplored possibilities.

18. AFTER

When she wakes, on the broken mattress in the corner of College's room, he's nowhere to be seen. She's alone, no company apart from the throb of bass through cracked windows, with the morning coffee craving that never leaves, even after all these years.

She sits for a few minutes, watching dust motes swirl like pixels in suspended sunlight. Self-doubt and regret. She could just stay, forget everything else. Make a life here, again. Start something new.

It sounds easy. But the ghosts will always be here, in the corners of the room. Out in the hallway. On the street, just beyond the window. They're dancing now, sunny carnival vibes, and she knows from there it's only a short time until the screaming and bleeding starts.

She pulls herself off the mattress, packs her bag quickly. Grabs the backpack College stuffed with spex for her last night, and heads out the door.

College is at the end of the street, on the corner of Ashley Road and the Croft, surrounded by kids. He's handing out spex to anyone that passes. And there's no shortage of anyones, a steady, thick stream of party people flooding in through the gates. She tries not to gaze too long into the crowds, knowing ghosts lurk.

He smiles as she approaches. "Ah. It lives."

"You should have woken me."

"Eh, you looked like you needed the sleep."

"Yeah. I did. So, how's your adoption rate?"

He laughs. "Pretty good. Gonna run out soon. Time to start scouring shops for more. Trying to get people to go home and look in their drawers, innit."

"People are into it?"

"Yeah. Yeah, appears so. Taking a bit of explaining. People think I'm bullshitting, some crazy man. Until I make them put on a pair. Those old enough to remember seem a bit freaked out. The kids, though . . . the kids fucking love it."

"So I see."

College sighs heavily, shakes his head. "He was right, though, wasn't he?"

She looks at him quizzically.

"Grids. He was right. About us not knowing what came next. That's why all this failed. We didn't have any vision, did we? Just some beliefs and some ideals. But no way of, y'know, making something solid out of them. No organizing, no planning. Instead we ended up just scrabbling around, trying to fix things, trying to keep them patched up." He looks out at the crowd streaming past. "It's no different to what it was like before, really."

"I guess not. But hey, you got another chance now. A whole new network."

"Yeah." He laughs. "I guess. Maybe. Just make sure we don't make the same mistakes as last time, huh?"

"Ah, we probably will."

"Yeah, probably. I just wonder if actually this is all just bullshit, y'know? Like maybe our brains just ain't designed to deal with networks. They're not going to evolve to interface with millions of other people. They're just not designed for that. And trying to force it just makes us angry and actually more alienated."

"I dunno. Didn't they say the same about television?"

"Yeah. Well." He laughs. "Television fucked things up pretty bad. You remember advertising? Politics?"

"Yeah. Good point."

They look at each other for a second.

"So what now?" he asks her.

"Me? I'm going back. Wales." She taps the shoulder strap of her bag. "Gotta get these back. People need them."

"For what? I mean . . . what's the plan?"

"I dunno." She looks off into the distance, down the street at the gathering crowds. "We're getting our asses kicked out there. Lots of little cells spread through the valleys, insiders working in farm camps. Trying to disrupt stuff as much as possible. The hope is we can set up a network, get everyone working together. Get everyone watching each other's backs. Coordinate. Give us a bit of an advantage over the army. The upper hand, for once."

College laughs. "So, despite everything, you've not given up, then? Right now you sound more positive than me."

"What d'you mean?"

He taps his spex. "This. You sound more positive about all this. I woke up this morning kinda defeated, worried we're just going to keep repeating mistakes, distractions. But you're all fired up again. You sound like the old days."

"Ha. I guess I do."

"You sound like you think you can make a difference."

"Yeah. I guess I do. I have to. People are dying." Awkwardness hangs in the air between them. She puts her hand on his shoulder, squeezes gently. "Look, don't let it get you down. Maybe Grids is right, maybe this is all a fucking waste of time. A huge distraction, and we're all going to make the same mistakes again. Thing is, College, at least you're trying. You want it to not fuck up? Then don't let it.

Take some ownership of it. Shape things. Talk to people. Organize. That's where we fucked up last time, we just burned everything down, didn't plan for afterwards. Grids was right about that."

"I guess."

"Look, I got faith in you. You know this place, you know these people. Help them. Give them what they need. Take the lead if they need you to. Don't be scared of power. That's the other way we fucked up before, we were always scared of power, of taking the lead. We just thought everything would sort itself out somehow. It won't. It's not enough to just take power away from those in charge. If we don't use it ourselves, they just take it back."

She pauses again. "Look. I've got faith in you. You'll do what's right. You've got this. And if you ever feel like you ain't, come find me in Wales, and I'll give you another patronizing pep talk."

College laughs. "Seriously, though. Thanks. I needed that. I feel better."

"Really?"

"Yeah, really." He sighs, low and deep. "So this is it, huh?"

"Yeah. This is it. Gotta catch my ride before he heads back."

"No convincing you to stay?"

"No. No, College."

"Then I won't try." Instead he smiles that big goofy smile of his, and hugs her. They hold each other tight, and when she speaks, it's into the warm, musky comfort of his chest.

"Thank you."

"Just fucking take care of yourself, yeah?"

"I will."

"You fucking promise me?"

"I fucking promise you," she says, holding back sobs. "Maybe I'll be back."

"Yeah. Maybe."

When they separate she holds his cheek for a second, then turns and leaves, walking against the tides of the crowd, not looking back.

The crowd flows around Grids like a stream around a rock, splitting itself naturally and re-forming behind him, keeping a respectable distance. They know who he is. At best they smile or nod, say a couple of words, but most drop their heads slightly, avoiding eye contact. Too hammered by a decade of chaos, uncertainty, of scraping around for shelter and existence in the shattered shell of the city, they know when to step aside, to stay quiet. So they make way, walk around. Flowing like air over a wing, effortlessly passing across the frictionless field of significance he projects around him.

But for the first time in a while he can feel that significance ebbing away. Too many motherfuckers in this crowd with College's damn spex on their faces. Walking past him, flowing past as part of some semiautonomous crowd dynamic, but not actually seeing him. Distracted.

He shakes his head. Can't deny them the distraction, he understands that. Damn, it's carnival day, distraction is what it's all about. Come down and get distracted. Smoke some bud, shake your ass. Escape. Forget the relentless fucking daily battle to stay alive that this city has become.

But he knows this is different. He's seen this before. Escape to him was getting away from this. Sure, he tore College and Anika off a strip for their idealism, for not having some plan for the aftermath—but really, to him it felt like the chains had come off when it all got ripped down. That world—the one behind those glasses, the one that beamed itself directly into your fucking retinas—he was pleased to see it fall, to see it burn. To see it stripped of its value, its systems, its endless fake fucking battles. Its baked-in hierarchies and structures. He didn't build it, it wasn't built for him—it was built by some cunts in some other country, built by some rich white motherfuckers that just wanted to get richer. That wanted to make money off him, by occupying his headspace, by taking his credit, by turning him into spectacle and entertainment, content for their advertising vectors.

He shakes his head again and remembers the crazy shit they did as kids. Cars on fire, shoe shops looking like a bulldozer had been through them, carpets compacted hard with crushed plastic and glass. The sound it made beneath his feet. Was fun back then, before he understood who it

was for. Who he was really doing it for, who was really ben-
efiting. Who was turning him and his postcode's dramas
and daily struggles into prime-time entertainment. Trending topics on the timelines. Algorithmically curated. The
filler between the ad breaks.

College understood that, that's why he came down to
the Croft and got with those guys all them years ago.

Melody got it too.

Melody got it more than anyone.

He reaches into his inside jacket pocket and pulls out
the spex Mary gave him. Laughs to himself. She picked
him out a nice pair, some old Nikes. Of course. Dirty and
busted up, sure. Tinted lenses, not too scratched. Check
mark logo on the arm. He touches it and it glows a dull
green. Charged.

He turns them over in his hands, looks out at the crowd.
Sighs and slips them onto his face.

The air around him fills with windows and doorways,
images and words, rumors and opinions, music and politics. Lies nestle with facts, jokes with atrocities, the exotic
with the mundane. As his eyes fall across any spex wearer
in the crowd the air around them explodes with data, tiny
blinkable squares orbiting their heads like unswattable flies.
Most of them have only been on the network for a few
hours max, but already they're broadcasting their own insignificance, filling their profiles with the trivial facets of
their lives, transmitting their half-formed thoughts and
feelings, insisting on becoming their own self-important

nodes in the network. Bubbles float up from skulls and hang above the crowd, trailing their owners like unwanted odors, filled with soundbites, video clips, unrequested proclamations. A never-ending spewing of content. It's too much for Grids, too much static, too much noise, already threatening to drown out what matters, what he's built—to distract these people from the stark reality he knows they need to face. It's almost like he can feel the radio signals being bounced between the wearers, see them polluting the air with triviality, like background radiation silently eating away at the order he's brought to the Croft. Too much insignificance, and it's contagious.

He rips them from his face, rubs his eyes, curses quietly to himself.

Fuck.

From down the street he hears music start up, a slo-mo dub rhythm. Synthetic bass rumbles, the tick of ancient, processed drums. Detuned 808 hits vibrate up through Grids's shins. Full-on nostalgia rush, threatening to sweep his legs from under him. Ghosts in the crowd, then he's back there, in the brutalist shadows of Barton Hill, waiting for her to call him, to yell his name. For a second he closes his eyes and lets himself drift, reverse vertigo, as the towers circle and sway around him, synced to the distant filtered breaks that ebb from unseen speakers.

He slips the spex back onto his face.

Avoiding looking at the crowd of insignificance, he instead pulls menus down from his periphery. Deep-diving options, it takes a few blinks to find what he wants. Dials in the day and time Mary told him.

The world around him starts to shimmer and flex. Architecture shifts, graffiti murals washing across walls, geometries shattered by stray tank shells fading back into existence, regrowing like lizard limbs. The crowd morphs, grows stronger, even more spex on faces that are smeared with that look everyone had those few, short days down in the Croft. A mix of confusion and relief, panic and liberation. Significance. He remembers it well, he'd seen it on everyone flooding in. He'd come down here with his crew to see what the fuck was going on, to see if the rumors were true.

Of course they were true. Of course she was already gone by then.

And then the sound comes in, that reverse-suck rush, like air refilling a vacuum. Sirens, distorted police announcements from orbiting quadcopters, the crowd chanting, air horns.

And then the beat hits, that first sub-bass analog kick, and in the long-drawn-out space filled with sampled air before the snare hits he knows it's her. It couldn't be anyone else. Nobody else could ever craft melancholy out of reverb like that, breathe that much soul into ping-pong echoes. And then her voice is here, not full words—never full words—just cut-up vowels and breaths, stutters and sighs. The crowd moves with her, hands in the air, ghost faces he recognizes between the raised limbs. Anika dancing, College nodding his head, joint hanging from his lips, stoned grin on his face.

Just not Melody, because by then Melody had already gone.

He lets it play out, the DJ slipping into another rhythm, and he reaches out for the nonexistent jog wheel. Rewind.

He lets it wash over him again, and for the first time that day he feels a smile crack across his face, the kind of smile he hasn't flexed in years. The smile he used to save for her. Involuntary, real. Like when he'd catch her looking at him, or when he'd tell a joke and she'd laugh. He can hear that now, her laughter, echoing through the waves of white-noise dub, the spaces between the beats. And for a few long minutes it's like she wasn't gone, like she was there, standing behind him, like she's got his back, and he feels one mile tall.

He finds himself drifting away from the crowd, drawn toward the secrets he has buried, toward the lies he's told. Toward the truth he's hidden for a decade, hidden from College and Mary and the whole city.

He stops in an alleyway, alone, the sound of the party almost fading away.

It was here, he tells himself.

He blinks in a date two days after that final show.

And then he can see himself, his own back to him now, hurrying up the alleyway. He glances back at himself, looking to make sure he's not being followed. He looks scared, worried, and young.

So very young.

He's got an arm around a shorter figure, a hood fully covering the head and face, as he guides them up the alleyway, to a parked car. He opens the rear door, takes a bag from the still-anonymous figure, throws it in.

Grids is standing behind them both now, close, struggling to breathe.

She's about to get in the car, when she pauses, turns back to young Grids, and pulls back her hood.

It's her, looking exactly like that last day, exactly like he remembers her. Tired, scared. But still alive.

It takes all Grids's strength to not pause it there, to not just stand and stare into her eyes.

"C'mon, you gotta go," *then* Grids says, gently.

"Come with me," she replies.

The sound of her voice. All the air leaves *now* Grids's lungs.

"I can't, Mel. I gotta stay. I got people I need to look after." Grids mouths the words, perfectly in time with the hidden memories, words that have echoed around his head every day for ten years, full of regret and self-doubt.

She'd come to him, a few days before that final show. Told him that things were going to get bad, that she was going to have to fake her death to keep the cops from coming after her again, that she was going to have to get out of the city. That he should too. She'd given him money, told him she needed a car—an old one, one that didn't drive itself—and someone to drive it, who wouldn't ask any questions, wouldn't breathe a word to anyone. And that he mustn't either, not tell a soul. Told him he was the only one she could trust, that nobody else knew what was going to happen. Nobody in her crew, nobody in her production team.

Now she's getting into the car, and *then* Grids is closing the door behind her and nodding to the unseen driver, as the car pulls away, and *now* Grids has to fight the urge to run after it, to follow it, to try to stop it.

Instead he, and his young self, stand together and watch it go, both consumed by regret and lost possibilities.

At the other end of the alley the car crosses the border of the Republic, escapes the recording's all-seeing eyes, and vanishes.

Grids instinctively reaches for a virtual jog wheel, starts to rewind it, then stops himself.

Not again, not now.

Some other time.

There'll be times when he'll need her back, but not now. Let her have her peace, let her be gone.

He taps the Nike logo, shuts down the simulation, steps back out onto Stokes Croft and watches the crowd flowing around him like a stream around a rock, splitting itself naturally and re-forming behind him, keeping a respectable distance while nodding back at his smile, but he keeps the spex on so they can't see his tears.

As Anika walks past the tank she pauses, glances over. Music she doesn't recognize reverberates from the huge speaker stacks that flank it. Something new, yet old at the same time. Hints of the grime and jungle she used to dance to, but somehow different, weirder time signatures and polyrhythms. Flexible tempos, the groove holding while the BPM noticeably shifts. Somewhere, amid the percussive cacophony, what sounds like rain. Wind passing by a high window. The distant sound of voices through urban spaces.

She peers over the swaying crowd and sees the kid, Tyrone, standing in the top of the tank's paint-splattered turret like a triumphant general, facedown over the decks, one headphone shell covering an ear, the other tucked behind. And as she squints against the sun she notices something else—spex on his face, some jury-rigged mass of cables tumbling from them into the mixer. She smiles. Clearly College's handiwork. What he must have been doing with that soldering iron when she passed out last night, high.

She thinks about stopping, dancing with the crowd, trying to pursue some lost memory of youth. When was the last time she danced? Maybe in Wales. Maybe in those long, boozy nights on the farm before the Land Army arrived, the silhouettes of trucks and troop carriers rising on the horizon. Dark angular shapes against dull, damp skies.

And then. In the crowd. She catches his face. A quick glance as he turns away from her. She knows it's him, the same guy she saw that first day here. The suit might be gone, but the baseball cap and spex are hiding nothing.

The same guy, the same VIP she'd seen when she first got here, the same potential target. The same chance to strike a blow for the resistance. And this time without his security detail.

Her hand goes into her bag.

She closes her eyes briefly, slows her breathing, recalls her Bloc training.

With zero bandwidth there is no calling for backup.

With zero bandwidth the advantage is ours.

With zero bandwidth there is no many.

With zero bandwidth there is no legion.

With zero bandwidth we are singular.

With zero bandwidth there is no time to hesitate.

With zero bandwidth there is only opportunity.

With zero bandwidth opportunity is our only weapon.

Eyes open again.

Not here. Too many people.

He's slipping away into the crowd now, heading out the gates, heading toward the Bearpit.

She breathes again. Repeats the mantra. Pulls her hoodie up over her head and follows him, leaving the last new music she's heard in a decade behind her.

Walker pauses in the shadows of the tunnel under the 5102, the darkness echoing with the chatter of the crowds still pouring into Stokes Croft. A quick glance over his shoulder, a paranoid flash of being watched. Maybe he shouldn't have come alone, maybe he should have brought his security detail with him. But then that would have alerted the LA, and they'd be down here trying to work out what was going on in their usual ham-fisted way. The time for their depressing bureaucracy and gunboat diplomacy would come. Maybe later today, maybe tomorrow. Maybe next month. He had no idea how the increasingly erratic Bristol command worked anymore, but when they did get down here they'd try to fuck everything up for everyone, including him.

He glances around again, reaches into his bag, takes out and unrolls the picture the girl had given him as they left the shop, stares at the sad eyes, feels the quality of the paper between finger and thumb.

Blinks.

The spex trace outlines of the drawn face, countless nodes where chalk and pen lines interact. A window pops out of the paper, floating a few inches in front of his face. A request for more details. He dials in the time, as best as he can figure.

The inside of the tunnel starts to shimmer and distort. The crowd disappears, replaced by the reflective glow of flashing blue lights. Silence at first, then the weird rush of sound. Music, police radio chatter, shouts. Behind him, somehow piercing it all, the whisper of panicked, scared voices.

They're not going to let us out
They will

Ahhh god my arm god I think it's broken

We're best just getting to some first aid

Ahhh please

Be careful

They'll let us out really trust me

"Jane!" he hears himself shout, as he spins around. His way is blocked by an impenetrable wall of armor-plated riot cops. Polycarbonate shields and science-fiction face masks, dystopian silhouettes against the whiteout of smoke-filtered daylight. And behind and between them, there she is, she and her friends, like tiny crumpled figures.

Please, my friend is injured, we need to get to safety.

Step back! Step back immediately!

Please

I'm sorry

Please, his arm is broken, look

Walker wants to grab the cops by the shoulders, pull them out of the way to make room for the kids to pass—

Step back!

Please! Look! I'm Jane Walker! Jane Walker! My dad is Chris Walker! Chief Constable Chris Walker!

I said, STEP BACK!

Chris Walker is my dad! I'm Chris Walker's daughter!

Sarge?

What?

Please!

Says she's the chief's daughter, Sarge?

What?

It's true! I'm Chris Walk—

Fuck. I don't know. Okay. Fine. Let 'em through.

Let them through! Make way and let them through!

And suddenly the wall parts, armored bodies shuffling aside, and she's there, Jane is there standing in front of him, and he starts to cry, tears rolling down his face from behind the spex. More than anything he wants to reach out, hold her to him, feel her—

Take your friend through to the Bearpit. There's first aid there. Should be, at least.

Thank you, thank you.

He watches them limp past him, and through the blur of tears follows them, stumbling into the bodies of party-goers intersecting his reality. Follows them through the dark, out into the light.

In the Bearpit he watches her, standing back and use-less, as she lowers her friend onto the ground. Around them all is chaos, injured and stunned-looking police, civilians. Exhausted-looking paramedics. Blood pooling in the gaps between paving slabs, concrete stained crimson.

I'm going to see if I can find someone to help.

The girl, Jane's friend—Walker faintly recognizes her: Gemma?—disappears off into the crowd, leaving Jane alone, crouching next to the boy. She holds his hand.

It's going to be okay.

My fucking arm—

Yeah. I think you broke it.

It's killing me.

He crouches next to her, unable to take his eyes off her. Tears still flow.

Hey, you're going to be fine. I promise.

Everything is so fucked-up—

It's fine. It's all fine. We got out and we're safe. We're going to get someone to check you out and then we'll get you back up to Clifton.

Time to go home?

Time to go home.

She smiles, and his heart flips. So much kindness. Who is this kid? Is that her boyfriend?

Something rips the sky above them apart, something screeching as it rips through the air, and then a boom that dulls eardrums.

He glances up—up through the geodesic dome, now (then) whole and complete—just in time to see the top corner of one of the nearby brutalist office towers dissolve into dust, a point cloud of masonry pixels.

What the fuck was that?

Running, screaming. Shouting.

Incoming!

Walker wonders who could have been responsible for shattering a building, the dread realization falling across him that it was probably friendly fire, or another rogue round from the malfunctioning drone.

Everyone is moving around him, but he's transfixed again, unable to take his eyes off her.

We need to go.

No, just stay here! Don't move!

But—

We're safe here, don't move! Just hold my hand.

Walker looks up again, through the geodesic lattice of the dome. It seems alien to him, like this. He got so used to seeing it shattered for the last decade. Through the recording it looks like an ode to a forgotten, lost future—smeared with bird shit and graffiti, glass panels missing here and there, CCTV cameras retrofitted to its frame. For some reason his mind fills with Buckminster Fuller, that book he read about him, the way he was heralded by designers and architects as a neglected hero, the one that would have built us a utopia if he'd been given half a chance.

And how someone had told him that was all bullshit, and people thought of him so well only because his plans never got built. If they had been, he would have made the same mistakes as Le Corbusier and Goldfinger and all the others—the mistake of believing the myth that architects can build futures full of people as simply as they make their little models, sketch their little plans.

He knows what comes next.

The air ripped open by screeching, the thunderclap, the ceiling above them exploding into a billion shards of glass and steel.

But he doesn't see it, because he's staring into her face when the rain hits.

---- ---- ----

Anika releases her grip on the gun, slips her hand back out of her bag.

She watches her target sprawl on the floor of the Bearpit, hammering concrete with fists, sobbing as the crowds heading into the Croft flow around him. Most of them barely see him, avoiding him on autopilot. They've had ten years of public nervous breakdowns, of people screaming at floors and architecture, of trying to fistfight the confusion and the chaos and the loss.

Most of them have probably done it themselves, she thinks.

PTSD on a civilization-wide scale.

She takes a deep breath, pulls her hood up tight. Adjusts the bag full of spex on her back, and heads into the crowd like a fish swimming upstream, not looking back, just heading for Cabot Circus and her ride back home.

EPILOGUE

Lajune climbs down from the jeep and steps over dead bodies in the parking lot, follows waypoints dropped by Kareem, pulsating pale blue arrows hanging in the air, pointing to the shattered glass of the low building's entrance. Five members of the assault squad are waiting there, their outlines made amorphous by what hangs from their bodies; armor, assault rifles, grenades. It's too much to fucking carry, she finds herself thinking. Need to sort this shit out.

Two of the squad are sitting on the floor, in the debris, and their leader orders them up as he sees her approach.

"On your feet, soldiers."

"Nah, it's okay, Kareem. You're good. Stay put. Sitrep?"

"Site secured, sir. Residents have been taken aside and are being processed for rehousing in NYC. Just waiting for the trucks."

Lajune glances around the parking lot, at bodies with missing arms, legs. Heads.

"Looks like you met some resistance."

Kareem smiles. "Nothing we couldn't handle."

"Any casualties on our side?"

"Nothing major. DeShaun and Williams received minor limb injuries. We got them patched up and waiting for evac."

"ETA?"

"Last I heard from Hoboken we're six hours out till the trucks arrive."

"Jesus. They'll be fine till then?"

"They'll be fine, sir."

Lajune nods through the shattered glass doors. "So what's the story here?"

Kareem takes a deep breath. "The usual, from what we can make out. Some prepper cult. Probably been holed up here damn near three years now. Came down when the crash happened, 'cause it still had power. Stayed here to shelter from the storms. They weren't, ah, in particularly good shape mentally, if you catch my drift."

"The place has power still?"

"Seems that way. Lots of solar on the roof, lots of backup batteries."

"You got them?"

"Yes, sir. Second squad got them out a couple of hours ago. Again, just waiting on the trucks."

"And this is a colo, right?"

"Right. Medium-sized. Modular, container-based design."

"Commander?" It's one of the girls sitting on the floor. Young. In her teens. Queens accent. Pretty, tired face almost drowned by the battle gear she's wearing. "Can I ask a question?"

"Go ahead, soldier."

"Why there so many damn colos around here? In Jersey, I mean?"

Lajune stamps one combat-boot-wrapped foot on the asphalt. "We sitting on one of the biggest data pipes in the world, buried right beneath our feet. Stretches all the way from here to Manhattan, and then out across the country. Real fast line. Back before the crash this was the best place you could put a data center if you didn't want it to be in the city. All those Wall Street motherfuckers, after nine-eleven, they moved their shit out here, hidden away in the middle of nowhere. And those big-data motherfuckers, too. They got backups here of all their stuff. All that cloud bullshit. When the crash happened, a lot of these centers automatically shut themselves off to avoid getting infected.

Looked like they'd been wiped but the data is still intact. That's why you're out here, soldier. To make sure they can't be started up again. To make sure everything gets wiped. You get me?"

"Yes, sir."

"Damn right, yes, sir. You doing the most important job there is for the Movement right now. We can't go back. No turning back. That data in there, it's slavery. It's oppression. It's greed. It's *me*, not *we*. We can't go back to that. Understand?"

"Yes, sir."

She turns back to Kareem. "Speaking of which, how did the wipe go?"

"Well, that's what I wanted to talk to you about, sir. We've not actually triggered it yet."

"The charges are set?"

"All set, sir. All in place."

"So?"

Kareem shrugs. "That's why I radioed you in. We got a situation."

"What situation?"

"Maybe it'd be best if you take a look yourself."

He leads her through the shattered entrance, the crunch of glass and exploded plastic strangely satisfying beneath her boots. He leads her through airlock after airlock, all filled with bodies, blood and bullet holes sprayed across Kubrickian white walls.

Eventually they emerge onto a gantry above the main hall. More blood, corpses, firefight traces. But the main features of the hall are the shipping containers, dozens of them, arranged in neat parallel rows. All must have been originally painted white, she sees, but have long since been encased in layer upon layer of graffiti. Scrawled letters, weird symbols, words Lajune doesn't recognize.

Kareem leads her down steel steps to the floor of the hall. "Usual, standard setup. Basic shipping containers reinforced for extra protection. Each one rented out to a client originally, I'd guess. Individual fire control and power."

"But not EMP shielded?"

"Not enough for what we're packing, nah."

"So I'm still not getting what the holdup is, Kareem."

"Sorry, sir, just a little farther."

He's leading her past the boxes, each one open. She glances inside. In some she sees bunk beds. In others, plants growing—fruits and vegetables. Another is full of what looks like dead children. She steadies herself, holds back the urge to vomit, and instead curses under her breath.

Eventually they stop, at a container that is almost at the dead center of the hall. The first thing she notices is that the door is shut.

"What's going on?"

"Take a look."

She steps up to the viewport, a small impact-proof glass slit in the door, and peers in.

Inside is dimly lit chaos.

The walls are lined with server racks, strobing with green and amber lights. Lajune is no expert, but she's seen inside plenty of colocation centers over the last year, and there are far more racks in this box than usual. It looks like somebody has moved them here, probably from some of the other boxes, so they can all be in the same place. Moreover, they're all wired together in some crazy-ass way, the box full of suspended cables, crisscrossing through the air from wall to wall, rack to rack, like a three-dimensional spiderweb. Infinite fucking detail. The box is littered with trash; food fragments, clothing, computer parts, those old-fashioned fold-up computers—so much crap she can't actually see the floor. She can feel heat coming from it all—even through the near airtight box she can smell the all-too-familiar stench of rotting organic matter and human excrement.

And, sitting in the middle of it all, cross-legged, is a man.

He's stripped to his waist, his brown skin covered in a thin layer of sweat. All she can see of his face is a long beard, graying into white, because his ears are covered with headphones, his eyes hidden by something else. Lajune isn't quite sure what it is, but some kind of technology, vaguely familiar-looking, like a boxy visor you can't see out of.

And he's waving his hands around in the space in front of him, like a slow-motion fucking madman.

"What the fuck is he doing?"

"No idea." Kareem shrugs. "Your guess is as good as mine."

"Get him out of there."

"That's the thing, we can't. It's locked."

"For fuck's sake." She peers back through the slit. "And he's just been sitting there, all the time you've been here?"

"Affirmative."

"You tried getting his attention?"

"Yeah. Nothing. Don't think he can hear us with all that shit strapped to his face."

Lajune starts hammering on the container door with her fist, yelling. "Hey! HEY!"

Nothing.

They both stand in silence for half a minute, staring at the guy in the box.

"What you think he's doing?" she asks Kareem.

"I dunno. He's jacked into all that shit . . . I mean, I've met people in these colos before, crazy people, saying they'd come here looking for something. Something they lost in the crash. Hoping they'd find it in here somehow. Mostly they'd just be going up to the racks, prodding at shit. Wide-eyed and strung out. Always thought they were crazy. But this guy . . . I dunno. Looks like he might know what's he's doing. Never seen anything like this before." He shrugs again. "Hence I pinged you."

Lajune sighs. "What happens if we wipe it now?"

"What happens to him, if we wipe with him in there?" Kareem sucks his teeth. "Shit, I dunno, sir. With that much

tech in there? He'll probably fry. The whole box is gonna
be lit up."

Lajune looks at him, then back to the guy in the box.
From the corner of her eye she can see blood and dead bodies. Casualties. "You got cutting gear with you?"

"Back on one of the trucks, out in the lot."

"Then what the fuck you waiting for, soldier? Cut
him out."

When he pulls back the kitchen cupboard doors with his
ghost hands, he can see what's inside. Brand names stacked
a little too perfectly, like video game items assembled in an
equipment menu.

It's not really what's in the cupboards, of course, just the
imprints made by data he found. An approximation, an
elaborate infographic, the representation of data he's spent
years mining from the server backups of the five data centers he trawled through before he got to this one. Amazon.
FreshDirect. Trader Joe's. Bank of America. The data trails
of Scott's grocery-buying habits. He found some data from
Seamless just a few months back, found Scott's record in
there. Cross-reference it with the right date and time and
then he can even open the fridge and see what his takeaway
leftovers are.

He turns his head, the headset tracking his eyes, scanning light across his retinas. The tiny apartment looks odd,
disjointed, nothing quite fitting. The lighting never looks

right. He's tried his best to make it work, but nothing quite stitches together properly. Mainly because it's been sourced from too many places, none of them quite high-res enough, lacking in details. Images captured by the smart TV and sent quietly back to Samsung. The video feed from the entry phone routed through a failed security start-up. Fragments of LIDAR taken by the motion tracker on a PlayStation that Sony lied about deleting. One badly taken photo on a rental agent's website. Disparate images assembled from the wreckage of the cloud.

He can put Scott's apartment back together, just not him.

He could pull open the apartment door right now, step outside. Float-walk down the stairs of the old Brooklyn brownstone, out and down the stoop, and wander around a similarly patched-together reconstruction of Park Slope. Walk into every shop and diner, every bar and restaurant. Peer into every alleyway and scour every backyard.

But Scott won't be there.

He knows, because he's looked.

Every day, seventeen hours a day, for the last two years.

Trawling through data, looking for him, like he spent twelve hours a day for a month trawling through the shattered architecture of Brooklyn, his hands bleeding as he moved rubble and masonry from the wreckage of the brownstone, leveled by explosions when the crash came and an automated gas pump failed.

But he'll find him yet.

He'll keep looking.

He just needs to scour the cupboards, the streets, the neighborhoods. Brooklyn. The five boroughs. Search every scrap of data, find a trace. A shadow on a CCTV camera feed, a reflection in a store window on Google Street View.

If it's not here it'll be in the next data center, or the one after that. He just needs to keep moving. Trawling. Mining. Searching.

He blinks open a window, intricate film systems and directory structures unwrapping themselves around him—
and
then
someone
rips the headset from his face
and drags him
kicking
and screaming
and blinking
into the light.

"I think he's finally calmed down," Kareem says.

They're both looking down at the guy, as he sits cross-legged at their feet, his head in his hands. Kareem had found a soiled blanket in the box among all the other detritus, and has draped it over his shoulders. He's calmer now, but Lajune can hear him gently sobbing.

"You want me to get one of the squad, get him loaded onto the truck?"

"Nah. Not yet. Give me some time with him alone."

Kareem flashes her a concerned look. "You sure, sir?"

"Yeah, you good. Go get your squad ready to bug out. I'll ping you when I need you."

Kareem nods, leaves. Lajune takes a knee in front of the guy. He stinks, but that ain't unusual these days. She can't remember the last time she took a shower. She probably doesn't smell too rosy herself.

"Hey." For the first time he looks up, slowly, from his hands, makes bloodshot eye contact with her. She unclips a canteen full of water from her armor, offers it to him. "You should drink."

Reluctantly he takes the canteen, takes a sip. "Thanks."

"You want some food? I can get one of my squad to bring you something from the truck if you want. We got some bread and—"

"No. No, it's fine. I'm good. Thanks."

"You don't look too good."

"I'm fine."

"What's your accent?"

She swears he almost smiles. "I'm British."

"Really? What the fuck are you doing all the way out here?"

"I'm looking for someone." Any hint of that smile is gone.

"Shit, we're all looking for people." She finds she has to

break eye contact, stare up into the corner of the room, choke back memories of the lost. "How you end up with these preppers, though?"

"Preppers? I dunno if I'd call them that. Dunno if they were ever that organized." He scratches at his overgrown beard. "They were certainly fucking weirdos. But hiding from storms in a data center for years will probably do that to you. They were into . . . some new religion? More like a cult, I guess. I've only been here a month or two. To be honest, they mainly left me to get on with shit. Minded their own business as long as I helped them keep the solar running."

"You know about keeping solar working?"

"Yeah. A bit."

"Then maybe you can help—" She's interrupted by a pinging sound. The spex hanging from her lapel. She takes them off, flips them open, peers through the lenses without fully putting them on. Notifications and messages. Distractions. She sighs. "Well, that can wait."

When she looks back at him it looks like he's just been given a bump of adrenaline. His eyes are wide, disbelief. Almost agitated. "Where . . . where the hell did you get those?"

"These? Back in the city. NYC."

"Can I see? Please?"

She hesitates, squints at him. Probably a bad idea, somehow. But she's intrigued by this weird fucking brown Englishman that's hiding out in a shipping container full of servers surrounded by hillbilly white supremacists. She hands them to him.

"No funny business," she says.

Rush puts on the spex this black woman in combat gear has given him and it's like being sucked back in time, across years and continents, through victories and mistakes.

Windows unfurl in the air around his face. Maps, data, incoming messages. Status reports.

It's Flex, there's no questioning that. He knows every retina-projected pixel and floating icon, barely changed from when he coded them. Tweaked maybe, but at surface level it looks identical, frozen in time.

Instinctively he blinks through menus, pulls up the version number.

His heart seems to stop, his throat dry.

"Holy shit."

FLEX OS. VERSION 4.027

Open source.

Built by Rush00.

This program is free software: you can redistribute it and/or modify it under the terms of the GNU General Public License as published by the Free Software Foundation.

This program is distributed in the hope that it will be useful, but WITHOUT ANY WARRANTY; without even the implied warranty of MERCHANTABILITY or FITNESS FOR A PARTICULAR PURPOSE. See the GNU General Public License for more details.

Flash back to the last time he'd seen those letters and numbers, arranged precisely like that, when he'd compiled this build, zipped it up, e-mailed it. To Scott.

He struggles for words. "I . . . where did, where did you get this, when?"

"The spex?"

"Yeah, I mean the software. The network. I thought it was all gone."

"Yeah, so did we. So did everyone." She sighs. "I dunno exactly. Seemed to spring up out of Brooklyn. Kinda like an underground thing. Stories of some guy walking around handing out working spex to people. Came in handy when the government and the militia rolled in to try to shut us down. Gave us an advantage."

"When was this?"

"I dunno, a year? Year and a half ago? It's all been a blur."

He blinks open a network map. It opens on a hyperlocal scale, pulsing blue dots representing the dozen or so troops in and around the data center, name tags floating alongside them. He zooms out hard, New Jersey laid out as a basic green wireframe map, few details apart from pixel-thin lines representing roads and the occasional town. None of this was built into Flex, of course, he knows that, imagines them building it themselves as they pushed their way out of NYC, brand-new maps drawn from the user level up through collaboration and exploration. He zooms out some more and scrolls east, following a line of pulsing dots—individual users, sometimes grouped together, sometimes on their own—spaced out just enough to keep the network connections to back home stable.

And then he hits it, New York City, mapped out in infinite detail, unlike the stark, unexplored wastelands of Jersey. A new map, not dictated by some distant conglomerate or orbiting, all-seeing satellite, but built from the ground up by the people that actually live there. And here the blue dots are so many, so close together, that they're one huge pulsating, growing mass, filling the outlines of Brooklyn and Queens, spilling over bridges into Staten Island, Manhattan, pushing up north into the Bronx and beyond.

At this distance names are obscured, as much as he tries to zoom in on individuals. Good, that's how he designed it, to protect anonymity at long range. But if he could get back there, back into Brooklyn, back to where he could find the source, the first nodes to join . . .

"Hey, you done?" The woman interrupts him. "Can I get them back?"

"Sorry." He hands them back to her, sees his hands are shaking. Excitement, disbelief. Embarrassment.

"You know about this stuff, huh?"

"You could say that, yeah."

"I can get you a pair, maybe. If you come with me."

"I need to get back to New York."

She laughs. "Oh, honey. Trust me, you're going back to NYC. I should be packing you into one of these trucks right now to send you back to work on the farms. To help rebuild Queens and Brooklyn. But you look like you know what you're doing with this . . . with this shit. We need people like you. Agree to help me and things can be a lot easier. So yeah, you're going back to NYC. It's just whether you want to ride in the back of the truck with those cracker freaks or in the jeep with me."

He smiles at her. "The jeep sounds more comfortable."

Out in the jeep Lajune unzips her flak jacket, throws it on the seat behind her. Stretches her arms, her neck. She's stiff, could do with a bath. A bed. Home.

She slips on her spex, opens a channel to Kareem.

"We got everybody clear? Safe distance?"

"Affirmative, commander. All operatives clear and at safe distance. Freed residents also at safe distance, awaiting pickup."

"Understood. Light her up. Over and out."

"Affirmative. Initiating EMP detonation now, sir. Have a good ride home."

She sits in silence. It takes about ten seconds. She can

imagine Kareem or one of his squad hitting the three primer buttons in sequence, then finally the detonator.

Then it starts, the brief, muted but still loud *click click click* of explosions from inside the low building, like someone letting off a stream of firecrackers in a steel box. The building, structurally unaffected, plunges into darkness.

She sighs again. Nervously she turns the jeep's ignition, relaxes as it springs into life. She does the same thing every time they do a wipe; panics that she's not gotten safe enough away, and that the electromagnetic pulse is going to fuck with the car. It's never happened. But it's become a ritual, reassuring, something she can't quite explain.

She turns to the weird, bedraggled British guy in the passenger seat, still unsure she's made the right decision letting him ride with her.

"You probably think we're crazy doing this, huh? Think we're barbaric."

He smiles back at her. "Actually, you couldn't be more wrong."

And she puts the jeep in drive and pulls away.

ACKNOWLEDGMENTS

This book would never have happened without the love and support of sava saheli singh and my parents.

Huge thanks also to my agent, Grainne Fox, for her belief, persistence, and always paying for the coffee. And to Sean McDonald for taking a gamble.

Beyond that there's an almost infinite list of friends and people who helped me, influenced me, paid me, bought me lunch, or encouraged me along the way—of which this is (in no particular order) just a tiny selection:

Simon Ings, Liam Young, Kate Davies, Lydia Nicholas, Sumit Paul-Choudhury, Brian Merchant, Brendan Byrne, Black Lives Matter, Ingrid Burrington, Frank Swain, Justin Pickard, Craig

Willingham, Mike Wolf, Cory Doctorow, Jack Womack, Alan Tabrett, Bobi Richardson, Forsaken, Superflux, Jonathan Wright, Urmilla Deshpande, the crew of the *Maersk Seletar* (July 2014), Veronica Goldstein, Daniel Vazquez, everyone at FSG.

And the people of Brooklyn and Bristol.